UNVEILED CONCEALMENT

UNVEILED CONCEALMENT

AMAAN SHABIR

Amaan Shabir

Contents

Thank You to Andre, Scarlet, Dan and Brad for reading pieces of this project that I probably annoyingly sent you at 3am.

Thank You to Rayane for supporting me when things got tough in my personal life as well as my writing life.

Thank You to Fin for making this project enjoyable, since we were both writing books and were 'on the same page' when it came to writers block.

Contact The Author

Instagram Handle: @amaanshabirofficial
Twitter Handle: @amaanshabiroff
Email: amaanshabir09876@outlook.com

Opening

It's been a while, reader, since you last heard from me. But fret not, for I am here now, ready to whisk you away on a whirlwind journey through a city of unrealistic perfections. Buckle up, tighten your grip on reality, and prepare yourself for a rollercoaster of love, lust, and pain. This is not a tale for the faint of heart, for the timid souls that cower in the shadows. No, this is a story that races through the veins like a wild stallion, a tempestuous symphony of contradictions.

In this city, where dreams dance with nightmares and beauty collides with decay, I shall guide you. Its streets pulsate with a vibrant energy that ignites the air, seducing all who wander within its grasp. Tall buildings reach for the skies, casting long shadows upon those below, like giants guarding secrets too precious to reveal. Neon lights flicker like shooting stars, casting their kaleidoscope glow upon the darkened pavements.

As I walk through this city, its heartbeat reverberates through my every step. I taste the bittersweet flavours of love and lust, blending on my tongue like forbidden elixirs. I see passion woven into the very fabric of its existence, in the way lovers embrace, their bodies melding together like two halves of a broken mirror.

This city, friend, is both a siren and a sanctuary. It is a paradoxical symphony of discordant harmonies. It whispers promises of purity, yet reveals the underbelly of shattered dreams. Its beauty can be blinding, intoxicating, like a mirage in the desert, promising salvation in the most barren of landscapes.

But amidst the chaos, the pain pulses. It's a relentless ache, an ever-present reminder that life's imperfections are as integral as the brushstrokes on a masterpiece. In this city, pain is a muse, a catalyst for growth, and a beacon of resilience. It lingers in the air, seeping into the cracks and crevices of broken hearts, leaving scars that tell tales of battles fought and won.

So hold on tight, reader, as we traverse this metropolis of contradictions. Love, lust, and pain intertwine, twirling in a dance of ecstasy and despair. Together, we shall uncover the hidden depths and explore the uncharted territories of the human heart. It's time to dive headfirst into the whirlpool of emotions, to embrace the kaleidoscope of sensations that await us in this city of unrealistic perfections.

****

The city of FleshBourne looms before me, a monument of paradoxical beauty and brutal judgment. Its architecture, a macabre fusion of fleshy hues and sinewy structures, invokes a sense of morbid fascination. Jagged spires rise like bones piercing the sky, casting eerie shadows over the streets below. The city seems to pulsate with a dark energy, as if it has a life of its own, throbbing with the weight of the sins it bears witness to.

In this unforgiving metropolis, the consequences of wrongdoing are etched upon one's very skin. Every misstep, every transgression is made visible to all, a raw wound exposed to the world. In FleshBourne, the authorities are not content with mere punishment—they thrive on the power to condemn and execute those marked by their sins. The city is a theatre of fear, where the display of wounds becomes a death sentence.

I, too, bear the weight of countless wounds upon my flesh, scars of past mistakes that I dare not reveal. Layers of clothing cloak my shame, veiling the evidence of my misdeeds from the prying eyes of both authority and citizenry. Scarves wrapped tightly around my neck, gloves encasing my hands, and long sleeves pulled down to conceal the map of my guilt. Each garment serves as armour, guarding me against the merciless scrutiny of a city that revels in the exposure of weakness.

FleshBourne is a grotesque tapestry of brutality and grandeur. Buildings, adorned with intricate carvings that resemble twisted veins and pulsating organs, line the streets. The marble façades, weathered and discoloured by the weight of collective sin, create an unsettling contrast against the blood-red sky that hangs overhead. The air carries a palpable tension, heavy with the scent of paranoia and the metallic tang of fear.

Society in FleshBourne is a dance of perpetual caution. Eyes, hardened and judgmental, scan the streets, dissecting every passerby for any sign of vulnerability. Trust is an illusion, a fleeting mirage that evaporates upon contact. Behind closed doors, whispered conversations betray a society in a state of constant surveillance, where secrets are currency and betrayal is a survival strategy.

The enforcers of this twisted order, known as the Scourge, prowl the streets like predators in search of prey. Cloaked in blood-red uniforms, their faces concealed by porcelain masks adorned with grotesque expressions, they wield their authority with ruthless efficiency. They are the embodiment of the city's collective wrath, the harbingers of punishment, and the purveyors of death.

Within the depths of my concealed wounds, a flicker of rebellion ignites. In the hidden corners of FleshBourne, a resistance brews, fuelled by the shared desire for liberation and justice. They operate in the shadows, their actions concealed by a veil of secrecy, for the consequences of discovery are dire. But the whispers of rebellion grow louder, a defiant anthem that resounds within the hearts of those who yearn for change.

As I traverse the dimly lit back alleys of FleshBourne, each step carries the weight of uncertainty. The scars beneath my garments throb with a mixture of shame and determination. The fear of discovery haunts my every move, a constant reminder that my facade is but a fragile shield against the merciless gaze of the Scourge.

In this city of twisted desires and hidden wounds, the rebellion finds solace amidst the decay. Underground chambers, nestled beneath the decaying underbelly of FleshBourne, become sanctuaries of defiance. Illuminated by flickering candlelight, the resistance members gather, their faces marked by scars openly displayed. Each wound becomes a symbol of defiance, a rallying cry against the tyranny of the city.

Within the hallowed halls of the resistance, plans are laid bare, and hope blooms like a fragile flower pushing through the cracks in the pavement. We devise strategies to dismantle the oppressive regime, to unveil the true face of FleshBourne to the world. In these clandestine gatherings, the strength of unity and the resilience of the human spirit rise, defying the darkness that surrounds us.

But caution remains our unwavering companion. The Scourge's grip on the city is unrelenting, their presence ever-ominous. We move in shadows, our steps shrouded in silence, knowing that a single misstep could extinguish the flame of rebellion and seal our collective fate.

Yet, as I stand on the precipice of revolution, my heart beats with a newfound courage. The scars on my skin pulse with an ancient resilience, urging me to shed the cloak of fear and embrace the vulnerability of truth. The time has come for FleshBourne to confront its own monstrosity, to realize that wounds, though visible, do not define our worth or our capacity for change.

Together, we shall rise, reclaiming the streets of FleshBourne with the power of unity and the indomitable spirit that resides within us all. The city that thrives on the exposure of weakness will crumble beneath the weight of our determination, and in its place, a new dawn shall break, where scars are no longer a source of shame but a testament to our resilience and the triumph of our shared humanity.

I

Another Wound

As I lie in bed, the oppressive darkness of my room envelopes me, with only slivers of moonlight daring to peek through the curtains. Sleep should be a respite, a sanctuary from the weariness of the world, but tonight, it eludes me. My mind races, tangled in a labyrinth of thoughts and regrets.

A subtle discomfort starts to stir at the base of my neck, a smouldering ember of unease that refuses to be ignored. It festers, growing into an inferno of burning sensations, as if a wrathful flame dances upon my very skin. Each flicker sends a shiver down my spine, an oxymoron of icy heat coursing through my veins.

Slowly, the scorching agony transforms, twisting its fiery tendrils into something far more sinister. The pain intensifies, morphing into a relentless stabbing, as though a thousand needles pierce my vulnerable flesh. I can't help but gasp, clutching at the torment radiating from the depths of my neck.

With trembling limbs, I must summon the courage to sit up, and as I do, my mattress creaks in protest, echoing the torment within me. It's then that I feel it—a disconcerting wetness against my fingers. Panic seizes my heart as I glance down, witnessing the rivulets of crimson snaking their way down my trembling palm.

The wound, once invisible, now reveals itself to me in all its grotesque splendour. It glows with an eerie crimson hue, casting a haunting illumination upon my very soul. It's as if the wound itself possesses a macabre sentience, mocking me for my transgressions. The glistening red takes on a life of its own, a malevolent light that mesmerizes and terrorizes simultaneously.

In this moment of visceral vulnerability, I am gripped by a terrible realization. This wound is no mere accident, no ordinary affliction. It is the physical manifestation of my own immorality, a damning consequence etched upon my skin. The very essence of my transgressions has erupted from the depths of my being, leaving me exposed and vulnerable in the pale moonlight.

Desperation takes hold, and I tremble with fear and regret. How did I allow myself to sink so deeply into this pit of moral decay? The wound, like a spectre of my conscience, throbs with a mocking pulse, its presence a constant reminder of my fall from grace.

As the wound's glistening glow begins to dim, my panic intensifies. Will it ever fade completely? Or is it now an indelible mark, forever etched upon my flesh, branding me as a captive to my own immorality? I am left to grapple with this revelation, the weight of my actions crushing down upon me in the suffocating darkness.

Oh, sleep, how I long for your solace. But tonight, I am left to wrestle with the consequences of my own demons, my room a dark battleground where morality and immorality collide.

I stand here, bathed in the pale moonlight, my heart pounding in my chest like a frantic bird trapped in a cage. The night is silent, save for the distant echo of my own guilt-ridden breaths. A shiver runs down my spine, as if a ghostly hand has grazed its icy fingers along my vulnerable flesh. But it is not a specter that haunts me; it is the fresh wound on the back of my neck, an unyielding reminder of the crime I have committed.

The wound throbs like a melancholic melody, each beat of pain resonating through my body. It is a paradoxical symphony of agony and relief, as if my very being is at odds with itself. The blood trickles down my skin, like scarlet tears of remorse, staining the fabric of my shirt. It weaves a macabre tapestry of my transgressions, forever etched upon the canvas of my existence.

My mind is a tempest, swirling with regret and self-condemnation. I am a marionette, dancing to the twisted strings of my own malevolence. The weight of my actions presses upon me like an anvil upon fragile bones, threatening to crush the remnants of my conscience. Guilt, an insidious demon, clings to my soul, its tendrils seeping into the deepest recesses of my being.

I peer into the mirror, and the reflection that stares back at me is a stranger, a fractured shadow of the person I once was. The eyes, once vibrant and full of life, now hold a haunting emptiness. They are windows to a broken soul, a soul burdened by the weight of sin. The face, once adorned with a smile, now bears the mark of a perpetual frown, etched by the lines of sorrow and regret.

The wound on my neck, a treacherous betrayal from my own hand, has taken on a life of its own. It whispers secrets only I can hear, a reminder of the irreparable damage I have caused. It is a living metaphor, a physical manifestation of the pain I have inflicted upon others. It throbs like a pulsating heart, a heart that beats in tandem with my own, as if my guilt has become a living entity, forever intertwined with my existence.

I long for redemption, a chance to scrub away the stains of my transgressions. But forgiveness eludes me like a mirage in the desert, forever out of reach. The weight of my guilt bears down upon me, like an anchor dragging me to the depths of despair. The wound on my neck is a scarlet badge of my shame, a permanent reminder of the darkness that dwells within.

As the night deepens, I find solace in the shadows, seeking refuge from the harsh light of truth. The wound on my neck, a wound both physical and metaphorical, serves as a constant reminder of my fall from grace. It is a wound that will never fully heal, a wound that will forever seep with the blood of remorse. And so, I carry it with me, like a penance, etching its mark upon my soul, forever condemned to live with the burden of my own sins.

2

Sunlight Kisses

Rays of sunlight caress my face in the most obscene manner as my eyelids flutter under the golden hue of disturbance.

The gentle tweeting of birds filters in from outside, like a symphony of tiny flutes in a melodious chorus. Yet, beneath their cheerful tunes, there lingers a faint note of something ominous, a subtle undertone that tugs at the edges of my awareness.

As the sun climbs higher, its golden rays stream through the window, casting a beam of light that tenderly caresses the room. The sunlight, like liquid honey, spills across the polished marble floor, illuminating every corner with a warm and inviting glow. But within those luminous rays, shadows flicker and dance, elongating and twisting as if they have a life of their own, hinting at secrets whispered by the shifting light.

Within this celestial embrace, the space of my bedroom unfolds, offering respite and solace. The bed, draped in sheets as soft as clouds, occupies the centre, beckoning me to sink into its embrace.

But sometimes, in the midst of midnight stillness, it feels as if unseen hands linger just beneath the surface, a chilling touch that sends shivers cascading down my spine.

Adjacent to the bed, a weathered oak nightstand stands tall, adorned with a flickering candle that casts dancing shadows upon its worn surface. The flame flickers and sways, its gentle dance an echo of unseen forces, as if it harbours a hidden knowledge that flickers just beyond the reach of understanding.

Against the far wall, a grand bookshelf stretches from floor to ceiling, cradling a treasure trove of knowledge within its polished wooden arms. The books, like loyal companions, lean against each other, whispering secrets and stories waiting to be explored. Yet, in the depths of their pages, ancient whispers stir, like a chorus of forgotten voices, their words hinting at worlds beyond our own, and truths that should remain buried.

On the opposite side of the room, a small writing desk stands, adorned with scattered papers and an antique inkwell. The inkwell, a relic of time, holds forgotten dreams and untold tales, patiently waiting for the moment they will flow onto the page. But sometimes, as I dip my quill into the ink, a chilling breeze whispers through the room, as if the stories long to break free from their confines, yearning to reveal the darkness that lies beneath the surface.

Near the desk, a cracked mirror leans against the wall, a silent witness to the passage of time. Its fractured surface reflects fragments of memories, distorting reality with its shattered perspective. And sometimes, when I gaze into its fractured depths, a fleeting glimpse of something otherworldly flashes before my eyes, a haunting image that leaves me questioning the true nature of the room I call my own.

In this haven of mine, where marble walls shelter dreams and sunlight embraces solitude, I find peace and inspiration. But amidst the pleasant facade, hints of something sinister lurk, weaving their way through the threads of my existence. The symphony of bird-song outside, the touch of sunlight, and the arrangement of objects within this sanctuary create an atmosphere both comforting and unsettling, a delicate balance between beauty and darkness.

****

I head downstairs, my footsteps echoing through the polished marble corridors, the sound seemingly swallowed by the ominous silence that pervades the building. I enter the washroom, splashing cool water on my face, hoping to wash away the lingering unease that the room had stirred within me.

As I gaze into the mirror, my reflection seems distorted, as if the cracks in the glass reflect not just my physical appearance but the fractures within my own soul. A shiver courses through me, a harbinger of the events to come. I try to push aside the haunting thoughts, focusing instead on preparing for the day that looms ahead. Today is Sunday. The day of the weekly spectacle.

In the city of FleshBourne, every week brings forth a dark and ominous ritual imposed by the Scourge, the tyrants ruling over our lives. It is a law, decreed without mercy, that each citizen must attend the public punishment of the criminals. With heavy hearts and trembling souls, we gather in the heart of our once vibrant town, our steps echoing on the bloodstained marble floor of the town centre.

In the dimly lit washroom, I carefully select my attire, ensuring that each garment serves a dual purpose - to mask the wound on my neck and to blend seamlessly with the crowd during the weekly public punishment of criminals. I choose a high-collared shirt, its fabric soft against my skin, its folds conspiring to shield the scar that betrays my secret. As I fasten the buttons, my fingers move with a practiced ease, securing the hidden truth beneath layers of fabric. A silk scarf becomes my ally, gracefully wrapped around my neck, obscuring any trace of the wound. Its intricate pattern offers a mere glimpse of the beauty that hides the horrors I carry.

The mirror reflects back an image of a face shrouded in mystery, a face that must navigate the treacherous paths of this fractured world.

Stepping outside, I walk the streets, my attire offering me a semblance of protection, a fragile shield against the relentless pursuit of the Scourge. The fabric embraces my body, whispering reassurances and blending seamlessly with the collective consciousness of those who gather for the public punishment.

The city of Fleshborne, with its towering edifices and bustling streets, transforms into a malevolent entity before my eyes. Its very essence seems to come alive, each element personified, a relentless observer intent on unmasking my hidden shame. The stone structures loom over me, their silent presence casting judgment like a sentinel guarding its post. They leer with disapproval, mocking my feeble attempts to conceal the burning wound etched upon my flesh.

Every step I take is shrouded in trepidation, as if the ground itself conspires to expose my transgressions. The labyrinthine alleys wind and twist, whispering secrets to one another, concealing the truth of my wrongdoing. I navigate this cityscape, burdened by the weight of my concealed sin, each breath a silent confession, a desperate plea for absolution in a realm where mercy seems an illusion.

Fear coils around me, a suffocating embrace, its tendrils seeping into my every thought. The city's denizens, draped in garments of self-righteousness, cast disapproving glances my way. Their eyes gleam with righteous indignation, their whispers like venomous serpents, hissing judgment and scorn. I become a solitary figure in this labyrinth of scrutiny, a target of their collective disdain.

Within this realm of paradoxical allure, the streets awaken with a symphony of contrasting elements. The distant rumble of thunder echoes through the city's veins, a primal rhythm that reverberates within my core. It mingles with the harmonious melody of raindrops cascading upon cobblestones, a soothing cadence that masks the turbulent storm within my soul.

The wind sighs through the narrow passages, its mournful whispers carrying the weight of hidden secrets. It dances through the labyrinth, rustling the leaves of ancient trees, and its melancholic melody becomes a lullaby for lost souls. I find solace in its gentle caress, a momentary respite from the relentless judgment that pervades the air.

As daylight envelops the city, a symphony of ambient sounds fills the atmosphere. The rhythmic fluttering of wings, as birds take flight, creates a delicate orchestra, their songs punctuating the silence. The distant chiming of church bells floats upon the breeze, carrying with it a sense of solemnity and reflection. The city breathes, its pulse resonating through the gentle hum of life, an intricate tapestry of existence woven with the threads of judgment and secrecy.

And through it all, the wound upon my neck throbs, a constant reminder of my inner turmoil, an ever-present companion on this journey of concealment. The city becomes my labyrinth, my captor and my captivated, an enigmatic realm where the mark of my sins remains concealed, forever hidden from the prying eyes of its inhabitants.

With each passing moment, I navigate the treacherous paths of Fleshborne, aware of the invisible weight upon my shoulders. I tread softly, my steps cautious and measured, my facade unyielding. In this city of contradictions, I am but a solitary figure, forever conscious of the wound that mars my existence, forever entwined within the enigma of Fleshborne's twisted embrace.

****

As the merciless rays beat down upon us, the air shimmers with heatwaves, mirroring the tension and apprehension that fills our souls. We stand shoulder to shoulder, perspiration clinging to our brows, our gazes fixated upon the chilling spectacle that awaits us. High above the marble floor, the gallows stand imposingly, casting long, ominous shadows.

Amidst the stifling silence, the Scourge drag forth the condemned, their faces etched with despair, bodies withered by anguish. These unfortunate souls, stripped of their humanity, are to endure a fate that defies comprehension. Their vacant eyes meet ours momentarily, an unspoken plea for mercy lost amidst the crowd's apathy.

The Scourge prepares for their grand proclamation. Clad in ebony armour, each member stands tall and resolute, their faces obscured by featureless masks that exude an air of authority and anonymity. The room is heavy with anticipation as they synchronize their movements, their collective presence radiating an aura of power and dominance.

In the silence that befalls the town square, the Scourge takes a collective breath, the air pregnant with the weight of their imminent words. Each member steps forward, their voices merging into a unified declaration. As their words echo through the chamber and beyond, they become an indomitable force, their conviction etched into the minds of all who listen:

Citizens of FleshBourne!

Today, we gather to witness the unyielding might of the Scourge, a group of soldiers dedicated to upholding order and justice in our beloved city. It is through their unwavering vigilance that we stand united against the forces that seek to sow chaos and discord.

These criminals before you, who have dared to disrupt the harmony of our society, shall face the consequences of their actions. The Scourge, with their unwavering resolve and unrelenting discipline, will ensure that justice is served.

Watch as these wretched souls are subjected to the punishment they so rightly deserve. Their bodies shall be broken, their spirits shattered, as a stark reminder to all who would dare challenge the authority and stability we have fought so hard to establish.

Let their suffering serve as a warning, a testament to the unwavering strength of the Scourge and the consequences that befall those who defy our order. May their cries echo through the streets, a reminder that none are above the law, and the Scourge will not falter in their duty to protect our city.

Rejoice, citizens of FleshBourne, for in the face of adversity, the Scourge stands as a beacon of order and righteousness. Embrace this display, for it is a testament to the power and unity that defines our great city.

Long live the Scourge, the protectors of FleshBourne, guardians of justice and bringers of order!

They get to work. The sweltering air carries the acrid scent of burning wood as they secure the convicts, their desperate cries for mercy blending with the relentless crackling of flames below. Beads of sweat trace winding paths down our faces as we bear witness to the horrors that unfold before us.

One by one, they sever flesh and sinew, each stroke an agonizing testament to the Scourges' reign of terror. The anguished screams of the condemned pierce the air, their pain reverberating through our very cores. Blood, thick and crimson, spills forth onto the marble below, mingling with the scalding heat of the midday sun.

Ashes rise like spectral phantoms, carried by the hot breeze to settle upon our sweat-drenched bodies. The crowd becomes a tableau of horror and resignation, marked by the sombre dance of crimson and grey. Each drop, each splatter, paints a sinister tapestry upon the marbled canvas, a permanent reminder of our powerlessness in the face of such brutality.

As the condemned bodies sway above the fire, the searing sun casts long shadows upon the square, distorting the grotesque spectacle into something out of a fevered nightmare. The once vibrant city of FleshBourne becomes a theatre of pain, its essence tainted by the suffering and torment that unfold before our helpless eyes.

The midday hours wane, and the life force slowly drains from the broken bodies. Their ravaged forms hang limp, stripped of flesh and dignity, a chilling tableau under the unrelenting sun. We disperse, aching and despondent, each carrying the weight of witnessing unspeakable horrors burned into our minds.

3

An Old Friend

I emerge from the chilling spectacle of the midday public executions, mingling with the restless crowds as we make our way back to our homes. The sweltering sun beats down upon us mercilessly, yet the wind gusts fiercely, carrying with it a haunting blend of scents. The pungent odour of decaying flesh and blood intertwines with the delicate fragrance of roses and flowers, creating a macabre symphony for my senses.

My heart flutters with a sense of relief, however slight, as I realize my choice of clothing has successfully concealed the damning wound upon my neck. Hidden beneath the fabric, the mark of my transgression remains concealed, protecting me from the fate that has befallen the wretched souls subjected to the Scourge's merciless judgment.

Every step I take is imbued with caution, as if the very ground beneath me may reveal my secrets. I navigate through the sea of faces, each person's eyes glazed with a mixture of fear, resignation, and curiosity. Whispers ripple through the crowd, rumours and hushed conversations about the fates of those condemned today, and the looming presence of the Scrouge itself.

The city bustles with activity as the midday crowds disperse, weaving their way through the labyrinthine streets. The air crackles with a vibrant energy, the echoes of conversations blending into a symphony of voices. Merchants call out their wares, their voices carrying through the narrow alleys, mingling with the laughter and footsteps of passersby.

As I navigate through the throngs of people, a sense of urgency pulses within me. The wind picks up, swirling around me in gusts that tangle my hair and whip at my clothing. It carries with it a welcome respite from the scorching sun, as if nature itself is signalling a change in the weather.

Overhead, rain clouds gather, shrouding the sky in a layer of darkening grey. The sun, once blazing with intensity, now struggles to pierce through the thickening veil. The atmosphere becomes pregnant with anticipation, as if the city itself holds its breath in anticipation of the impending storm.

The first few drops of rain descend, landing softly on the cobblestone streets and the upturned faces of the weary travellers. The sound of the rain is a gentle patter, a symphony of nature's rhythm, gradually intensifying into a melodic chorus. The droplets cascade from rooftops, spattering against awnings and creating a harmonious symphony of nature's percussions.

Determined to reach the safety of home before the rain intensifies, I quicken my pace. Each step becomes a deliberate stride, my focus honed on the path ahead. The streets, once bustling, begin to thin as people seek shelter from the impending downpour. Umbrellas unfurl, dotting the landscape with bursts of colour, as the city transforms into a refuge for those seeking respite from the rain.

Suddenly, a tap on my shoulder interrupts my determined stride. Startled, I pivot around, expecting to meet a familiar face or perhaps a friendly neighbour seeking a moment's respite from the bustling city. To my astonishment, it is Joseph, a dear friend whom I haven't seen in what feels like an eternity.

Recognition flickers in our eyes, a moment of shared surprise and joy amidst the confusion. Before either of us can speak, however, Joseph's hand jerks back from my shoulder as if singed by an invisible flame. Bewilderment registers on his face, and he takes a few steps back, needing a moment to recompose himself.

The reunion between Joseph and me had taken an unexpected turn, plunging us into an abyss of confusion and frustration. As I tried to engage in casual small talk, Joseph remained hesitant, his unease palpable.

"Hey, Joseph! It's been ages," I greeted him, attempting to mask the unease that now clouded the atmosphere between us. "How have you been?"

Joseph's response was hesitant, his voice laced with uncertainty. "Hello. I... I've been alright. Busy with work, you know."

I pressed on, hoping to break through the tension that hung heavily in the air. "Oh, I understand. Life can get pretty hectic. So, how's everything else? How's your family?"

But instead of engaging in the usual pleasantries, Joseph seemed consumed by a singular thought. He cut straight to the heart of the matter, his anxiety thinly veiled. "They're fine. Look, when I touched your shoulder, I felt this strange burn. It startled me. Do you have any idea why that happened?"

Taken aback by his directness, I searched for an answer, my mind racing to make sense of the perplexing situation. "I... I honestly have no clue, Joseph," I admitted, my voice tinged with genuine confusion. "It's as baffling to me as it is to you. I can assure you I haven't done anything to intentionally cause such a sensation."

But Joseph's frustration grew, his tone sharpening with each word. "But there must be some reason! I've never experienced anything like that before, and it happened the moment I touched you. You have to give me an answer."

Feeling unjustly accused, I couldn't help but grow defensive. "Joseph, I wish I had an answer for you, but I genuinely don't know what could have caused it. It's not fair for you to expect me to explain something that is beyond my understanding."

The anger in Joseph's voice was now unmistakable. "Not fair? We've known each other for years, and suddenly, this strange occurrence happens when I touch you? How can you expect me to just brush it off? I deserve an explanation!"

Frustration welled up within me, the weight of the unexplained burden pressing heavily upon my shoulders. "I understand that it's unsettling, Joseph, but getting angry at me won't solve anything," I shot back, my own voice tinged with exasperation. "I'm just as confused and concerned as you are. Maybe it was a random occurrence, a bizarre coincidence. Can we not argue about this?"

Sarcasm dripped from Joseph's words as he retorted, "A coincidence? You expect me to believe that? There's something you're not telling me, and it's tearing me apart. I thought we were friends, but you won't even be honest with me."

The accusation cut deep, a pang of hurt mingling with my frustration. "I am being honest! I don't have an answer for you, and it's unfair for you to accuse me of keeping something from you," I defended myself, my voice wavering with a mix of emotions. "If I knew what caused it, I would tell you, but I don't, and it's frustrating for both of us."

Trembling with a mix of anger and betrayal, Joseph's voice quivered as he uttered his next words. "I thought I could trust you.

I thought you would understand. But it seems like you're hiding something, and I don't know if I can trust you anymore."

As his words hung in the air, a heavy silence settled between us, suffocating any remnants of the warmth that had once defined our friendship. A mix of sadness and frustration washed over me, the realization sinking in that our bond had been shattered by a mystery we couldn't unravel. With a heavy heart, I made a final plea. "Joseph, I never wanted our friendship to be strained like this. I genuinely don't have an answer for you. If you can't believe me or trust me on that, then maybe we need some time apart to figure things out."

With those words, the tension reached its breaking point, leaving us standing at a precipice, uncertain if our friendship could withstand the weight of the unexplained phenomenon that had driven us apart.

As I walked away from the confrontation with Joseph, anger and emotional hurt swirled within me, mingling with a sense of incredulity. How could he start an argument over something so seemingly trivial? The accusations felt petty, an unnecessary strain on our friendship. Resentment simmered beneath the surface, and I couldn't shake the lingering bitterness that hung in the air.

Lost in my thoughts and seething with frustration, I continued my journey through the city streets. The atmosphere seemed to mirror my inner turmoil. Dark clouds loomed overhead, mirroring the storm brewing within me, as the wind whipped through the narrow alleys, carrying with it a haunting whisper of discontent. The once vibrant streets now appeared desolate, as if reflecting the cracks forming in my relationship with Joseph.

Finally, I reached my house, a grand structure of pristine marble that stood as a testament to my aspirations and accomplishments. Yet, even in the familiarity of my own abode, the anger within me refused to dissipate. With a surge of pent-up energy, I slammed the door shut, the reverberating sound echoing through the silence, emphasizing the finality of the argument.

Inside, the atmosphere was a stark contrast to the chaos outside. The calmness of the interior offered a momentary respite, but my mind continued to churn with questions and doubts. The eerie sense of the burn lingered, gnawing at the edges of my consciousness, refusing to be dismissed as mere coincidence.

As I paced the hallways of my home, the polished marble floors cool beneath my feet, a profound unease settled within me. It was as if the house itself mirrored my internal turmoil, each corner hiding secrets yet to be uncovered. The air felt heavy, as if carrying an invisible weight that strained my every step.

Lost in my thoughts, I retraced the events in my mind, searching for answers that seemed elusive. What had caused Joseph's reaction? Why had the simple act of his touch triggered such a sensation? The more I pondered, the more I realized that there was a hidden truth lurking beneath the surface, waiting to be unveiled.

The argument still echoed in my mind, the hurt and confusion refusing to subside. But amidst the storm of emotions, a flicker of unease emerged. The burn, the peculiar reaction Joseph had experienced, hinted at something more profound than a simple disagreement between friends. It carried an undercurrent of mystery, a whisper of a secret that needed to be unravelled.

As I contemplated the enigma, a sense of trepidation crept over me. There was something inexplicably wrong, something sinister that lingered just beyond my grasp. The air seemed to hold its breath, as if the house itself sensed the impending revelation.

In the midst of my emotional turmoil and the mysterious burn, I couldn't shake the feeling that I had stumbled upon a truth that went far beyond my understanding. The argument with Joseph, petty as it seemed, now held a greater significance, its roots entangled with an ominous secret that had yet to be unveiled.

With a mixture of anger, confusion, and a growing sense of foreboding, I vowed to uncover the truth, to confront the eerie sense of the burn that clung to me like an invisible mark. Little did I know that my quest for answers would plunge me into a web of intrigue and danger, where the line between reality and the supernatural would blur, and the true nature of the burn would reveal itself in ways I could never have imagined.

4

It Is Better To Not Burn A Bridge

Days had slipped by in a haze of lingering tension since the argument with Joseph, and the weight of the unresolved conflict sat heavy on my shoulders. As the passing hours transformed into days, a growing sense of remorse began to replace my initial anger. Perhaps it was time to mend the rift that had formed between us, to bridge the gap that had opened up in our once-solid friendship.

The eerie sensation of the burn had not dissipated, and in the solitude of my thoughts, I began to realize that it wasn't just Joseph who had felt it. I, too, had experienced the inexplicable searing touch when our paths briefly intersected. The memory of that strange encounter replayed in my mind like a haunting refrain, leaving me with a nagging sense of unease. What had caused it? And why were we both plagued by its ghostly presence?

With a determined resolve, I decided to reach out to Joseph. It was time to set aside our differences and seek understanding, to unravel the enigma that had driven us apart. The desire for reconciliation mingled with the curiosity to unearth the truth, creating a complex blend of emotions that propelled me forward.

The hours ticked away, the weight of anticipation growing heavier with each passing minute. The public execution was still a few days away, and the decision to confront Joseph at the event remained steadfast in my mind. I couldn't shake the sense that this gathering held the potential to bridge the divide between us, to set things right.

As the sun began its descent, casting long shadows across the city streets, a mixture of restlessness and anxiety pulsed through my veins. The wind, now cooler and more insistent, whispered secrets and carried the scent of impending rain. The atmosphere crackled with a palpable energy, a blend of excitement and foreboding that mirrored my own internal turmoil.

Unable to quell the turmoil within, I found myself pacing back and forth in my house. The polished marble floors echoed my restless footsteps, a rhythm that mirrored the rapid beating of my heart. I glanced at the clock on the wall, the hands ticking away relentlessly, marking the passage of time, drawing me ever closer to the pivotal moment.

With a mixture of trepidation and determination, I made my way to the mirror hanging in the hallway. I stared at my own reflection, searching for signs of resolve, steeling myself for the encounter that awaited. The wound on my neck, a painful reminder of my transgressions, began to glow with an eerie light, and fresh blood trickled down my skin. I remained calm, knowing this was not the first time such wounds had opened. With practiced ease, I reached for a nearby cloth, pressing it gently against the wound to staunch the bleeding. The rhythmic pulsation of the wound matched the beat of my heart, a reminder of the consequences of my actions. Though I carried numerous wounds like this on my back and chest, their presence did not incite panic within me. I had learned to tend to them, to conceal them beneath layers of resolve and determination. With practiced precision, I applied steady pressure to the glowing wound on my neck. The bleeding gradually subsided, the flow reduced to a trickle, until it ceased altogether. The cloth absorbed the blood, turning a deep shade of red.

The decision to seek Joseph out at the public execution weighed heavily on my mind. It was a risk, a leap of faith into the unknown, but the opportunity for reconciliation outweighed the fear of further conflict. I yearned to bridge the gap that had formed between us, to find understanding amidst the chaos of our shared experience.

With each passing minute, the resolve within me solidified. I knew I couldn't let this opportunity slip through my fingers, for the chance to rebuild what had been shattered was too precious to ignore. The public execution, with its charged atmosphere and communal gathering, felt like the perfect stage to confront the past and pave the way for a brighter future.

5

The Reason

In the solitude of my bedroom, I lay naked in bed, allowing my skin to breathe, seeking solace in the cool night air that caressed my wounds. Sleep evaded me, as restlessness gripped my mind, stirring questions that spun in relentless circles.

Why did I bear these wounds upon my body? Though I did not recall causing harm to anyone, a nagging sense of responsibility gnawed at the edges of my consciousness. The scars etched upon my skin were a haunting reminder of past wrongdoings, yet the memories eluded me. It was as if my transgressions had been buried deep within my subconscious, waiting to be unearthed.

With a sigh, I untangled myself from the sheets, my bare feet meeting the cool wooden floor as I stood and made my way to the window. The darkness outside was illuminated by the shimmering stars that adorned the night sky, their distant light casting an ethereal glow upon my skin.

In the soft embrace of starlight, a gradual realization began to take hold. The wounds that adorned my body were not random markings of fate, but rather manifestations of a deeper conflict within my heart. They were the physical toll of my dissent, a reflection of the disapproval that simmered within me for the ways of Fleshbourne.

As I stood by the window, bathed in the gentle radiance of the stars, I traced the intricate patterns of my scars. The realization unfolded slowly, like a delicate dance between memory and understanding. It became clear that my wounds were not inflicted by external forces, but by the very core of my being—the disapproval that coursed through my heart.

This gradual revelation weighed heavily upon me, settling like a heavy fog within my thoughts. I grappled with the knowledge that my opposition to the traditions of Fleshbourne had left its mark upon my skin. The scars, a physical reminder of my dissent, had become a secret I guarded fiercely, for fear of the consequences they might bring.

Yet, the sleepless nights, the questions that spun relentlessly, and the gentle touch of starlight had stripped away the layers of denial. They had urged me to confront the truth that had eluded me for so long. The wounds I bore were not simply a consequence of unknown actions, but a result of my unwavering disapproval for the ways of Fleshbourne.

In the quiet of the night, surrounded by the stars that whispered tales of distant galaxies, I grappled with the weight of this newfound understanding. The scars upon my skin became symbols of the internal conflict I waged, the battle between my dissenting heart and the society that deemed me a wrongdoer.

With each passing moment, the gravity of my realization intensified, fuelling the fire of resistance within me. The forthcoming public execution, a recurring ritual that perpetuated the violence I disdained, loomed on the horizon. It would serve as the stage upon which I would confront the traditions that clashed with my beliefs, to challenge the status quo and seek a path toward a more compassionate future.

With newfound clarity, I began to prepare, harnessing the strength derived from my understanding of the wounds that adorned my body. The sleepless night had birthed a revelation, awakening a defiant spirit within me that would not be silenced. The scars, once concealed, became symbols of resilience and determination, driving me forward on a journey to reshape the narrative that had cast me as a wrongdoer.

In the embrace of the starlit night, I resolved to navigate the uncertain path that lay ahead, guided by the unwavering beat of my dissenting heart. The sleepless night had birthed a profound realization—an understanding that the scars I carried were not just marks of past transgressions, but reminders of my unwavering commitment to reshape the world around me.

With conviction pulsating through my veins, I returned to the bed, the coolness of the sheets now a sanctuary for my weary body. A renewed sense of purpose coursed through me, aligning with the echoes of dissent that reverberated within my heart.

As I closed my eyes, a kaleidoscope of images danced behind my eyelids. Visions of the public execution, the gathering storm of condemnation, and the intricate web of traditions that governed Fleshbourne played out in my mind. It was within this vivid tapestry that I understood the true significance of my wounds. They were not simply physical marks, but the embodiment of my resistance against the oppressive norms and the violence that plagued our society.

The scars, etched upon my skin like a map of rebellion, symbolized the price I had paid for holding true to my dissenting beliefs. Each mark spoke volumes of the battles fought within the depths of my soul, battles that sought to challenge the unjust practices that had shaped our lives. In a world that condemned those who dared to question, my wounds became a defiant testament to the unwavering flame of defiance that burned within me.

With every heartbeat, the memory of my past transgressions, though still clouded, grew clearer. I had not caused physical harm to others, but my refusal to conform to the traditions of Fleshbourne was considered a transgression in itself. The disapproval that simmered within my heart, the vehement dissent against the violence we perpetuated, had manifested in these scars.

The weight of responsibility settled upon me, an acknowledgement of the role I played in challenging the status quo. Though my memories remained fragmented, the undeniable truth of my defiance pulsed through my veins. I was a disruptor of the established order, a catalyst for change amidst a sea of conformity.

Yet, even as the fire of resistance burned bright within me, a flicker of apprehension flickered in the depths of my consciousness. What would this newfound clarity mean for my meeting with Joseph? Would he understand the depths of my dissent, or would he be caught in the crossfire of my defiance?

Questions spun in relentless circles, intermingling with the certainty that burned within me. But I knew that I could not waver in my resolve. The forthcoming public execution would serve as the stage upon which I would confront the traditions that suffocated our souls. It would be an act of defiance and an opportunity to sow the seeds of change, to rally others who silently shared my dissent.

As I surrendered to the embrace of sleep, I carried with me a sense of purpose and a determination that transcended the realm of dreams. The scars upon my skin, now more than ever, held a profound significance. They were a visual testament to the battles fought, the price paid, and the unwavering commitment to reshape the world around me.

In the depths of the night, I found solace in the knowledge that I was not alone. There were others who shared my dissent, others who longed for a world free from the cycle of violence and condemnation. With their silent support, and the strength born from the understanding of my wounds, I was ready to face the forthcoming storm, to challenge the traditions that had cast me as a wrongdoer, and to ignite the spark of change in the hearts of those who dared to dream of a better future.

6

The Second Execution

As the days melted into one another, a week had passed since the last public execution, and the city of Fleshbourne had continued its relentless march forward. In the wake of that fateful day, the ebb and flow of life had carried on, marking the passage of time with a tapestry of ordinary events.

The streets had witnessed a parade of faces, each one a mere fragment of a story, lost among the multitude. Conversations had been exchanged in hushed tones, a symphony of whispers that fluttered through the air, their secrets hidden within the folds of anonymity.

In the days that followed, the sun had risen and set, casting its golden hues upon the cityscape. Shopkeepers had opened their doors, their wares enticing passersby with promises of novelty and escape. Laughter and the clinking of glasses had spilled out from the taverns, intertwining with the melodies that drifted from street musicians, creating a vibrant harmony that momentarily drowned the echoes of dissent.

Life had continued its relentless dance, seemingly unfazed by the undercurrent of tension that swirled beneath its surface. Yet, for those with a keen eye, glimpses of restlessness flickered like sparks in the darkened corners. The city's inhabitants had grappled with their own inner turmoil, their hopes and fears entangled in a delicate balance.

Amidst the backdrop of these mundane events, I had watched the days pass with a growing sense of purpose. The forthcoming public execution loomed on the horizon, a looming spectre that hung heavy in the collective consciousness. Its approach had stirred a renewed determination within me, fuelling my resolve to seek out Joseph, to mend the wounds that had severed our friendship, and to find solace in the midst of uncertainty.

With each passing day, my thoughts had been consumed by the questions that plagued my mind. What had become of Joseph? How had the burn we both felt affected him? These inquiries had become a steady rhythm, pulsating in the depths of my being, driving me to embark on a quest for answers.

In the quiet solitude of my thoughts, I had imagined our encounter, replaying different scenarios in my mind. I yearned for the opportunity to bridge the chasm that had separated us, to find forgiveness in his eyes and offer my own. The desire to see him had become intertwined with the urgency to make amends, to rekindle the bonds that had once tethered us together.

Now, as the day of the execution dawned, a blend of anticipation and anxiety coursed through my veins. The clock ticked relentlessly, its steady rhythm echoing the fleeting moments that remained before the event would unfold. The city seemed to hold its breath, as if bracing for the climax of the ritual that had become a recurring spectacle.

In the depths of my being, the desire to find Joseph burned brighter than ever. It mingled with the resolve to challenge the traditions that had cast us as wrongdoers, to confront the cycle of violence that had permeated our lives. The forthcoming public execution would be more than a display of judgment; it would serve as a crucible where the embers of friendship and dissent could be reignited.

With these thoughts as my guide, I ventured forth into the city streets, my footsteps measured and purposeful. The echoes of the past week's events reverberated within me, painting a backdrop of memories and emotions. As the world around me prepared for the unfolding spectacle, I remained steadfast in my determination to seek out Joseph, to mend what had been broken, and to uncover the truth behind the burn that had united us in an enigmatic bond.

As the city awakened to the day's crescendo, I embarked upon my journey, propelled by a singular purpose. The sun's gentle rays bathed the streets in a golden glow, as if illuminating the path that lay ahead. The stage was set, the pieces were in motion, and the convergence of fate and reconciliation beckoned from beyond the horizon.

In the midst of the preparations for the impending public execution, a surge of determination and a glimmer of hope propelled me forward. This time, I chose a different ensemble, carefully selecting an outfit that would veil the wounds etched upon my skin, while still allowing me to move with a sense of purpose.

The clothing I chose was an intricately designed cloak, adorned with flowing sleeves and a high collar that gracefully framed my face. Its deep, rich hues mirrored the shadows that danced beneath the surface of my scars, a secret language shared only between me and the fabric that enveloped my body. The cloak, though concealing, also carried an air of mystery and resilience, its layers whispering of the battles fought and the strength that pulsed within.

As I stood before the bathroom mirror, the room bathed in soft, diffused light, I watched my reflection with a mix of trepidation and hope. The scars, now concealed beneath the layers of my chosen attire, were hidden from view but ever present, serving as a reminder of the journey I had undertaken. With each careful adjustment, I ensured the fabric fell just so, veiling the marks of dissent that adorned my body.

The reflection that stared back at me bore the weight of a broken friendship, the remnants of a connection that had been strained by the burn we both felt. In the depths of my being, I carried a yearning to mend what had been fractured, to find Joseph and seek solace in the possibility of making amends. But amidst these hopes, there lingered an underlying worry, a gnawing concern that his touch had sparked a painful realization of the wounds I carried.

As I gazed into my own eyes, searching for the strength to face the impending public execution, a sense of déjà vu washed over me. The mirror, once again, became a threshold between worlds. In its reflection, I glimpsed the echoes of the past preparations, the layers of concealment and the spirit of defiance that had burned within me. It was a familiar dance, yet imbued with the renewed determination that now coursed through my veins.

With a steadying breath, I steeled myself for the journey ahead. The execution grounds awaited, a convergence of fates and a stage for transformation. But before stepping into the tumultuous current of the city streets, I whispered a silent plea to the universe, hoping that fate would guide my path to Joseph, granting us the opportunity to heal the wounds of our broken friendship.

As I left the sanctuary of the bathroom, the echoes of my

hopes resonated within me. The cloak, a shroud of concealment and strength, flowed around me as I stepped into the world outside. The streets of Fleshbourne greeted me once more, their familiar tapestry of life and anticipation. The scent of freshly bloomed roses mingled with the subtle undertone of anxiety that lingered in the air.

I walked among the bustling crowds, a solitary figure cloaked in the embrace of my chosen attire. The layers of fabric shielded my scars from prying eyes, preserving the secrets they held within. Each step carried a mixture of purpose and anticipation, as I weaved through the throng, searching for any sign of Joseph.

The forthcoming public execution loomed on the horizon, an occasion that held both the weight of tradition and the possibility of redemption. With each passing moment, my heart beat with renewed determination, fuelled by the desire to find Joseph, to mend the rift that had torn us apart, and to ensure his well-being in the face of the burning touch that had shaken us both.

As I navigated the streets, glimpses of familiar faces danced at the periphery of my vision, but none belonged to Joseph. The search for him became an undercurrent within the tide of anticipation, a whisper of longing that threaded through my thoughts. And though uncertainty lingered, the determination to confront the traditions that had cast us as wrongdoers remained steadfast.

With each step toward the execution grounds, the weight of anticipation settled upon my shoulders, mingling with the echoes of hope and reconciliation. The cloak I wore, a symbol of resilience and concealment, held within its folds the dreams of redemption and the yearning to find solace in the presence of a once cherished friend.

As the final moments before the execution drew near, I steeled myself for the convergence of fate and resolution. The scars concealed beneath my chosen attire pulsated, reminding me of the battles fought, the wounds borne, and the strength that resided within. The forthcoming spectacle would be an opportunity for transformation, a stage where the threads of broken friendships and defiant dissent would intertwine.

With each passing heartbeat, I prepared myself to face the storm that awaited, driven by a burning resolve to challenge the traditions that suffocated our souls. The search for Joseph would continue, woven into the fabric of my purpose. For in his presence, I hoped to find not only the chance to mend our fractured connection but also a glimpse of understanding—a glimpse that would shed light on the burn we both felt and the wounds that bound us in a shared destiny.

7

Trapped In A Spider's Web

As I made my way towards the site of the second public execution, the atmosphere buzzed with a mix of curiosity and trepidation. The weather, too, played its part in setting the tone. Dark clouds loomed overhead, casting intermittent shadows over the streets, while gusts of wind swept through, tugging at coats and scarves.

The town centre was a whirlwind of activity, bustling with the townspeople who had gathered to witness the unfolding spectacle. The streets were alive with the hum of conversation, a tapestry of voices that blended into a vibrant mosaic of everyday life. Families strolled hand-in-hand, their children's eyes wide with a mix of wonder and innocence.

I caught snippets of dialogue as I navigated the crowded thoroughfares. A group of friends chatted animatedly about the upcoming event, their voices filled with a mixture of curiosity and unease. "I heard there are multiple wrongdoers this time," one of them whispered conspiratorially. "Their identities are hidden behind masks until the Scourge reveals them on the stage."

A couple walking arm in arm exchanged nervous glances. "It's unsettling, isn't it?" the woman remarked, her voice tinged with uncertainty. "I wonder what they've done to deserve such a fate."

As we inched closer to the town centre, the crowd grew denser. The sound of footsteps echoed in harmony with the distant rumble of thunder. The anticipation was palpable, a tangible energy that filled the air. Strangers stood shoulder to shoulder, their gazes fixed on the central stage, awaiting the arrival of the Scourge and the masked wrongdoers.

My thoughts, however, were consumed with the hope of finding Joseph among the sea of faces. I yearned for the opportunity to mend the frayed threads of our friendship, to understand the pain that had driven us apart. Yet, as the crowd pressed closer, I found myself caught in a river of anonymous souls, their identities hidden behind masks, blending into a collective mass.

With every step, the weight of the occasion settled upon me. The impending public execution represented more than just the punishment of a few individuals—it was a stark reminder of the delicate balance between order and chaos that governed our lives. The swirling emotions within me mirrored the tempestuous sky above, both filled with a sense of gravity and uncertainty.

As we finally reached the town centre, the stage stood as a grand centrepiece, adorned with banners and symbols of authority. The crowd hushed, a collective silence descending upon us. All eyes turned toward the stage, awaiting the arrival of the Scourge and the masked wrongdoers to face judgment.

In that moment, I stood amidst a sea of strangers, united in our shared fascination and curiosity. The imminent execution, with its inherent gravity, loomed before us like a spectre. It was a stark reminder of the power held by the Scourge and the consequences that awaited those who strayed from the accepted path.

My heart raced with a mix of anticipation and apprehension.

The stage was set, and the unfolding drama would reveal the truths hidden within the shadows of Fleshbourne. Amidst the multiple masked wrongdoers, I hoped to find not only the answers to the mysteries surrounding them but also the opportunity to rekindle a fractured friendship and seek redemption for the dissent that simmered within my own heart.

****

"Ladies and gentlemen of Fleshbourne, today, gathered under the bright gaze of the sun, we, the Scourge, stand before you on this solemn occasion—the second public execution. As stewards of justice, bound by the laws and traditions that have safeguarded the sanctity of our city for generations, we address you with a shared purpose.

In the grand tapestry of Fleshbourne's history, our laws have been etched as the foundation of our society. They stand as a beacon of order, ensuring that harmony prevails and that transgressors face their rightful fate. Our ways may seem harsh to some, but they are the necessary fabric that weaves us together as a united community.

Today, there is a transgressor among us, one who has committed the gravest of actions. You may wonder how we, the Scourge, have come to know of this transgressor, hidden in plain sight among the crowd. The answer lies in the depth of their dissent—their hatred for the ways of Fleshbourne.

To hate the very essence of our city, to harbour feelings of disdain for our traditions and laws, is the greatest transgression one can commit. It is a venom that seeps into the heart and festers, threatening the unity that holds our community together.

It is this hatred, this defiance against our way of life, that allowed us, the Scourge, to discern the presence of the biggest transgressor among you.

We bear the mark of knowledge, a keen insight into the souls of the citizens of Fleshbourne. And with this mark, we have found those who associate with the biggest transgressor, for they bear a unique wound, a symbol of their connection.

As we stand here today, ready to unveil the transgressor's identity, we implore you to heed the warning. For anyone found to be in association with the biggest transgressor shall be marked as well, a scarlet letter of sorts, highlighting the presence of this defiance in our midst.

In the face of such hatred, it is our solemn duty to preserve the harmony that defines us. The path to redemption lies in loyalty and submission to the ways of Fleshbourne. Those who dare to defy, who harbour rebellion within their hearts, shall face the consequences of their actions.

And so, citizens of Fleshbourne, we beseech you to remain vigilant. Let the fate of this wrongdoer serve as a warning, a reminder that our city's laws are immutable, and our traditions are sacrosanct. Let this day be etched into your memory, a testament to the consequences that await those who dare to challenge the very fabric of our existence.

As the Scourge, we pledge to uphold the laws that have guided us for generations. We will ensure that order is preserved, that justice is meted out, and that dissent is quelled. Let this execution be a solemn reminder that the path to redemption lies in loyalty and submission to the ways of Fleshbourne.

May the brightness of the sun bear witness to our unwavering commitment to these principles. May its rays illuminate our path, guiding us towards a future where harmony prevails, and the dark whispers of rebellion are silenced.

And to the biggest transgressor who stands among us, may you finally come to understand the gravity of your transgression. Your fate awaits you, and there shall be no escape from the web of justice that now ensnares you. May this execution be a sobering reminder of the consequences that await those who dare to defy the traditions of Fleshbourne."

****

As the words of the Scourge echo through the air, a surge of panic courses through me. My heart pounds in my chest, and a cold sweat breaks out on my forehead. They know. They know about my dissent, my defiance against the ways of Fleshbourne. The realization hits me like a hammer, and I feel exposed, vulnerable in a sea of onlookers.

The crowd around me begins to murmur, their voices a cacophony of curiosity and fear. Whispers float through the air, eyes darting around, searching for any signs of guilt. I keep my head down, trying to appear inconspicuous, but inside, I am trembling with trepidation.

"Silence!" The Scourge shouts, their voices amplified by a strange sense of authority that compels the crowd to hush. "Let the justice of Fleshbourne prevail."

The crowd falls silent, but their eyes remain fixated on the line of wrongdoers on the stage. The Scourge moves with a deliberate pace, their dark cloaks swirling like shadows as they approach the first person to the right.

With a swift motion, the Scourge removes the mask, and a gasp ripples through the crowd. It's someone else, a wrongdoer with a face unknown to me. The Scourge continues down the line, unveiling one wrongdoer after another, each face distinct from the last.

The stage before me feels like an abyss, and my mind swirls

with a mixture of emotions—regret, fear, and a glimmer of hope. Hope that somehow, amidst the darkness and uncertainty, a sliver of redemption might still be possible.

And in that moment, as the dramatic scene unfolds, I can't help but wonder what lies ahead—what price must be paid for daring to defy the ways of Fleshbourne.

Then, the Scourge's hand hovers over the next mask, and with a breath held tight, they slowly lift it, exposing the face beneath.

It's Joseph.

8

Unveiled Concealment

As the mask falls away, revealing Joseph's face, the crowd gasps in surprise and shock. Joseph stands on the stage, trembling with fear and sorrow etched across his features. His deep-set eyes, usually warm and welcoming, now appear clouded with anguish and vulnerability. They speak of a soul burdened by the weight of the world and a spirit crushed by the fear of the Scourge's judgment.

His hair, usually neatly combed, now appears dishevelled, mirroring the tumultuous emotions he must be experiencing. Each strand seems to tremble with his unease, as if trying to convey the overwhelming fear that grips his heart.

Joseph's once sturdy physique now appears frail, as if the weight of the city's condemnation has taken a physical toll on him. His shoulders slump under the weight of his despair, and his once-confident stance is now replaced by a posture of defeat.

But it is not just Joseph's fearful demeanour that captivates the crowd; it is the extraordinary wound that slithers around his torso and chest that leaves us in awe and disbelief. The wound, shaped like a serpent, serves as a haunting reminder of his transgression. It coils around him like a spectre, a constant reminder of the consequences that await those who challenge the city's authority.

The serpent-like wound appears to move almost imperceptibly, as if in sync with Joseph's trembling breaths, intensifying the eerie and sombre atmosphere that surrounds him. It is a sight that evokes sympathy and sorrow, a stark reminder of the price he must pay for dissent.

As Joseph stands there, his wound exposed for all to see, the crowd is filled with a mixture of curiosity and compassion. We are witness to a man who once lived among us, now marked by a punishment unlike any other, a symbol of the sorrowful path he now walks.

The revelation of Joseph's wound only deepens the sense of sorrow among the spectators. His terror and sorrow resonate with the collective conscience of the crowd, reminding us all of the fragility of life and the relentless grip of the city's traditions.

As the truth of Joseph's identity sinks in, a chilling realization washes over me like an icy wave. I am the biggest transgressor—the one who dares to hate the rules of Fleshbourne. The gravity of my dissent, my disapproval of the city's traditions, has marked me as the very embodiment of defiance.

The burn I felt when Joseph touched me, now I understand its significance. It was a warning, a symbolic manifestation of the consequences of associating with me. Joseph's betrayal to the Scourge is now laid bare before my eyes. By befriending me, he too has become entangled in the web of transgression.

I can feel Joseph's stare burning into my soul, his eyes like an abyss of sorrow and betrayal. It sends shivers down my spine, for I know that he holds the truth of my identity—the biggest transgressor, the one who hates the ways of Fleshbourne.

The air is thick with tension and anticipation as the Scourge makes their cruel decision. They decide to begin with Joseph's execution, using him as a warning to anyone who would dare associate with the biggest transgressor.

The masked figures surround Joseph, their cold eyes locked on his trembling form. One of them taunts him with a sardonic smirk, asking, "Any last words?"

Joseph's voice quivers with fear and defiance as he responds, "I know who the biggest transgressor is."

****

As Joseph's revelation hangs in the air, a heavy silence envelops the stage. The Scourge, taken aback by his words, exchange glances, their masked faces betraying no emotion. They seem momentarily uncertain, as if grappling with the unexpected turn of events.

In an instant, Joseph is dragged to the centre of the stage, his trembling form now framed against the backdrop of darkness and despair. The Scourge's cruel intentions are evident as they brandish a burning hot metal rod, a menacing threat placed mere inches away from him.

"Who is the biggest transgressor?" one of the Scourge demands, their voice laced with cold malice.

Joseph's gaze, now filled with a mixture of sorrow and hatred, locks onto me. His arm trembles as he lifts it, attempting to point in my direction. His intent is clear, and his final act is one of betrayal—a desperate attempt to save himself at the cost of exposing me.

But just before his finger can reach the direction of where I stand in the crowd, the Scourge show no hesitation. The metal rod is brutally shoved into Joseph's torso, the searing pain piercing his body. A gut-wrenching cry escapes his lips as he writhes in agony.

The crowd watches in horror, their faces contorted with shock and terror at the brutal display before them. In that moment, Joseph's act of betrayal is halted, his attempt to save himself from the Scourge's wrath silenced by their merciless response.

As the metal rod is withdrawn, Joseph slumps to the ground, blood pooling around him. The Scourge's message is clear—there is no escape from the consequences of dissent, no sanctuary for those who dare to oppose the ways of Fleshbourne.

As Joseph's lifeless body lies on the stage, the weight of his sacrifice suffocates me, and a wave of overwhelming sorrow crashes over my soul. The Scourge's harsh shouts pierce through the air, demanding that I be seized, as there are still others yet to witness their merciless fate.

The urgency to escape grips me, and I turn on my heels, desperately pushing through the dense crowd that surrounds me. Panic courses through my veins, and I feel the hands of strangers reaching out, attempting to stop me. With every step I take, more grasp onto me, their desperate grip tearing at my cloak and clothes.

"Stop! Seize him!" the Scourge's voices ring out, fuelling the frenzy around me. The crowd, once docile witnesses to the public execution, transforms into a sea of chaos and confusion. Fear paints their faces, but I cannot be deterred—I must flee this nightmarish scene.

With a heart pounding like a drum, I fight against the tide of people, my breaths coming in ragged gasps. Sweat beads on my forehead, mixing with tears of grief and terror. The world around me blurs, my vision narrowed by the desperate need to escape the clutches of the Scourge.

The once pristine streets of Fleshbourne now become a

treacherous maze, my path obstructed by the very people I once called neighbours. Some try to reason with me, believing my escape to be futile, but I push forward, fuelled by the memory of Joseph's haunting stare and the torment of his final moments.

As the crowd's desperation intensifies, so does mine. I break free from one grip only to be ensnared by another, my cloak and clothes tattered from the relentless hands that grasp at me. Each tear in my garments echoes the breaking of my heart—Joseph's sacrifice tearing at the very fabric of my soul.

In my frantic attempt to escape, I stumble and trip over a protruding cobblestone, and before I can regain my footing, a Scourge seizes me by my torn shirt. The force of their grip causes an even bigger rip, and in that moment, my concealed wounds are exposed to the world.

Gasps and murmurs ripple through the crowd as my secret is laid bare. I feel a burning sensation, not just from the exposed wound, but from the crowd's realization that I am the biggest transgressor—the one who dares to hate the ways of Fleshbourne.

The Scourge's grip on my shirt tightens, their masked faces filled with malice and glee at having caught the elusive wrongdoer. Fear courses through me, and I struggle to break free, but his hold is unyielding.

"Look! The biggest transgressor stands before us!" he shouts, his voice dripping with triumph.

As the crowd's attention shifts to me, I am enveloped in a mix of shame, defiance, and a resolve to escape their clutches. But it is too late. The revelation of my true identity as the one who despises the ways of Fleshbourne seals my fate.

In the distance, I catch a glimpse of a narrow alleyway, a sanctuary away from the brutal scene that unfolds before me. My heart soars with hope, but the rest of the Scourges' shouts grow louder, their footsteps closing in. I cannot afford to falter, for to be captured now would mean sharing Joseph's tragic fate.

Summoning every ounce of strength and determination within me, I surge forward once more, this time fuelled not just by the need to escape but also by the burden of my dissent. The alleyway draws nearer, a glimmer of hope amidst the darkness that engulfs me.

The crowd becomes a blur of faces, each pair of eyes reflecting both fear and condemnation. I am not alone in my desire to distance myself from the execution, but in this moment of frantic escape, I feel the weight of the city's judgment pressing upon me. The world seems to shrink around me, the walls of Fleshbourne closing in as if to suffocate the life out of me.

As I dash towards the narrow alleyway, my heart pounding in my chest, the scourge that had seized me shouts at the top of their lungs, "After them! Do not let the biggest transgressor escape!" Their voice reverberates through the chaos, and three other scourge spring into action, their eyes ablaze with determination.

"Get them! Catch the transgressor!" one of the pursuing scourge yells, their masked face twisted in fury.

The crowd erupts into a frenzy, parting to make way for the scourge as they chase after me. Fear and panic spread like wildfire, and I can hear the desperate murmurs of onlookers as they try to make sense of the sudden chaos.

The pursuing scourge are swift, their movements honed by years of enforcing the city's oppressive laws. They are cloaked in dark, tattered garments, their faces hidden behind intimidating masks that embody the cruelty of their role. Their footsteps echo in the narrow streets, driving me to run even faster.

I can feel their presence closing in, their determination to capture the biggest transgressor evident in every step they take. Their footsteps seem to resonate through the very ground, as if the city itself aids them in their relentless pursuit.

The alleyway beckons to me like a fleeting sanctuary, but I know I cannot afford to slow down. I must stay ahead of my pursuers, no matter the cost. My body aches, and my breaths are ragged, but the fear of capture propels me forward.

"Stop! You cannot escape the Scourge!" one of the pursuing scourge calls out, their voice laced with malice.

Their threats only fuel my resolve, and I push myself to the limit, my legs carrying me faster and faster. The cityscape blurs around me as I navigate through the winding alleys, my every sense attuned to the pursuit behind me.

The narrow passageways seem to close in on me, the walls and buildings towering like menacing sentinels. My cloak flutters behind me, a torn remnant of my previous life. The pursuit is relentless, the scourge showing no signs of relenting in their quest to capture the biggest transgressor.

"Corner them! Don't let them escape!" another scourge commands, their voice harsh and unforgiving.

As I turn a sharp corner, my eyes widen in terror. The path ahead leads to a dead end—a wall of bricks and mortar sealing my fate. The realization that there is no escape sets in, and a sense of resignation washes over me.

In this moment of despair, I glance around, hoping for a miracle or a hidden escape route. But there is none. I am cornered, surrounded by the very embodiment of the city's oppressive laws.

The pursuing scourge approach with predatory grace, their faces masked, and their movements calculated. I can see the flicker of sadistic satisfaction in their eyes, relishing the capture of the biggest transgressor.

Fear consumes me, but it is not just for my own life—it is for the fate that awaits me and the city that seeks to crush all those who dare to dissent. In this moment of desperation, I know that my fate is sealed, but the fire of dissent within me refuses to be extinguished.

In the midst of the chaos and frenzy, my eyes catch a glimmer of hope—a narrow gap between the buildings on either side of the dead-end alleyway. Without a moment's hesitation, I throw myself towards the tight space, feeling the rough bricks scrape against my skin. The pursuing scourge are momentarily caught off guard, providing me with a precious few seconds of advantage.

I wriggle and wiggle through the confined passageway, my heart pounding in my chest and my breaths coming in short gasps. The narrowness of the path threatens to suffocate me, but I refuse to be defeated. Adrenaline courses through my veins, propelling me onward, my determination unyielding.

In the midst of my desperate escape, the narrow gap between the buildings proves to be both a lifeline and a torment. As I wriggle and squeeze through, the rough bricks scrape against my skin, causing my exposed wounds to reopen. A searing pain shoots through me as fresh blood trickles from the wounds, leaving a trail behind me.

With every movement, the bleeding worsens, creating a crimson testimony to the intensity of my pursuit. Each drop of blood feels like a weight, a reminder of the sacrifices made in the name of rebellion.

Despite the pain, I refuse to slow down. The determination to escape the scourge and the oppressive grip of Fleshbourne propels me forward, even as my body protests. The adrenaline and urgency coursing through my veins drown out the discomfort, and I continue to press on.

Emerging on the other side of the narrow passageway, I find

myself gasping for breath. The wounds on my skin throb with pain, but I dare not stop to tend to them. The pursuing scourge are relentless, and the sense of danger pushes me to keep running.

As I sprint through the labyrinthine streets, the bleeding becomes a stark reminder of the cost of my dissent. The cityscape blurs around me, but the pain serves as a constant companion, urging me to remain vigilant and resolute.

Each step takes me further from the clutches of the scourge, but the weight of my defiance grows heavier with each passing moment. The bleeding wounds symbolize the sacrifices made in the pursuit of change, a vivid representation of the struggles endured by those who dare to challenge the oppressive norms.

I can feel the gazes of the pursuing scourge on my back, and the knowledge that I am being hunted adds an additional layer of urgency to my escape.

As I run through the labyrinthine streets of Fleshbourne, my mind races with a singular focus—to escape the clutches of the scourge and the oppressive grip of the city. With each step, my heart pounds in my chest, and the pain of my bleeding wounds serves as a constant reminder of the sacrifices made in the name of dissent.

I have no destination in mind, no plan or route to follow. All I know is that I must keep running, keep moving forward, away from the dangers that lurk behind me. The city seems to close in on me, its towering structures and claustrophobic alleyways becoming a labyrinth of confusion and fear.

But just when I feel the weight of hopelessness bearing down on me, a sight emerges on the horizon—Fleshbourne's imposing gates. They stand tall and formidable, a testament to the city's determination to keep its inhabitants in and the world outside at bay.

The gates are massive, adorned with intricate carvings and engravings that depict the city's history and traditions. They loom over me like guardians, silent sentinels that have witnessed countless executions and acts of compliance.

Stretching on either side of the gates are towering walls that encircle the parameters of the city. They seem to extend infinitely, an unyielding barrier that holds the city's secrets and horrors within its grasp. The walls, too, bear scars of past transgressions—perhaps even echoes of dissenters who dared to challenge the city's ways.

As I draw closer to the gates, the sheer size of them fills me with both awe and dread. They serve as a symbol of my confinement, a reminder of the oppressive rules and traditions that have cast me as the biggest transgressor.

Yet, as my eyes settle on the gates, a flicker of determination ignites within me. Beyond those walls lies the world outside—a world free from the cycle of violence and condemnation. With each step, I move closer to the possibility of a new beginning, a chance to reshape my fate and challenge the oppressive norms that have suffocated me for so long.

The gates of Fleshbourne come into clearer view, and as I approach them, I can almost feel the weight of history pressing down upon me. But I do not falter. I run with a renewed sense of purpose, with the conviction that there is more to life than the suffocating confines of this city.

As I near the gates, a mix of emotions swirl within me—fear and hope, uncertainty and determination. But one thing is certain—I will not be silenced, and I will not back down. The sight of the gates spurs me on, pushing me to break free from the shackles of the past and embrace the unknown that lies beyond.

With a final burst of energy, I reach the gates, my breaths ragged and my heart pounding. I pause for a moment, my hand reaching out to touch the cold metal, as if seeking reassurance and strength.

The imposing structure looms before me, a threshold between the world I've known and the unknown that beckons beyond.

But as I grasp the cold metal bars of the gate, a sudden chill runs down my spine. I glance back, and to my horror, the Scourge are only a few meters away, closing in with determined glares and weapons gleaming menacingly in the fading light.

Their faces betray emotions of anger and frustration, their furious pursuit betraying the gravity of my transgression. The urgency in their shouts pierces the air like thunder, warning me that my defiance will not go unpunished.

"Stop right there, transgressor!"

"Your fate is sealed!"

Their words fuel my desperation to escape, knowing that they will show no mercy. I have become the embodiment of their fear—the biggest transgressor, an enemy of the city's oppressive traditions.

With trembling hands, I fumble with the lock of the gate, pushing it open with all my strength. The metal creaks in protest, as if resisting my departure, but I refuse to be deterred.

As I step beyond the city's walls, a mix of fear and hope courses through me. The world outside is vast and unknown, but it also promises the chance to be free from the violence and condemnation of Fleshbourne.

But just as I dare to imagine a life beyond, I feel a searing pain on my back. A Scourge had managed to catch up and slashed me with their weapon, leaving a painful wound that burns like fire.

Ignoring the pain, I push forward, knowing that I can't slow down. The gates behind me seem to taunt me, the opening closing in slow motion as the Scourge draw near.

In this moment of frantic escape, I can't help but wonder if I'll ever truly be free from the city's grasp. The pain in my back serves as a constant reminder that the scars of my dissent will not be easily forgotten...

As I run into the unknown, the world blurs around me, my mind consumed by the chase and the hope of salvation. I can only pray that my defiance will not be in vain, and that the scars of my escape will eventually heal, leaving me with the freedom to shape my own destiny.

9

Ruins

My heart races like a wild stallion as I continue my mad dash away from the gates of Fleshbourne. Every beat echoes in my ears, a relentless reminder of the danger that lurks behind me. I dare not slow my pace, for I know that the Scourge's watchful eyes are fixed on my every move. Despite their momentary hesitation, I cannot afford to underestimate their tenacity.

As I steal a glance over my shoulder, my breath catches in my throat. The Scourge stand motionless, like dark sentinels guarding the city's boundaries. It's as if they are taunting me, knowing that I can't outrun them forever. Though they haven't taken a step past the gates, their ominous presence looms over me like a shadow.

"They will surely find a way to get me," I mutter to myself, my voice barely audible against the sound of my frantic footsteps. I have dared to challenge the ways of Fleshbourne, to question the authority of the Scourge, and now I must face the consequences of my defiance.

With renewed determination, I push myself to run even faster, my legs burning with exhaustion. I try to put as much distance between me and the city as possible, hoping that the vast and desolate lands beyond will offer some semblance of sanctuary.

The landscape around me is a blur of earth and sky, the colours blending together in a dizzying whirlwind. The once familiar path is now unrecognizable, an endless expanse of barren wasteland that stretches into the horizon. The world around me seems to shrink, focusing only on the single objective of escape.

I can still feel the Scourge's gaze upon me, their watchful eyes like daggers piercing through the distance. It's only a matter of time before they decide to pursue me, and I must find a way to evade their relentless pursuit.

Every ounce of my being is focused on survival, on finding a way to outwit the Scourge and forge a new path beyond the city's grasp. The adrenaline coursing through my veins fuels my determination, driving me forward even as fatigue threatens to consume me.

As I continue to run, the landscape changes once again. The barren wasteland gives way to a rugged terrain, dotted with rocky outcrops and ancient ruins. The ruins loom like silent witnesses of a forgotten past, offering a glimpse into a history that has long been erased from the collective memory.

With each step, the sense of isolation deepens, and I can't help but feel like a lone wanderer in a world devoid of life. Yet, amidst the desolation, there is a glimmer of hope. Perhaps the ruins hold secrets that can aid my escape, or perhaps there are others who have also sought refuge beyond the city's walls.

Driven by a potent mix of fear and determination, I push myself to keep running, to keep searching for a sanctuary that will shield me from the relentless pursuit of the Scourge. I know that the path ahead is fraught with uncertainty, but I refuse to surrender to the darkness that threatens to consume me.

As I run, the echoes of my own footsteps become a symphony of defiance, a testament to the strength of my will and the unyielding spirit that refuses to be broken. With each stride, I carve my own path, determined to find a future free from the shackles of Fleshbourne's oppressive rule.

As I run, fatigue creeps up on me like a relentless spectre, its icy fingers gripping at the edges of my consciousness. My breaths become ragged gasps, and the ground beneath my feet seems to sway like a ship lost at sea. The world around me blurs into a hazy fog, and my mind is filled with a cacophony of thoughts that seem to echo and twist like ethereal whispers.

Light-headedness embraces me, swirling like a wisp of smoke, clouding my vision and leaving me disoriented. It's as if reality itself has become a distant dream, and I am merely a fleeting shadow chasing after elusive hopes. My body feels weightless, and my movements become erratic, like a marionette with frayed strings.

Amidst this surreal haze, my attention is drawn to my bleeding wounds and torn clothing. The wounds, like crimson petals unfurling, paint a vivid tapestry of pain and resilience upon my skin. Each drop of blood becomes a poignant storyteller, tracing the paths of suffering etched across my body. They fall like heavy raindrops, merging with the dusty ground, leaving a trail of distress in their wake.

The thick, oozing blood seems to have a life of its own, a dark and relentless force that defies my attempts to staunch its flow. It seeps from the wounds like molten rivers, eager to escape their confines and find release upon the unforgiving terrain. With each heartbeat, the crimson rivulets glisten in the fading light, a poignant reminder of my vulnerability and the battle I wage within.

The pain becomes an unyielding adversary, relentless in its pursuit to dominate my senses. It wraps its gnarled fingers around my body, squeezing every ounce of strength from my trembling form. My breaths become shallow gasps, as if I am inhaling the very essence of suffering itself.

I know I must tend to these wounds, for an infection is a brewing promise, a sinister spectre that lurks just beyond the horizon. But with my torn clothing barely clinging to my skin, there is nothing I can use to seize the relentless rivulets of blood oozing from my wounds. My desperate attempts to stem the flow are futile, like trying to quell a tempest with the mere flutter of a butterfly's wings.

In this desolate expanse, I am a solitary figure of anguish, a fragile soul battling against the relentless forces of nature and circumstance. The world around me seems to close in, the shadows growing taller, as if to claim me for their own.

As the blood continues to drip onto the ground, the earth seems to drink in my pain, bearing witness to the price of my defiance and the weight of my transgressions. The once-dusty ground now bears the mark of my journey, stained with the essence of my suffering.

Amidst the surreal haze of pain and fatigue, my attention shifts from my bleeding wounds to the vast and arid surroundings that stretch before me. The crimson rivers flowing down my skin become a mere backdrop to the unforgiving landscape that now captures my focus.

The ground beneath my weary feet feels dry and cracked, as if it hasn't tasted the touch of rain in eons. Each step I take sends tiny clouds of dust swirling around my ankles, a dance of desperation in this parched land.

The sun, high and mighty, reigns supreme in the cloudless sky, casting its scorching rays upon the earth like an unyielding judge. The air is thick with heat, and I feel beads of sweat forming on my forehead and back, testament to the relentless onslaught of the sun's fiery gaze.

In this harsh environment, my eyes scan the surroundings in search of anything that could serve as a makeshift bandage for my wounds. But the land offers little respite – the plants around me, with their thorns and dry leaves, seem as unforgiving as the sun itself.

As I continue my search, the world around me comes alive in its own unique way. The plants, though withered and parched, display a resilience that mirrors my own. They stand tall, defying the odds, and I find a strange kinship with their struggle.

In the distance, a rocky outcrop rises like a weathered sentinel, a testament to the enduring power of nature's forces. The landscape seems to pulse with a hidden energy, as if there are secrets buried within the earth, waiting to be unearthed.

The silence that envelopes this desolate land is both eerie and haunting, broken only by the occasional rustle of leaves in the dry wind. The absence of life is palpable, yet there is a certain beauty in the starkness of it all.

As I take in the scene before me, a sense of awe and trepidation washes over me. I am but a speck in this vast and untamed wilderness, a witness to the grandeur and harshness of nature's design.

With the sun as my relentless companion and the wounds as a reminder of my vulnerability, I press on into the unknown. The land stretches endlessly before me, a canvas of contradictions – beautiful yet brutal, inviting yet treacherous.

In this moment of solitude and self-discovery, I find myself drawn deeper into the mysteries of the landscape. The surroundings become a canvas for introspection, a reflection of my own journey – a quest for healing and a desire to uncover the secrets hidden within both the world and my own wounded soul.

****

As the sun blazes its relentless path across the sky, each day unfolds like a scorching tapestry of torment and endurance. My body, like a weathered canvas, bears the crimson brushstrokes of my daring escape, where rivulets of blood have now transformed into a patchwork of scabs, a mosaic of resilience.

In this desolate realm, the land stretches out like a canvas painted in hues of sepia and gold. The earth beneath my bare feet feels like ancient parchment, parched and cracked, a testament to the unforgiving nature of this untamed expanse.

The sun becomes a relentless artist, its fiery brushstrokes searing the landscape with a fiery intensity. The passing of days becomes an ever-changing palette, shifting from vibrant oranges to soft pinks, and finally surrendering to the cool embrace of twilight.

In the dark of night, the stars shimmer above like celestial fireflies, guiding my path through the darkness. They seem like distant beacons of hope, illuminating the way forward in this vast expanse of solitude.

The nights become a canvas of uncertainty, where the howling winds paint eerie melodies across the barren land. The silence takes on a life of its own, whispering secrets of ancient tales and long-forgotten civilizations.

Time becomes an elusive artist, its brushstrokes blurring the days together into a surreal blur. Each moment feels like an eternity, and yet the days slip through my fingers like grains of sand, leaving me adrift in the endless expanse of time.

As I wander through this barren realm, I feel like a lone reed swaying in the wind, bending but not breaking. The land seems to breathe around me, the earth heaving with every step, as if it, too, is alive and yearning for something more.

In the stillness of the night, I become one with the landscape, a mere whisper in the vastness of this untouched canvas. I am both a wanderer and a part of the land, connected by an invisible thread that weaves through the fabric of time.

Yet, amidst this harsh beauty, my body becomes a battleground of weariness and longing. Hunger gnaws at my belly like a relentless predator, while fatigue wraps its suffocating embrace around me like a heavy shroud.

The days become a slow dance with exhaustion, as I trudge forward with each footfall echoing like a heartbeat in my ears. My wounds, like delicate blooms of pain, refuse to heal, their crimson petals a testament to the struggle and the price of my defiance.

In the midst of this vast emptiness, I search for a glimmer of hope, like a lone firefly dancing in the night. My footsteps become an echo of determination, each one carrying me closer to the unknown, closer to the possibility of a new beginning.

As I journey through this desolate realm, I am both an explorer and a captive of fate. The land becomes a living canvas, revealing its secrets one brushstroke at a time. With each step, I uncover the beauty and brutality of this untamed world, and in the reflection of its landscape, I glimpse the depths of my own soul.

Yet, amidst this harsh beauty, the reality of my predicament becomes ever more apparent. I am a lone figure in a vast canvas of solitude, a wandering soul caught in the brushstrokes of destiny...

****

As days stretch into an undulating journey, I find myself drawn to the enigmatic embrace of ancient ruins that have withstood the ravages of time. The once towering structures now stand humbled, their grandiosity diminished by the hands of history. Broken remnants of clay buildings create a scattered landscape, like a mosaic of forgotten memories.

Seeking refuge from the scorching sun, I find solace under the remnants of a clay building, its once strong walls now crumbling and surrendering to the inexorable march of nature. Vines, like emerald serpents, writhe and coil around the weathered stone, reclaiming the land that was once usurped by human hands.

Amidst this ruinscape, nature and time have woven a dance of silent beauty. Tender tendrils of green foliage reach out, caressing the desolate stones with gentle fingers, as if seeking to heal the wounds of history. The once vibrant colours of the clay buildings have faded with age, now bathed in the warm hues of sunset.

As the day wanes, the cool touch of twilight descends upon this ancient sanctuary. The air is tinged with a nostalgic sweetness, carrying whispers of forgotten voices and long-lost dreams. The breeze rustles the leaves of the surrounding trees, a gentle symphony that echoes the passage of centuries.

In the hushed stillness, I find myself both in awe and trepidation. The allure of making a home amidst the ruins that are untouched by human life beckons, yet a sense of cautious hesitation pulls at my heart. The possibility of encountering another soul in this silent abode leaves me haunted by uncertainty.

The weathered buildings, standing like stoic sentinels, guard their secrets with an air of mystery. The ancient stones seem to bear witness to the ebb and flow of time, their silent resilience narrating tales of forgotten civilizations. Each crack and crevice holds a story, and I, like an eager explorer, yearn to decipher their long-lost histories.

Amidst this captivating symphony of ruins and nature, I find myself captivated by the enigma that lies before me. The passage of time has lent an ethereal charm to this place, where the remnants of human existence now interlace with the wild embrace of nature.

As the sun sets and the stars emerge, I feel a sense of serenity enveloping me. This place, though steeped in ancient history, holds an aura of tranquillity, offering a respite from the relentless pursuit of the Scourge. In the arms of these ruins, I find a moment of reprieve, a chance to contemplate my journey and the path that lies ahead.

10

A Familiar Encounter

As the first rays of sunlight gently caress the ancient ruins, I awaken from my slumber under the broken remains of a clay building. My body feels stiff, and my throat is parched with thirst. The need for water beckons me to begin my journey through this forgotten world in search of the life-giving elixir.

As I step out into the maze of ruins, I am greeted by a breathtaking sight. Nature has embraced this once-thriving civilization with an artistic touch. Vines and foliage weave through the decaying structures, reclaiming what was once lost to time. The buildings stand like sentinels of a distant past, whispering tales of grandeur and glory.

As I walk past the ancient ruins, my eyes are drawn to the intriguing markings etched onto the sides of each building, as if a secret language had been woven into their very stones. They appear like cryptic glyphs, the inscriptions of a forgotten civilization, waiting for someone to decipher their hidden meaning.

The walls bear witness to the passage of time, and these enigmatic markings are like whispered confessions, shared only with those who possess the curiosity to listen. Each symbol tells a story of its own, an untold narrative that spans centuries, waiting for a discerning eye to unveil its secrets.

As I run my fingers along the stone, I can almost feel the weight of history lingering within the lines. It's as if the walls hold a treasure trove of knowledge, locked away from the world, and I have stumbled upon the key to unlock their mysteries.

The marks are not random, but a deliberate language crafted by an ancient hand, a language that transcends spoken words. They weave a tale of forgotten wisdom, hidden knowledge, and perhaps even warnings from a bygone era.

With each building I pass, I feel a deeper connection to the past, as if the secrets they hold are seeping into my very being. It's as if the ruins themselves are whispering to me, revealing fragments of a lost world that existed long before I was born.

The beauty of these markings lies not in their intricacy, but in the mystery they evoke. They beckon me to unravel their riddles, to embark on a journey of discovery that could reshape my understanding of history itself.

As I continue my exploration, I can't help but feel a sense of reverence for the architects of this forgotten world. They have left behind a legacy of wonder and intrigue, a legacy that continues to captivate and inspire all those who dare to venture into these ancient ruins.

In the midst of nature's reclamation, the markings remain untouched, like sacred inscriptions preserved for eternity. They serve as a testament to the resilience of human creativity, a testament that even in the face of oblivion, our stories endure.

The ancient ruins have become more than just a backdrop for my journey; they have become living witnesses to the human spirit. The markings are a bridge that spans time and space, connecting me to a past that I never knew, yet now feel an intimate part of.

With each step, I uncover more of these hidden symbols, each one adding to the tapestry of mystery that surrounds me. As I continue my quest for water, the allure of the enigmatic markings pulls me deeper into this forgotten world, igniting a fire of curiosity within me that refuses to be extinguished.

As I walk through the labyrinth of crumbling walls, I feel a mix of awe and reverence. Each step is an exploration of history, a journey through the echoes of a forgotten civilization. My emotions are a blend of curiosity and trepidation, wondering what secrets this place holds and what mysteries I might uncover.

I follow the meandering paths, guided by an instinctual sense that water would not be far away. And just as nature has intertwined with the ruins, so has water found its way through the ancient structures. The soft sound of trickling water becomes my beacon, leading me towards the life-giving source.

As I draw nearer to the water's edge, I am met with a breathtaking sight. A small spring emerges from the heart of the ruins, surrounded by lush greenery. The water glistens like a precious gem, promising relief to my parched throat.

I cup my hands and take my first sip, feeling the coolness of the water flow through me like a revitalizing force. It is a moment of pure communion with nature, a profound connection to this forgotten realm that has become my sanctuary.

In this oasis of life amidst the ruins, I find solace and a sense of belonging. The ancient spirits seem to watch over me, their whispers carried on the gentle breeze. I feel as though I have become a part of the very fabric of this place, entwined with its history and secrets.

With my thirst quenched, I take a moment to sit by the spring, immersing myself in the serenity of the moment. The sights, sounds, and smells of the ruins envelop me, a symphony of nature and time that stirs something deep within my soul.

In this enigmatic world of ancient wonders, I am humbled by the realization that I am but a fleeting visitor, a mere fragment in the tapestry of history. Yet, I know that this place holds the answers I seek, the truths that will guide me on my journey beyond the crumbling walls.

As I stand by the spring, quenching my thirst and feeling the cool water soothe my parched throat, I catch a glimpse of my reflection in a small puddle nearby. To my astonishment, the image staring back at me looks nothing like the wounded, torn individual I had become accustomed to seeing.

In the reflection, my skin is unblemished and radiant, without a trace of the wounds that had covered my body just moments ago. Not a single scar or scab mars the surface, and the sight leaves me perplexed and bewildered. I mutter aloud, my words barely audible above the gentle rustling of leaves around me.

"How is this possible? How can my wounds vanish in this reflection?"

I trace my fingers over my skin while looking at the reflection, half-expecting to find that it was all an illusion, that the wounds still lingered beneath the surface.

I wince slightly as I feel my wounds, the pain a stark contrast to the illusion I witness in the reflection. It is as if I exist in two worlds simultaneously – one where my wounds are real and painful, and another where they have vanished without a trace.

As I continue to gaze into the reflection, a myriad of thoughts race through my mind. Could this be some ancient magic woven into the waters of the spring? Or perhaps it's a glimpse into an alternate reality, where my wounds have never existed?

A part of me wants to believe that this newfound reflection is the truth, that the wounds were merely a nightmare from which I have now awakened. But the pain in my body reminds me that the reality I face is far from an illusion.

****

As I stand by the spring, my gaze fixated on the reflection that defies reality, a chilling silence envelops the ancient ruins. But that silence is abruptly shattered as a taunting voice pierces through the stillness, sending shivers down my spine.

"Thought you could get away?" the voice sneers, mocking my feeble attempt to escape the clutches of the scourge. Panic surges through me, and I instinctively turn towards the source of the voice.

There, emerging from the shadows, are the scourge, their sinister masks obscuring their faces, but their eyes gleaming with malevolence. They have found me, and there is no escape from their relentless pursuit.

"I-I don't mean to cause any trouble. Please, just let me go," I stammer, feeling the weight of their judgment bearing down on me.

"Trouble? Oh, you've caused quite a bit of it, haven't you? And I don't think we're in the business of letting transgressors like you go," the scourge retorts with a mocking tone.

"I-I didn't cause any chaos. I just want to leave, that's all," I reply, my voice trembling with fear.

"Leave? Leave Fleshbourne and its sacred laws? That's not how things work here, pal. You will face justice for your defiance," the scourge taunts.

"But what harm have I really done? I just disagree with the ways of Fleshbourne," I say, mustering a bit of courage.

"Disagree? Oh, I'm sure that's a convincing excuse. You're not the first to try and play innocent, you know," the scourge scoffs.

In that moment, something within me snaps. A surge of defiance rushes through my veins, and I can't hold back the retort, "Innocent? I may not be innocent, but neither are you, enforcing such twisted justice."

The scourge's eyes narrow with anger. "Watch your tongue, transgressor! You have no idea what you're talking about."

"Oh, I have a pretty good idea, actually. You scourge are just as trapped in this cruel system as the rest of us," I fire back, unable to contain my frustration.

"How dare you speak to me like that! You'll pay for your insolence," the scourge growls, taking a step closer.

"Pay? What, like how Joseph paid for associating with me?" I say, challenging them further.

A flicker of surprise crosses the scourge's masked face, and I can sense that I've hit a nerve.

"Joseph's fate is of no concern to you. You should be more worried about your own," the scourge retorts coldly.

"Oh, I am, believe me. But I can't help but wonder, are you all wearing those cloaks to hide the possibility of having wounds too? Or are you just afraid of something else?" I taunt, my words laced with bitterness.

"That's enough! We're not here to exchange words with the likes of you. Grab him!" another scourge interjects, their patience clearly wearing thin.

As I dart towards the archways, the scourge are hot on my heels, their angry shouts echoing through the ancient ruins. My heart pounds in my chest, and with every stride, my fatigue threatens to slow me down. But I refuse to let fear overpower me.

Reaching the base of a crumbling building, I clamber upward, my hands finding purchase on the rough, weathered stones. As I ascend to the rooftop, I cast a quick glance back at my pursuers, their masked faces contorted with frustration. A smirk creeps across my lips, and I can't resist the urge to taunt them.

"Come on, you lot! Can't keep up with a simple escapee like me?" I jeer, reveling in the adrenaline-fueled defiance that surges through me.

"You won't escape us for long, transgressor!" one of the scourge barks in response, his voice laced with irritation.

"Guess you'll just have to try harder, then!" I shoot back, my voice dripping with sarcasm.

With a burst of energy, I leap from the rooftop, my feet landing gracefully on the crumbling remains of another building. My heart hammers in my chest as I balance precariously on the narrow ledge, my arms flailing for balance. The scourge below clamour after me, their weapons glinting in the dappled sunlight that filters through the vines.

"Give up now, and we promise a swift and merciful end!" another scourge calls out, their words meant to intimidate.

"Oh, I'm sure you do," I reply, my voice tinged with mock sincerity. "But I think I'll pass on that offer."

As I sprint across the rooftops, I can hear the thud of heavy boots behind me. The scourge are skilled in their pursuit, agile and determined in their quest to apprehend me. Leaping from rooftop to rooftop, they follow me with uncanny precision, their cloaks billowing in the wind like dark wings.

Their presence is a constant reminder of the danger I face, the consequences that await if they capture me. Yet, I can't let their looming figures break my focus. My heart races, not only from the exertion but from the thrill of outwitting my relentless pursuers.

With each daring move, I feel a fleeting sense of freedom, a momentary escape from the weight of my transgressions. The ancient ruins become my labyrinth, and in this reckless dance of evasion,

I feel a surge of adrenaline that pushes me beyond the limits of my fear.

But the scourge are relentless, their pursuit unyielding. They leap from rooftops with a deadly grace, their masked faces shadowed with determination. I can feel their breath on my neck, their presence like a dark cloud that threatens to engulf me.

As I navigate the precarious terrain, my surroundings blur into a dizzying whirlwind of decay and shadows. My focus narrows to the next ledge, the next leap, the next escape. With each daring move, I push myself to the limit, driven by the desperate need to stay one step ahead.

In this heart-pounding chase, I can't help but marvel at the scourge's tenacity, their unyielding pursuit of a single transgressor. But I refuse to succumb to their taunts and threats. I will not be a prisoner of their oppressive world.

With a surge of determination, I dash forward, my breaths coming in ragged gasps. The chase continues, an exhilarating dance between predator and prey, and I will not rest until I break free from their grasp.

As I continue running along the rooftops, the ancient city sprawls beneath me like a forgotten realm frozen in time. From this vantage point, the ruins take on an otherworldly beauty, their crumbling facades adorned with clinging vines and the hues of dusk casting a surreal glow upon the decaying architecture. But there's no time to marvel at the sight as I race against the scourge, my heart pounding with each stride.

At last, I reach the edge of a rooftop, and my heart sinks as I realize there is no other building for me to leap onto. I'm cornered, surrounded by the scourge who have closed in, their mocking smirks casting shadows on their masked faces.

"Well, well, looks like the little transgressor has run out of rooftops to hop," one of the scourge jeers, his voice laced with triumph.

I turn around, facing the encircling foe with a defiant glare. "You must be so proud, trapping a single unarmed individual like me. How courageous of you," I snap, my voice tinged with anger.

"Courageous enough to deal with the likes of you," another scourge sneers.

"Likes of me? You know nothing about me," I retort, my defiance fueling my boldness.

"Oh, we know enough. You're just another fool who thought they could challenge the order of Fleshbourne," a third scourge adds, amusement dancing in their eyes.

"Order? More like a twisted system of oppression," I shoot back, my frustration reaching its peak.

"You should have stayed within the city walls, where you belong," the first scourge taunts.

"Belong? I don't belong anywhere that suppresses the very essence of freedom!" I exclaim, my voice echoing through the ancient ruins.

The scourge's sniggers turn into infuriated glares, and I can feel the tension thickening in the air. But I'm done being passive, done being afraid of their intimidation tactics.

"You know what I think?" I continue, my voice steady and resolute. "I think you're all afraid. Afraid of what might happen if the people dared to question your so-called justice. Afraid of your own vulnerability."

The air crackles with tension as the scourge's anger ignites, and they take a step closer, their weapons drawn.

"You're nothing more than a pest, a disobedient little worm," one of them spits.

"Then prove it. If I'm just a pest, why do you all surround me like this? Afraid to face me one-on-one?" I challenge, my pulse racing.

The scourge exchange glances, their eyes narrowing with resentment. "You're not worth our time," one of them sneers.

"Ah, so you admit it! You're afraid I might just beat you," I retort, a smirk playing on my lips.

The nearest scourge, a burly figure with a menacing aura, steps forward, his lips curling into a wicked grin. "Foolish bravery," he mocks, gripping his sword tightly. "I'll be more than happy to show you what a true scourge can do."

I ready myself, my heart pounding, but determination surging through my veins. "Let's dance then," I quip, my voice dripping with sarcasm.

As the other scourge form a tight circle around us, I face my opponent with unwavering focus. The weight of my defiance and the stakes of this one-on-one clash press upon my shoulders. But I refuse to be intimidated.

With a sudden surge of energy, the scourge charges at me, his sword raised high, gleaming in the dim light. I know I have no weapon to counter him, but I rely on my wits and quick reflexes.

As he swings his blade, I swiftly duck to the side, avoiding the lethal arc. His attack slices through the air where I once stood, leaving behind a chilling reminder of his deadly intent.

"You're quick, but not quick enough," the scourge taunts, his voice laced with arrogance.

I don't let his words deter me. I've faced adversity before, and this battle is no different. With a deep breath, I steady myself and prepare for the next move.

He lunges again, and this time, I manage to dodge his strike by mere inches. His sword grazes my arm, leaving a shallow cut, but I don't falter. The pain only fuels my determination.

I use my agility to my advantage, darting around him, looking for any opportunity to strike. But he's experienced, and he parries my attempts with ease. Each time my fist nears his body, he sidesteps, deflecting my blows effortlessly.

I know I need to be strategic. I can't afford to make any mistakes. My mind races as I search for a weakness in his defences. He's strong and skilled, but I must find a way to outsmart him.

As we continue to engage in this dance of defiance, my adrenaline surges, heightening my senses. I anticipate his next move, but it's not enough. His sword finds its mark, landing a glancing blow on my shoulder, causing me to wince in pain.

The scourge smirks, seeing the effect of his strike. "You're just delaying the inevitable," he sneers.

As the scourge's sword removes itself from my shoulder, a sharp jolt of pain shoots through me, causing me to gasp. Panic surges within me as the throbbing ache intensifies. My mind races, knowing that my bare hands are no match for his lethal weapon.

But in that moment of desperation, something within me snaps. An unyielding anger takes hold, and I decide to seize any advantage I can find. With a surge of determination, I reach for his mask, my fingers wrapping around the edges.

With a swift motion, I rip off the scourge's mask, revealing his face underneath. His features are stern, with cold eyes that bear the weight of the oppressive system he serves. A scar runs across his brow, a mark of battles fought and endured. But it's the wound on his cheek that catches my attention.

It glows with an eerie light, pulsating like a serpent's slithering movement. The jagged scar begins to twist and writhe, as if it holds a life of its own. The sight is both mesmerizing and unsettling, and I can't help but notice the strange similarity to Joseph's wound.

For a moment, we lock eyes, and there's a flicker of recognition in his gaze. Does he see the connection too? Or does he merely see a defiant transgressor, someone who dares to challenge his authority?

But there's no time to ponder further. The other scourge close in, sensing my momentary distraction. They're quick to react, their weapons at the ready. I take a step back, my mind still reeling from the revelation.

The wounded scourge raises his sword, a snarl on his lips. "You've crossed the line, transgressor. Now you'll pay."

I gather my resolve, pushing aside the shock, and ready myself for the next strike. As the scourge lunges at me again, I narrowly evade his blade, my focus sharpened by the newfound knowledge of our shared past.

With each passing moment, the weight of this revelation fuels my determination to escape their grasp. I can't let them win, not when there's a truth hidden in the ruins of this city, a truth that may unravel the very fabric of the scourge's power.

In this dance of defiance, I use my agility to my advantage, evading their attacks, my eyes never leaving the wounded scourge. His scar serves as a reminder of the bond between us, a bond forged through shared hardship and pain.

But his anger grows with every missed strike, and his movements become more erratic, fuelled by the burning need to subdue me. With a ferocious roar, he lunges forward again, his sword aimed for my chest.

I react instinctively, moving out of the way, but he uses his momentum from the lunge to push me.

As the scourge's furious lunge propels me backward, I feel my feet slipping at the edge of the rooftop. Time seems to slow down, and a rush of adrenaline floods my veins. My heart pounds in my chest as I desperately try to regain my balance.

For a split second, I teeter on the brink, my body swaying precariously in mid-air. In that moment, the world blurs around me, and all that remains is the haunting realization that I am about to fall.

My fingers claw at the rough surface of the rooftop, but there's nothing to hold onto. The wind whistles in my ears, and I catch a fleeting glimpse of the ancient ruins below, their shadows stretching like beckoning arms.

Then, with a sickening lurch, I lose my footing entirely. The ground rushes up to meet me, and a cacophony of thoughts and emotions swirl within me. Fear, regret, defiance—all collide in a chaotic symphony.

I plummet through the air, my heartache echoing in my ears. The world spins around me, and for an instant, everything is a blur of crumbling stones and twisted vines. Time seems to stretch indefinitely, each second an eternity of falling.

As I hurtle downward, the realization dawns on me that there is no escape from this impending pain. I brace myself for impact, knowing that the ground below will not yield to my defiance. The pain will be relentless, unforgiving.

And then, with a heart-wrenching thud, I hit the ground. Agony courses through my body, shooting up from the impact point. Every nerve feels ablaze, every muscle contorted in pain. My breath is stolen from my lungs, and darkness encroaches on the edges of my vision.

In that moment, all defiance and determination seem to dissipate, consumed by the overwhelming physical torment. I can hear the scourge's laughter above, but it feels distant and distorted, drowned out by the throbbing pain in my head.

My consciousness wavers, a flickering flame on the verge of extinguishing. I fight to stay awake, to not surrender to the darkness that threatens to claim me. But the pain is relentless, unyielding, and my body feels like it's being torn apart.

And then, like a flickering candle finally extinguishing, I succumb to the darkness. Unconsciousness wraps its cold embrace around me, pulling me into oblivion. The world around me fades to black, leaving me adrift in a sea of pain and dreams.

In that void of unconsciousness, time loses all meaning. I am suspended in a state of hazy existence, where the line between reality and dreams blurs. Images flicker through my mind like fragmented memories, leaving trails of emotions in their wake.

But amidst the chaos, one image remains vivid—the face of the wounded scourge. His serpent-like scar seems to writhe and glow with an eerie light, an enigma wrapped in darkness. His eyes hold a haunting intensity, a mixture of anger and something else, something unspoken.

And then, even that image fades away, swallowed by the abyss of unconsciousness. The pain, the struggle, and the defiance all dissolve into an uncharted void. I am left drifting in a limbo of oblivion, waiting for the currents of consciousness to carry me back to the waking world.

11

Hope

As I gradually regain consciousness, a disorienting dizziness washes over me, like being lost in a turbulent sea. I attempt to open my eyes, but the darkness remains impenetrable. My vision is blurred, leaving me unable to decipher anything in this pitch-black void.

The absence of natural sounds and the unfamiliar sensation beneath me indicate that I'm no longer outdoors. The air feels confined, suffocating, as if I'm confined within the depths of a cavern or some hidden chamber.

As my mind struggles to piece together the events leading up to this moment, a vivid flashback of my fall from the rooftop floods my thoughts. The image of the scourge's gleaming sword and the sharp pain in my shoulder plays like a haunting echo, reminding me of the perilous struggle that brought me to this state.

Fear and confusion gnaw at the edges of my consciousness. Questions swirl in my mind like restless spirits—where am I? What happened after the fall? Did someone find me, or am I still alone in this desolate darkness?

The effort of trying to make sense of my surroundings is overwhelming, and I'm overcome by exhaustion and pain. My body feels like a canvas of bruises and aching wounds, and every movement sends a jolt of agony through me.

The memory of the scourge's face flashes in my mind, their taunting words, and the gleam of the sword. Did they leave me here, left to die in the shadows? Or did someone else find me, someone with far more sinister intentions?

Unable to see and struggling to gather my strength, I reach out blindly, hoping to touch something that might offer a clue to my whereabouts. My fingers graze against a cold, rough surface—a stone wall, perhaps, or an ancient relic of this mysterious place.

But the darkness remains unyielding, and my attempts to discern my surroundings are futile. There's an unsettling stillness, an eerie silence that leaves me feeling isolated and vulnerable.

As I lie there, disoriented and in pain, unconsciousness lingers at the edges of my mind, threatening to pull me back into its embrace. My body is drained, my spirit faltering.

Despite my best efforts to stay awake and alert, the allure of oblivion is irresistible, and I surrender to the depths of unconsciousness once more. In this inky void, I drift away, my mind becoming untethered from the tangible world, as I surrender to the uncertain embrace of darkness.

My eyes flutter open, and I find myself in a dimly lit room. The air feels stale and heavy, and the scent of dampness hangs in the air. My head throbs with pain, and I wince as I try to sit up. My body feels bruised and battered, each movement sending a jolt of agony through my veins.

As my vision adjusts to the dimness, I notice the faint glow of a small oil lamp in the corner of the room. Shadows dance on the walls, and I catch glimpses of wooden shelves filled with dusty books and mysterious artifacts. It appears to be some sort of hidden chamber, tucked away from the world.

Trying to remember how I ended up here, flashes of the rooftop clash with the scourge come rushing back. The pain in my shoulder where the scourge landed a blow is a constant reminder of the encounter. But what happened after that? How did I end up in this hidden sanctuary?

As I try to piece together the events, I hear a soft creak, and the door to the chamber opens slightly. A slender figure slips inside, and my eyes strain to make out their features in the low light. The figure moves with a gentle grace, and a sense of familiarity washes over me.

"Who's there?" I croak, my voice hoarse from the fall and the struggle.

"Don't be afraid," a soft voice replies. "You're safe now."

As the figure approaches, I can make out the outline of a face, framed by unruly locks of hair. The person kneels beside me, and I see a pair of warm, concerned eyes peering back at me. Recognition dawns upon me, and a wave of relief washes over my weary body.

"Lia?" I murmur, my voice barely audible.

"Yes, it's me," she whispers, her voice tinged with relief. "You took quite a fall, but luckily, I found you just in time."

Lia and I were once close friends in the tightly-knit community of Fleshbourne, sharing laughter and dreams under the sun's warm embrace. But as our paths diverged, she became entangled in the clutches of the scourge, embodying their iron-fisted justice. I watched, horrified and heartbroken, as she donned the mask of her new identity, executing my neighbours and fellow citizens without mercy. One fateful day, she vanished without a trace, leaving behind a void of uncertainty, and her absence cast a long shadow over our once vibrant bond. . The unexpected connection we shared was a glimmer of hope in this desolate world of secrets and oppression.

Lia's face is a portrait of strength and resilience, with high cheekbones that add a touch of elegance to her features. Her skin is kissed by the sun, bearing faint traces of the life she lived as a scourge before seeking freedom. A few scattered freckles adorn her nose and cheeks, giving her a youthful charm that belies the weight of her experiences.

Her eyes, the colour of deep emeralds, hold a mix of determination and vulnerability. They seem to carry the weight of the world, reflecting the pain and sorrow she has witnessed. Yet, there's a spark of hope flickering within them—a reminder of the unyielding spirit that drove her to break free from her past.

Lia's hair cascades in wild waves of chestnut brown, falling just past her shoulders. It seems to echo her untamed spirit, refusing to be confined by the shackles of her past. Strands of hair often escape the constraints of her makeshift ponytail, framing her face in a captivating, windswept way.

Her clothes bear the marks of practicality and adaptability. She wears a faded, dark green tunic, its sleeves rolled up to her elbows, allowing for ease of movement. A tattered brown cloak drapes over her shoulders, its edges frayed with age, providing some semblance of camouflage in the shadows.

Around her neck, a pendant of intertwined silver and amethyst hangs, its significance known only to her. The delicate chain rests against the hollow of her throat, a constant reminder of her quest for truth and redemption.

As I look at her now, the dim light of the chamber casting shadows across her face, I can't help but marvel at her strength and resilience. She may bear the scars of her past, but they do not define her. Instead, they have shaped her into the person she is today—a warrior with a heart of gold, fiercely committed to righting the wrongs of the world.

"How did you find me?" I manage to ask, my curiosity overshadowing the pain.

She smiles gently. "After you fell, I saw the scourge leave you there, thinking you were defeated. But I couldn't just let you die. So, I followed them to this hidden chamber they call the Archive. It's a place where they store their knowledge and secrets."

My heart swells with gratitude, knowing that she risked everything to save me. But there's something else I need to know—the reason behind her knowledge of this hidden sanctuary.

"How do you know about this place?" I inquire, my eyes searching hers for answers.

She hesitates for a moment before speaking. "I... I used to be one of them—a scourge. But I couldn't bear the cruelty and oppression anymore. I escaped, and I've been hiding here ever since, trying to uncover their secrets and put an end to their tyranny."

The pain in her eyes, the weariness in her voice—it all aligns with someone who has lived a life of conflict and turmoil.

"I don't know if I can trust you," I admit, the uncertainty clouding my thoughts.

She nods understandingly. "I understand. But for what it's worth, I saved you because I believe in your cause—to challenge the ways of Fleshbourne and the scourge. And I can't do it alone."

As I lay there, my eyes gradually adjusting to the dimness, I noticed Lia's silhouette moving gracefully through the darkness. She took a few steps towards a tall bookshelf, her figure illuminated by a faint, flickering light. With a delicate touch, she retrieved a piece of paper from the top shelf, carefully folding it and slipping it into her pocket.

The room around us was a symphony of shadows and ancient relics. The walls were adorned with faded tapestries depicting long-forgotten tales, and the air carried a musty scent of old books and history. The dim glow emanating from a solitary lantern cast eerie patterns across the cracked stone floor, revealing layers of dust that had settled over ages past.

As my eyesight continued to adjust, I could now make out Lia's facial features more clearly. Her eyes, once full of laughter and life, now held a weariness that spoke of the burden she carried. Her clothes were simple, a dark cloak that blended seamlessly with the shadows, and her long, dark hair cascaded down her shoulders, framing her face with an air of mystery.

With a soft sigh, Lia turned to face me, and a bittersweet smile danced upon her lips. "It's been a long time, hasn't it?" she spoke, her voice tinged with both relief and sorrow. "I never thought we would meet again like this."

Struggling to sit up, I managed to nod, the memory of her transformation haunting my thoughts. "I never expected to see you like this either," I replied, my voice heavy with emotion. "How did you end up as one of them, Lia? And why have you been hiding here?"

Lia's gaze softened, and she took a seat on a nearby broken chair. "After that night when everything changed, I couldn't bear to stay in Fleshbourne," she began, her eyes cast downward as if reliving painful memories. "I couldn't face what I had become, what I had done. So, I fled, seeking solace in these ancient ruins, hidden from both the scourge and the ones I used to call friends."

Her words hung heavily in the air, and I could sense the weight of her regret and remorse. "But why did you become one of them in the first place?" I pressed, needing to understand the path she had taken.

Lia hesitated for a moment before looking up, her eyes locking with mine. "I thought I could change things from within, protect you and others like us from the scourge's tyranny," she confessed.

"But I was naive and foolish. The power they offered came with a price I hadn't fully grasped."

As the truth unravelled, I felt a mix of empathy and anger swelling within me. Lia had once been a beacon of light in my life, and her fall from grace pained me deeply. Yet, as she sat there, vulnerable and burdened, I couldn't help but see the glimmer of the friend I had once known, hidden beneath the cloak of the scourge.

In the embrace of the dark room, we continued our conversation, unravelling the tangled threads of our shared past and the enigma of the ancient ruins that now held us both captive.

With a determined glint in her eyes, Lia slowly withdrew the piece of paper from her pocket and unfolded it, revealing a worn and weathered map. The parchment was covered with intricate notes and annotations, marking paths through treacherous terrains and ancient landmarks. The map seemed to hold secrets of a world beyond the confines of the dark room.

"There's hope, my friend," Lia said, her voice laced with excitement and urgency. "Up North, past the city of AshWays, lies a civilization of wealth and power. They have the resources to challenge the oppressive force of Fleshbourne and dismantle the scourge's rule."

Her finger traced the map's markings, guiding me through the twists and turns of a journey yet to be taken. "I've ventured there myself, seeking their alliance," Lia continued. "But my past as a former scourge met with suspicion and hostility. They threatened to expose me, to tear down any hope of assistance."

She paused, her gaze locked with mine, as if seeking my understanding and trust. "But I won't be deterred. We have a chance to change everything, to free our people from the chains of tyranny," Lia declared, her voice strong with conviction.

As I looked at the map, I saw the paths she had traversed, the obstacles she had faced, and the risks she had taken to secure a better future. Lia's bravery and determination stirred a sense of purpose within me, igniting a flicker of hope in the midst of darkness.

With an earnest gleam in her eyes, Lia extended the map towards me. "I need you to come with me," she implored. "The people of that civilization might not trust a former scourge like me, but you, you were never one of them. They might be more willing to listen to someone untainted by their oppressive ways."

Her words hung in the air, and I could feel the weight of the decision ahead. Going with Lia meant leaving behind the familiarity of the dark room, embarking on a perilous journey into the unknown. Yet, I also understood the significance of her plea. If there was a chance that my past as a free soul in Fleshbourne could bridge the gap between Lia and the potential allies, it was a risk worth taking.

The map seemed to beckon, its paths leading towards a destiny that could change everything. A future where the scourge's grip on the people of Fleshbourne might finally be loosened, and hope could bloom once more. The thought of being a part of this pivotal quest filled me with a sense of purpose I had never felt before.

My heart wavered in uncertainty as I gazed at the map Lia held out to me. The idea of leaving the safety of the dark room, venturing into the world beyond, and confronting the powerful forces that held Fleshbourne in their grip sent a shiver down my spine. It wasn't just fear that gripped me; it was also the weight of my own doubts.

"I appreciate your trust in me," I began, my voice tinged with hesitance. "But this journey you're proposing, it's not just dangerous. It's a leap into the unknown. And what if we fail? What if those people up North turn us away just like they did to you?"

Lia's gaze remained unwavering, her eyes filled with a mixture of determination and empathy. "I won't deny that the path ahead is uncertain," she admitted. "But I've seen what you're capable of. You defied the scourge and escaped Fleshbourne. You carry a resilience and a spark of defiance that could be the key to changing our fate."

I sighed, torn between the safety of my refuge and the prospect of making a difference in a world that had turned its back on me. "It's not just about me, Lia. It's about the people I've left behind in Fleshbourne. What if they need me too? What if I abandon them?"

Lia's voice softened, her understanding palpable. "I know it's a difficult choice, and I wouldn't ask it of you if I didn't believe it was our best chance. But think about it, if we succeed, if we manage to rally these people of power against the scourge's tyranny, imagine the lives we could change. The suffering we could end."

I lowered my gaze to the map, my fingers tracing the intricate paths and symbols. Each line seemed to represent not just a route, but a choice. A choice that could alter the course of not only my life but the lives of those still trapped in the clutches of oppression. The prospect was overwhelming, yet somehow, it felt like a responsibility I couldn't ignore.

Lia's eyes bore into mine, her sincerity shining through. "I'm not asking you to make this choice lightly. But I am asking you to consider the potential, the hope we could bring. Together."

Her words resonated deeply within me. As I met her gaze, a sense of clarity washed over me. My reluctance began to crumble under the weight of possibility, replaced by a newfound determination.

"You're right," I said, my voice stronger. "If there's even a chance that we can make a difference, then I can't turn my back on it. I won't."

Lia's face broke into a genuine smile, relief and gratitude evident in her expression. "Thank you," she whispered, her voice carrying a world of meaning.

With a steady resolve, I reached out and took the map from her hand. The decision was made. The journey ahead would be treacherous, and the challenges daunting, but alongside Lia, I felt a surge of courage and purpose that I hadn't felt in a long time. Together, we would face the uncertainties of the world beyond, armed not just with determination, but with the belief that change was possible, even in the darkest of times.

****

Over the course of the next two days, Lia and I embark on a journey that leads us through the heart of the ancient ruins. With each step, we seem to waltz through history, as we navigate the remnants of a civilization long forgotten. Broken statues and weathered walls stand as quiet witnesses to the passage of countless years, while tendrils of ivy reach out like nature's tentative fingers, reclaiming what time had taken away. Our footfalls, mingling with the susurrus of the past, create a symphony of echoes, as the ruins themselves seem to exhale the weight of memories.

As we venture further into the unknown, the landscape undergoes a metamorphosis. The familiar structures fade into the backdrop, and the terrain's starkness mirrors the uncertainty of our quest. We are met only by the occasional shrill cries of eagles circling high above, their voices carrying a hint of liberation that we crave. The land stretches out, an undulating canvas of golden savannah, occasionally interrupted by clusters of resilient flora, tenaciously thriving despite the harsh surroundings.

The sun bears down relentlessly, casting elongated shadows that appear to stretch indefinitely. It's a stark reminder of the trials that lie ahead, and every step forward feels like an affirmation of our resolve. Lia's guidance becomes our compass in this featureless expanse, her understanding of the land offering a thread of certainty in the face of the unknown.

Among the modest possessions Lia has provided, a fresh set of attire and bandages becomes a lifeline. The fabric adheres to my skin like a second chance, while the bandages provide both a soothing embrace and a promise of healing. With each stride, the discomfort from my wounds and injuries gradually fades, replaced by a newfound inner fortitude.

Beside Lia, our journey's rhythm transforms into a shared harmony of purpose. Our quiet moments are punctuated by conversations, the exchange of words like pebbles skimming the surface of a pond, revealing the depth beneath. As Lia spins tales of distant places and the people she has encountered beyond Fleshbourne, I offer fragments of my own past, memories that had been buried by time.

The days blend together, each one forming a mosaic of challenges and fleeting instances of beauty. We traverse the physical landscape as well as the corridors of our minds, linked by a common goal and a resolute defiance against the oppressive forces that once held us captive. In the midst of the boundless savannah, where the horizon stretches infinitely, I find solace in life's simplicity. The unending plains remind us that the world is vast, and our trials are mere threads in the tapestry of existence. Amid the cries of eagles and the whispers of the wind, I understand that no matter how formidable the path, Lia and I stand together, ready to confront the enigma that awaits.

In this journey through the heart of ancient ruins and the expanse of a relentless savannah, Lia proves to be a unique kind of companion. Her wit and sarcasm are like sparks that ignite our interactions, sometimes lighting up my annoyance, and other times, making me crack a reluctant smile.

As we navigate the ruins, I stumble upon a cracked stone, and Lia raises an eyebrow, her lips curling into a smirk. "Graceful as always," she remarks, her tone dripping with playful sarcasm.

I shoot her a wry look, my annoyance feigning seriousness. "Oh yes, because everyone knows tripping over ancient debris is an art form."

She chuckles, a melodic sound that seems out of place amidst the desolate surroundings. "You're right, we should probably alert the critics."

Our banter becomes a rhythm, a backdrop to our journey. When we stop to rest, Lia lounges against a weathered pillar, studying me with an appraising look. "You know, you wear that 'grumpy wanderer' look quite well. Have you considered a career in it?"

I roll my eyes, though I can't help the corner of my lips twitching upward. "Maybe it's my true calling."

She grins mischievously. "Ah, a man of many talents, then."

As we tread through the savannah, the monotonous landscape stretching endlessly before us, Lia's humour becomes a lifeline. When I express doubt about the path ahead, she smirks. "Don't worry, I'm pretty sure ancient explorers had Google Maps too."

I let out a chuckle, the tension easing. "I'm pretty sure Google Maps didn't account for ruins and gaping pits."

She waves a dismissive hand. "Details, details. Just follow the invisible unicorn trail, and we'll be fine."

Her quips, born from a blend of confidence and self-assuredness, manage to break through the sombreness that can sometimes hang over our journey. Even in the face of challenges, her witty retorts remind me that the world is still capable of humour.

Lia's unique brand of companionship doesn't just light up the moments, it becomes a symbol of our resilience. Amidst ruins and across vast savannahs, her sarcasm and my retorts forge a bond that transcends the bleakness around us. In her company, I realize that even in the darkest of times, a touch of humour can be a beacon of hope.

The sun beats down on us relentlessly as we trek through the seemingly endless savannah. I wipe my forehead with the back of my hand, feeling the sting of the sunburn starting to settle in. Lia, seemingly unfazed, glances at me with a playful grin.

"Well, aren't you a picture of radiant health?" she quips, a hint of sarcasm dripping from her words.

I give her a wry smile. "Hey, I'm cultivating that 'sun-kissed' look, you know."

Her laughter rings out, a sound that somehow manages to cut through the heat. "Oh yes, absolutely nailing it. Next, you'll be auditioning for the role of a roasted tomato."

I roll my eyes, but can't help but chuckle. "You're one to talk. I can practically see steam coming off you."

She waves a hand dramatically in front of her face. "Ah, yes, I'm just exuding glamour. It's called the 'sweat and sass' look. Very in this season."

We share a laugh, the levity a welcome relief from the harsh surroundings. The savannah stretches out before us, a seemingly infinite sea of golden grass. Lia points to a distant rise on the horizon.

"See that hill over there? It's our grand destination for the day."

I raise an eyebrow, a mock dramatic gasp escaping me. "A hill, you say? Truly, Lia, you know how to show a person a good time."

She feigns an offended gasp. "Excuse you, that hill happens to be the most captivating hill in a twenty-mile radius."

I nod sagely. "Of course, how could I doubt its allure?"

As we trudge forward, the breeze carries the distant call of a bird. Lia tilts her head, a mischievous glint in her eyes. "Did you hear that? The call of the wild!"

I play along, cupping a hand to my ear. "Ah, yes, the majestic squawk of the majestic... something."

Lia bursts into laughter, her voice carrying across the open expanse. "Truly, the animal kingdom trembles at our presence."

We continue our banter, each quip and sarcastic remark a small victory against the sweltering heat and the seemingly unending savannah. In the midst of our light-hearted exchange, I catch a glimpse of a far-off silhouette, a hint of a structure that breaks the monotony of the landscape.

"Hey, is that what I think it is?" I point towards the shape.

Lia squints, shading her eyes with her hand. "I think you're right. Civilization beckons."

We quicken our pace, a renewed energy propelling us towards the distant sight. As we get closer, the outline becomes clearer - a small structure, an oasis of sorts in the midst of the savannah's expanse.

Lia throws me a sideways glance, her lips curving into a grin. "Well, what do you know? Turns out our sun-kissed adventure just got a little less tomato-like."

I shake my head, laughing. "And here I was, thinking that hills were the epitome of excitement."

"Who knew that a building in the middle of nowhere could be our saviour?" she retorts with a wink.

As we approach the structure, our banter fades into the background, replaced by the anticipation of rest and respite. The savannah might be endless, but at least it's not devoid of surprises - and a healthy dose of sarcasm to keep things interesting.

As we continue our journey, the distant silhouette solidifies into a tangible structure. The oasis emerges like a mirage brought to life, a sanctuary of respite amid the relentless savannah. Its walls rise like protective arms, welcoming travellers with an embrace of cool shade. The wind, once a mere bystander, now plays a symphony as it rustles the oasis's leafy hair.

Lia's grin widens as we draw closer, and her steps quicken, like a child reaching for a long-awaited treat. "Behold, our oasis of comfort and splendour."

I can't help but smile. "The way you describe it, I half expect a royal feast waiting inside."

She playfully rolls her eyes. "Well, we do have our very own feast of dried fruit and questionable jerky."

As we approach, the oasis's secrets unfold. Its entrance stands like an ancient guardian, the door a portal to a world unseen. Faint shadows dance within, casting a tantalizing invitation. And like a whispered promise, the scent of damp earth and something sweet drifts from within, urging us forward.

We step inside, and it's as if the world hushes its breath. The oasis envelops us, a gentle embrace that shields us from the outside heat. Sunlight filters through the leaves, painting dappled patterns on the ground, a natural mosaic of warmth and comfort. Nearby, a small pond glistens like a jewel, its waters a cool reprieve from the sun's unrelenting glare.

Lia sinks onto a cushioned corner, a satisfied sigh escaping her lips. "Ah, the wonders of civilization."

I chuckle, following suit. "I must admit, this is far more inviting than our conversation with the savannah."

She smirks, raising an eyebrow. "Oh, so you're saying you don't find my wild survival tips helpful?"

Our laughter fills the oasis, echoing off the walls like a melody that nature herself composes. "Well, let's just say your tips add a certain... flavour to survival," I reply with a grin.

With an air of practiced camaraderie, Lia and I set to work, our makeshift 'five-star dining' unfolding beneath the oasis's tranquil canopy. We gather fallen branches and leaves, fashioning a simple fire pit near the water's edge. The anticipation of a warm meal fuels our efforts, the promise of sustenance a reward for our journey through the savannah's expanse.

The flames leap to life, casting a flickering glow upon our surroundings, illuminating the oasis with an enchanting radiance. As the fire crackles and dances, we arrange stones to create a stable cooking surface, the natural elements becoming our impromptu kitchen.

I pull a bundle of dried herbs from my bag, their earthy aroma infusing the air. "Found these while we were trudging through that golden sea."

Lia smirks, her eyes gleaming with approval. "Well, who knew our adventure would yield some hidden treasures?"

The oasis seems to hold its breath, the flames casting playful shadows upon our preparations. Lia retrieves a small pot from her bag, the metal cool to the touch. She fills it with water from the oasis, the liquid reflecting the dancing firelight like liquid gold.

As the water begins to heat, I take charge of the makeshift skewers we've crafted from twigs, carefully threading pieces of food onto them. The oasis's spirit seems to guide our hands, a reminder that even in the wild, there's an innate rhythm to life that we can tap into.

Lia adds the dried herbs to the pot, the fragrance enveloping us in a sense of comfort and anticipation. "Ah, the scent of our culinary masterpiece."

I chuckle, turning my attention to the skewers. "Just wait until you taste it. Then you'll be calling it a masterpiece."

With a quick glance exchanged, we both know it's not just about the meal. It's about the companionship, the shared experience that turns a simple act into a memory etched in time.

The pot simmers, its contents swirling with the promise of flavour. Lia reaches into her bag and retrieves a small container of grains, pouring them into the water with a practiced hand. The aroma of the cooked herbs and grains intermingle, a symphony of scents that permeates the oasis's air.

We sit back, our hearts light and our souls nourished by more than just the meal before us. The oasis watches over us, its presence a reminder that even in the wild, there are pockets of respite, moments of connection that transcend the challenges of the journey.

As the meal finally comes together, we share a knowing smile. The oasis has provided more than a place to rest; it's offered a sanctuary where friendship thrives, where sustenance is more than just food—it's the thread that weaves us into the tapestry of this untamed world.

Lia's eyes dance with amusement. "Ah, flavour, you say? My dear companion, consider your taste buds officially enlightened."

As our banter tapers off, I take a moment to absorb the oasis's embrace. The air is a gentle caress, a soft breath of relief after the savannah's oppressive embrace. The scent carries the earth's secrets, mingling with the subtle sweetness of nearby blossoms. The oasis's symphony continues, leaves whispering secrets and the water's gentle lapping composing a harmonious lullaby.

I reach out to touch the leaves that brush against my hand, their texture a testament to resilience and endurance. The vibrant green of their souls adds life to the oasis, a lush palette against the arid world outside. And just as our laughter lingers, the oasis's spirit remains, an invitation to pause, to rest, to find solace in nature's gentle arms.

The oasis is a canvas painted by time, its colours rich and layered like a tapestry woven from moments of solace. And as I close my eyes, I can almost taste the stories it whispers, tales of travellers who found haven here, weary souls who discovered sanctuary amid the wild.

With a contented sigh, I lean back against the cushioned corner, feeling the oasis cradle me like a cherished friend. The sun's fingers continue to weave patterns through the leaves, casting intricate shadows that dance upon my skin. The air, alive with the oasis's essence, is a balm that soothes both body and spirit.

Lia's voice breaks the peaceful stillness. "Well, aren't you just the picture of zen?"

I open my eyes, meeting her gaze. "Who knew an oasis could be such a haven?"

She smirks, a glint of mischief in her eyes. "Oh, this is just the beginning. Wait till you experience the 'five-star dining'."

As we prepare to savor our makeshift feast, the oasis's embrace remains, a timeless refuge that bridges the gaps between worlds. Here, amidst nature's gentle whispers and the symphony of water and leaves, we find ourselves entwined in a moment that is both fleeting and eternal.

As the first bite touches my tongue, a burst of flavours unfolds like a symphony of tastes. The grains, infused with the essence of the dried herbs, carry an earthy warmth that wraps around my palate. Each chew releases a subtle nuttiness, a reminder of the journey these humble ingredients have taken to reach our makeshift oasis haven.

The herbs themselves provide a symphony of notes. There's the gentle, minty undertone, cooling and soothing like a gentle breeze that rustles the leaves of the nearby trees. Then comes the hint of thyme, adding a savoury depth that resonates like the whispered secrets of the land itself. And amidst it all, a delicate touch of rosemary, its piney essence carrying the promise of adventure and exploration.

Lia's laughter dances through the air, her enjoyment mirroring my own. "Who knew a few twigs and herbs could taste this good?"

I nod in agreement, my mouth too full to respond. The grains and herbs work in perfect harmony, each bite a journey through the savannah, a taste of the wild made deliciously tangible. The oasis's spirit seems to linger in the flavours, a reminder that even in this far-off corner of the world, there's a connection that transcends the confines of geography.

As the meal continues, the firelight casts a warm glow upon us, turning the simple act of eating into a memory etched in amber hues. The oasis's tranquillity wraps around us, a cocoon of serenity that feels worlds away from the challenges we've faced and the journey that still lies ahead.

With each bite, the flavours deepen, the experience becoming more than just sustenance. It's a reminder that even in the untamed wild, there's a beauty that can be savoured, a connection that can be forged through something as simple as a shared meal. As the last remnants of our feast disappear, the flavours linger on my palate, a reminder of this oasis oasis—a moment of respite and nourishment that will remain imprinted on my senses.

As the last of the food disappears from our makeshift plates, a comfortable fullness settles over me. I lean back on my makeshift seat, a rock that's been worn smooth by the passage of time, and sigh contentedly. Lia's grin matches my satisfaction, and I can't help but feel a sense of camaraderie, a bond forged over a shared meal in the heart of the savannah.

With a stretch and a satisfied pat on my stomach, I turn to Lia. "So, how long do you plan on calling this oasis home?"

Lia glances around, her gaze lingering on the tranquil surroundings. "A day, maybe. It's a good spot to rest, let our bodies recover a bit."

I nod, taking in the oasis once more. "And what's the next course of action after this little oasis interlude?"

Lia's lips curve into a thoughtful smile. "Tomorrow morning, we move out. We'll head further north, through the savannah. It's a couple of days' journey, but it should bring us closer to AshWays."

Her words spark a mix of excitement and trepidation within me. "AshWays, huh? You think they'll be more welcoming than your last visit?"

Lia chuckles, a sound that ripples like a hidden stream. "Let's just say I'm hoping that your presence might help smooth things over."

With that, she rises from her seat and heads towards the small basin of water, the oasis's lifeblood that mirrors our own need for sustenance. "Mind getting the map from my bag?" she asks, her voice carrying a hint of mischief.

I oblige, rummaging through her bag until I find the folded piece of parchment. Handing it to her, I watch as she unfolds it, the paper crinkling softly like a whispered secret. With a careful finger, she traces the lines and annotations, her focus unwavering.

"Here," she says, tapping a point on the map.

I lean closer, my eyes following the trail of her finger. "That's where we are?"

Lia nods. "Exactly. The oasis is a good spot to rest, but it's not too far from the path we'll take tomorrow. Once we leave here, we'll continue north. There's a rhythm to the land, a flow of time and distance."

I watch as she delicately folds the map back up, her movements almost reverent. "So, we spend the rest of the day here, then move out tomorrow?"

Lia smiles, her eyes gleaming with a mixture of determination and hope. "That's the plan. A moment of respite, a chance to gather our strength, and then we keep pushing forward."

As she speaks, I find myself nodding, a surge of determination rising within me. The savannah might be vast and unyielding, but with Lia by my side, and the promise of AshWays beckoning like a distant beacon, I'm ready to face whatever challenges lie ahead.

The hours stretch lazily, like a cat basking in the warmth of the sun. As the day wears on, the oasis becomes our haven, a sanctuary of peace amidst the vast savannah. With the map safely stowed away, Lia and I find ourselves engaged in a myriad of activities to pass the time and prepare for the journey ahead.

We sit by the water's edge, our fingers skimming the cool surface as we talk and share stories. There's an ease to our conversation, a natural rhythm that we've settled into. It's as if the weight of the world has been lifted, if only for a while, and all that matters is this oasis and the companionship it offers.

Lia unfolds a piece of cloth, revealing an assortment of herbs and leaves she had collected during our journey. With a knowing smile, she starts to mix them, a concoction that fills the air with a soothing aroma. I watch with curiosity as she explains their properties and the benefits they offer, a lesson in survival and resourcefulness.

As the sun begins its descent, casting a warm golden glow across the savannah, Lia and I decide to gather some firewood. We scour the oasis's edges, collecting dry branches and fallen leaves. Our teamwork is seamless, a dance of coordination as we gather what we need for the night ahead.

With the fire crackling to life, its warm embrace fending off the encroaching night chill, we sit close, our backs against a large rock that serves as a natural barrier. The flames flicker like old stories whispered by the ancestors, casting playful shadows that dance along the oasis's walls.

As the stars emerge in the inky sky, we share a quiet moment of reflection. The savannah stretches out before us, a vast canvas that holds the promise of the unknown. I can't help but marvel at the contrast - the untamed expanse and the tiny oasis, a reminder that even in the harshest of landscapes, life finds a way to thrive.

The night wears on, and fatigue slowly settles in. We retreat to our makeshift resting spots, finding solace in the comfort of knowing we're not alone. The sounds of the savannah, once foreign, now become a lullaby, a symphony of crickets and distant calls that serenades us into sleep.

As I close my eyes, I'm filled with a sense of gratitude - for the oasis that cradles us, for the companionship that warms the night, and for the journey that lies ahead, promising adventure, challenge, and perhaps, the liberation we both seek.

****

The first rays of dawn pierce through the darkness, heralding the birth of a new day. As I lay nestled in my makeshift resting spot, a sudden cascade of cold water splashes onto me, jolting me awake. I sputter and sit up, blinking in shock as Lia stands before me, a triumphant grin on her face.

"Well, good morning to you too," I mutter, my voice dripping with sarcasm.

Lia laughs, a sound that's like a mischievous melody in the early morning stillness. "Oh, don't mention it. Just ensuring you're fully awake for the day's grand adventures."

I glare at her playfully, wiping droplets of water from my face. "You're lucky we're friends."

She raises an eyebrow. "Friends? Is that what they're calling it these days?"

We exchange a few more sarcastic remarks, a dance we've perfected over the course of our journey. But beneath the banter, there's an unspoken camaraderie, a bond that's been forged through challenges and shared experiences.

With a sigh, I stretch and start gathering my belongings, preparing for the day's journey. Lia watches with amusement, her lips quirking into a smirk.

"Ready to face the world, tomato boy?"

I roll my eyes, playfully exasperated. "Don't you have anything better to call me?"

She chuckles, the morning sunlight dancing in her eyes. "Not yet, I'm afraid. But I'll keep working on it."

I secure my bag and turn to Lia, a glint of determination in my eyes. "Alright, let's get moving."

She nods, her gaze lingering on me for a moment before she retrieves the map from her bag. As she unfurls it, I take a step closer.

"Mind if I hold the map this time?" I ask, a hint of mischief in my tone.

Lia scoffs, her fingers tracing the markings on the map. "Oh, of course. Because reading squiggly lines and figuring out where we are is child's play, right?"

I grin, undeterred by her sarcasm. "Well, I did ace Connect the Dots when I was a kid."

She rolls her eyes, but a small smile tugs at the corner of her lips. "Fine, fine. Here you go, oh great master of navigation."

I take the map from her with a flourish, a mock bow accompanying the gesture. "Why, thank you, Lia. Your faith in my navigational prowess is truly heartwarming."

We share a laugh, a final exchange of banter before we set out once more. The savannah stretches before us, a landscape of promise and possibility. As we step forward, side by side, I can't help but feel a surge of excitement. With Lia by my side, the journey ahead holds the allure of the unknown, and I'm ready to face it, squiggly lines and all.

Lia's gaze remains fixed on the horizon, her voice carrying a mix of fascination and wariness. "You know, what's most fascinating is that AshWays is the antithesis of Fleshbourne in every way. Where Fleshbourne is regal and sophisticated, AshWays is a vivid eruption of cyberpunk aesthetics. Imagine neon lights whizzing through the air like shooting stars, shopping malls made from jewels and crystals that shimmer like galaxies."

I can't help but visualize the stark contrast she's describing. "Sounds like a complete departure from the opulence of Fleshbourne."

"Absolutely," Lia confirms with a nod. "But despite its divided segments - North, East, South, and West - each part of the city carries the same frenzied atmosphere. It's like an ecstatic dystopian dream come to life."

The idea of a city divided into such distinct quadrants, yet unified in its eccentricity, both intrigues and unnerves me. "So, which part are we headed to?"

Lia chuckles softly. "West. It's known for its lush foliage and areas of thick forests. It's the only segment of AshWays that offers a respite from the city's manic energy. A bit ironic, isn't it?"

The anticipation of entering a world so different from any I've known ignites a spark of excitement within me. "Sounds like a sensory overload."

"Oh, it absolutely is," Lia agrees, her eyes glinting with a mixture of anticipation and a touch of mischief. "But don't worry, I'll be your guide to this vibrant maze."

The rhythmic beat of our footsteps on the path continues, punctuating our conversation. I glance up at the sky, noticing a few dark clouds gathering on the horizon. "Looks like rain might be on the way," I comment, pointing towards the gradually darkening sky.

Lia follows my gaze, a wry smile playing on her lips. "Ah, the joys of unpredictable weather. Truly, the savannah's version of a spa treatment."

I chuckle, a sense of camaraderie building between us. "I must admit, I could use a little refreshment."

As if in response to our conversation, the first droplets of rain begin to fall, creating dark spots on the dusty ground. The scent of earth and moisture hangs in the air, mingling with the sharp fragrance of the savannah's grass.

Lia lets out a half-laugh, half-sigh as the raindrops gently splatter across her clothes. "Well, at least it's not tomato-red this time."

We both quicken our pace, seeking shelter from the rain. A nearby cluster of trees offers some respite, their leaves already glistening with raindrops. With a shared glance, we break into a sprint, racing towards the natural cover.

"Rain might be refreshing, but I'm not exactly a fan of getting drenched," I admit, shaking my head to flick off a few errant drops.

Lia nods, brushing the rain-soaked strands of hair away from her face. "Agreed. Euphoria or not, I'd rather not resemble a drowned rat."

Under the canopy of leaves, the rain's intensity lessens, casting a gentle patter that provides a soothing backdrop to our conversation. We lean against the trees, both of us breathing a sigh of relief as the rain cools the air around us.

"So, what's the plan now?" I ask, peering out from under the trees at the rain-drenched landscape.

Lia tilts her head, her expression thoughtful. "Well, since we're already sheltered here, how about we wait until the rain stops? It shouldn't be too long."

I give her a wry grin. "Sounds like a plan. Beats being a part of a real-life water show."

She smirks in return, her eyes glinting with a playful challenge. "True. At least our fashion choices won't be the talk of the season."

As the rain continues to fall, we share a moment of shared humour, our determination to stay dry unshaken by the unexpected weather. The savannah's rain-soaked embrace has a way of emphasizing the unpredictability of our journey - a journey that now includes the vibrant enigma that is AshWays, waiting for us beyond the horizon.

Time trickles on, each raindrop a metronome marking its passage. The persistent rain shows no signs of letting up, and the meagre protection the trees offer is quickly proving insufficient. The gentle pattering that had initially soothed us has transformed into a constant, cold drizzle that seeps through our clothes and sends shivers down our spines.

Lia's patience, once unyielding, is now wearing thin. She lets out an exasperated sigh, casting an annoyed glance towards the sky. "Oh, fantastic. I've always wanted to experience life as a half-drowned rat."

I can't help but chuckle at her dramatic display of frustration. "Well, look on the bright side. At least you're getting that much-needed spa treatment after all."

Her response is a pointed glare that doesn't hide her dissatisfaction. "Ah, yes, the rejuvenating experience of feeling like a soggy piece of bread. Truly, I'm living my best life."

Despite her grumbling, I can't deny the truth in her words. The rain might be an inconvenience, but it's also a reminder of the unpredictability of nature. It's as if the savannah itself is testing our resilience, challenging us to adapt and find humour even in the most uncomfortable of situations.

I lean back against the tree, feeling the dampness of the bark seep into my clothes. "Well, at least we won't forget this leg of the journey anytime soon."

Lia's gaze softens as she looks at me, her annoyance momentarily replaced by a hint of amusement. "You always manage to find the silver lining, don't you?"

I shrug, a smile playing on my lips. "Someone's got to keep the optimism alive, right?"

She shakes her head, a small laugh escaping her. "You're something else, you know that?"

As we share a laugh amidst the rain-soaked surroundings, the realization hits me that even in the midst of discomfort, camaraderie is what makes the journey worthwhile. The savannah might be testing our patience, but it's also forging a bond between us that goes beyond the unpredictable weather. And as the rain continues to fall, I find myself grateful for this unexpected moment of connection amidst the drizzle.

Time stretches on, and with every passing minute, Lia finds a new reason to grumble. She paces beneath the trees, casting disdainful looks at the sky, as if she could bully the clouds into submission.

"Great, just great. Now my boots are caked in mud," she declares, hoisting one foot to inspect the mess as if it's personally offended her.

"I mean, who needs dry feet, right?" I reply with a playful smirk.

She shoots me a withering glance, her sarcasm undeterred by the rain. "Because nothing says 'jungle expedition' like fashionable boots, right?"

I let out an involuntary chuckle, watching her single-handed war against the raindrops. Her litany of complaints becomes a symphony of irritation, each grievance punctuated by an exaggerated gesture or a theatrical sigh.

"Honestly, if I ever track down whoever's responsible for this rain, they'll be in for an earful," she mutters, annoyance and wry humour mixing in her voice.

I can't help but laugh, my amusement blending with the sound of rain pattering on leaves. Lia's attention pivots to me, her brows furrowing.

"What's so funny?" she demands, a mix of exasperation and curiosity lacing her tone.

I manage to rein in my laughter, grinning at her. "Your talent for complaining is truly something."

She crosses her arms, faux-glaring at me. "Oh, you haven't seen anything yet. There's a whole symphony of complaints I've yet to unleash."

Raising my hands in mock surrender, I chuckle. "By all means, I'm here for the performance."

And perform she does, each grievance outdoing the last in terms of creativity.

"My hair is going to turn into a permanent frizz factory!" she announces, running her fingers through her damp locks as if they've betrayed her.

"I hear frizz is in this season," I reply with a grin.

Lia rolls her eyes, continuing her comedic monologue. "And don't even get me started on these clothes. I look like a wet cat."

"Well, you're a very fashionable wet cat," I tease.

She huffs, shaking her head in mock exasperation. "Oh, and let's not forget the pièce de résistance - soaked snacks. Nothing screams 'culinary delight' quite like wet crackers."

I laugh outright at that. "Ah yes, the pinnacle of gourmet cuisine."

As the rain persists, I realize that sometimes, the best response to adversity is to meet it with a dose of humour. So, I listen to Lia's ever-evolving catalogue of complaints, the rain adding its own percussion to our impromptu rainy day comedy show.

As the rain gradually begins to taper off, Lia's commentary doesn't miss a beat. If anything, her sarcasm seems to gain momentum along with the clearing sky.

"Well, would you look at that," she quips, eyeing the retreating rainclouds. "Even the rain decided to pack up and leave, probably tired of my rants."

I chuckle, shaking my head. "I'm sure the raindrops were hanging onto your every word."

She grins, a mischievous glint in her eyes. "Oh, absolutely. I've got quite the fan base among the precipitation."

We share a laugh, and the atmosphere lightens with the receding rain. Yet, Lia doesn't seem ready to let go of her witty tirade just yet.

"I mean, I must be the rain's personal critic if it's in such a hurry to escape," she continues, her tone dripping with mock self-importance.

I play along, feigning awe. "A true talent indeed. The rain should be honoured to receive your feedback."

She takes an exaggerated bow, her dripping hair sending tiny droplets flying. "Thank you, thank you. Don't worry, I'll be back for an encore."

As Lia and I press on through the changing landscape, the passage of time is marked by the gradual descent of the sun. The brilliant blue sky gives way to warm hues of orange and pink, painting the horizon with a breathtaking display. Shadows grow longer, and the golden expanse of the savannah takes on a softer, more subdued glow.

As daylight wanes, the pressing question becomes where we might find shelter for the night. The recent rain has transformed the terrain, leaving patches of mud that cling to our boots as we walk. The once-dry grass now glistens with dew, and the earth seems to hold onto the memory of the rain in its every pore.

The absence of an oasis this time around doesn't dampen our spirits, though it does present a challenge. With the savannah turned into a sea of mud, our options for rest are limited. Lia glances around, her expression thoughtful.

"Well, this is quite the conundrum," she muses, her eyes scanning the landscape.

I nod in agreement. "Seems like the mud had its own party after the rain."

She chuckles, then points to a slightly elevated area nearby. "How about that spot? It looks like the mud might be a bit less... enthusiastic."

I follow her gaze, studying the patch of ground she's indicated. It does appear to be marginally drier, the mud there more of a patchwork than a swamp. "Sounds like a plan," I reply, adjusting my steps to head in that direction.

As the sun dips lower, casting long shadows across the savannah, we finally reach the relatively drier ground. We set about gathering some of the drier grass to create a makeshift bedding, a small but welcome barrier between us and the mud.

Lia brushes off her hands, glancing around with a satisfied grin. "Well, I must say, we've turned mud into a five-star accommodation."

I chuckle, joining in her light-hearted tone. "Who needs luxury when you've got good ol' savannah mud?"

With our simple bedding prepared and the sun now resting just above the horizon, the world takes on a serene quality. The gentle rustle of the grass and the distant calls of unseen creatures blend into a soothing symphony. As darkness approaches, the stars begin to peek out one by one, adorning the night sky like scattered jewels.

My sleep shatters in an instant, Lia's voice urgent and panicked. "Wake up! We need to move, now!"

I jolt awake, confusion and adrenaline coursing through me. "What's going on?" I manage to get out, still disoriented from sleep.

Lia's eyes are wide with anxiety, her voice clipped and flustered. "No time for questions! Just get up and get your things. The scourge are near, and we have to go."

I scramble to my feet, her urgency infectious. My heart pounds as I gather my belongings, the reality of the situation hitting me like a wave. The scourge, relentless as ever, are dangerously close.

"How did they find us?" I ask, my mind racing to catch up.

Lia snaps, her tone tense. "I don't know, and it doesn't matter right now. We have to move!"

Her sharpness startles me into action. We can't afford to stand around pondering how they tracked us. As we hurriedly begin to move, Lia's agitation is palpable, her movements quick and determined.

"We need to distance ourselves from them," she urges, her voice on edge.

I nod, adrenaline pumping through my veins. The once calm

savannah now feels like a trap, danger lurking in every shadow. Lia glances over her shoulder, her face tense with worry.

"Keep moving, and don't ask so many questions!" she snaps, frustration evident in her voice.

I swallow my inquiries, understanding that her focus is solely on getting us to safety. The specter of the scourge's pursuit adds a new layer of urgency to our journey. We forge ahead, each step a deliberate move away from the looming threat.

Lia's flustered urgency is a stark reminder of the danger we're in. With every footfall, her desperation becomes more evident. The once serene landscape now feels hostile, our escape route narrowing to a treacherous path.

"We have to keep going," she urges, her voice a mixture of anxiety and determination.

The rhythm of our footsteps matches the pounding in my chest as we navigate the unforgiving terrain. Lia's hurried glances and sharp instructions keep me focused, driving me to match her urgency.

As dawn breaks, we press on, the savannah stretching endlessly before us. Lia's urgency is a constant reminder of the peril we're facing. Every second counts, and her frustration is a testament to the stakes of our escape.

Breathless and anxious, I manage to match Lia's hurried pace. The tension in the air is palpable, and my curiosity gets the better of me.

"How do you know they're near?" I ask, my voice a mixture of concern and curiosity.

Lia's face is a mask of panic, her eyes darting around as if expecting to see the scourge emerge from the landscape itself. She takes a quick, shallow breath before answering, her words rushed and tinged with fear.

"I heard voices, faint but unmistakable. They're spreading out, searching for us. They... they assumed you were dead after the fall. They must have tracked me, thinking I'd lead them to you."

Her words hit me like a blow. The realization that they believed me dead and that they're closing in with the intent to capture or worse sends a chill down my spine. Lia's panic is contagious, and I feel a knot of anxiety forming in my own chest.

"We can't let them catch us," she adds, her voice shaky.

I nod, a sense of urgency overriding any lingering traces of sleep. As we press forward, each step becomes a testament to our determination to escape this relentless pursuit. The fear in Lia's eyes is a reminder that there's no room for complacency - only swift, calculated movement to outpace the threat that draws ever closer.

The distant sound of hooves galloping cuts through the tension-laden air, confirming the relentless pursuit of the scourge. Lia's frustration bubbles over, her sarcastic exclamations mingling with the urgency of the situation. With a quick exchange of glances, we abandon our brisk walk for a full-on run, the wet mud beneath our feet making each step slippery and treacherous.

"Of course they have horses! It's not like we're just fleeing for our lives or anything!" Lia's voice drips with sarcasm, her annoyance evident even in the midst of our escape.

I can't help but chuckle, despite the circumstances. "Wouldn't be a proper pursuit without a little dramatic flair, right?"

Lia glances at me, her eyes a mix of anxiety and exasperation. "Oh, absolutely. Horses, masks, the whole villainous package."

We sprint through the muddy terrain, the echoes of the approaching hooves growing louder with every passing second. It's a desperate race against time, our feet slipping and sliding in the mud, our breaths coming in ragged gasps. But beneath the surface layer of panic, there's an odd sense of camaraderie in the face of danger, a shared understanding that we're in this together.

As we continue our mad dash, the galloping hooves draw nearer, the sound mingling with the pounding of our hearts. The savannah stretches out before us, seemingly endless, but every step takes us further from the encroaching danger. Our escape becomes a dance with adrenaline, a wild chase against the odds. And in the midst of it all, Lia's sarcastic outbursts serve as a strange but strangely effective motivator, pushing us forward with a mix of frustration and determination.

As we race forward, Lia's panicked urgency fills the air. I manage to squeeze out my question between breaths, "Lia, that scourge I fought on the rooftops... Why did he have a wound like Joseph's? And why do scourge have wounds themselves?"

Lia starts to explain, her words a mix of hurriedness and desperation, but her sentence is abruptly cut short as she shouts, "Look out!"

Reacting instinctively, I veer to the side, just in time to avoid colliding with a low-hanging branch. My heart thuds wildly as I cast a quick glance back at Lia, her eyes wide with alarm.

"Thanks for the heads up," I pant, my breaths ragged from both the sprint and the close call.

Lia nods, her expression still tense. "Sorry for the interruption. To answer your question, those wounds are... complicated. There's more to the scourge than meets the eye, but now's not the time to dive into it."

Our conversation is abruptly halted as a deafening sound of hooves reaches our ears, and my heart sinks as a scourge on horseback appears before us, blocking our path. Adrenaline surges through me, and I skid to a halt, my eyes locked onto the mounted figure.

Lia's frustration bursts forth in an exasperated breath, her brows knitting together in irritation. "I assumed they were tailing us from the rear. Yet, this one blocking our path suggests they've orchestrated a ring around our resting spot while we were vulnerable. Crafty move."

The realization hits me like a splash of cold water. "So, we're cornered then?"

Lia's lips tighten into a tense line, her gaze flickering around as if calculating our options. "Not necessarily. There might be a chance to shake them off if we backtrack and find an alternate route. But we can't linger here."

Her urgency resonates, and the gravity of our situation is palpable. The sun, now hugging the horizon, stretches shadows across the muddy savannah, casting an ominous hue over our dilemma. The sound of approaching hooves grows louder, a stark reminder that time is slipping through our fingers.

As the scourge in front of us dismounts, his horse comes into clearer view. The animal is a powerful, sleek beast, its ebony coat gleaming in the fading light. Its eyes are keen and alert, nostrils flaring as it paws at the damp earth. The scourge himself is draped in dark attire, a twisted symbol of his allegiance. His features are obscured by a mask, his eyes glinting with determination as he takes purposeful steps toward us, a chilling embodiment of the threat we face.

Lia's voice drips with sarcasm. "Oh, look who decided to join the party. Did the dramatic entrance class finally pay off?"

The scourge's eyes narrow beneath his mask, his steps deliberate as he moves closer. "I see your tongue is as sharp as ever, Lia."

She feigns surprise, her hand pressed to her chest. "Oh, you remember my name. Must be a special occasion."

He ignores her barb, his gaze fixed on her. "You've always had a way of stirring things up. Running away was a bold move."

Lia smirks, unfazed. "You know, leaving the circus can be quite liberating."

The scourge's tone grows colder. "You're not as free as you think. Fleshbourne's reach is long."

She rolls her eyes dramatically. "Ah, the Fleshbourne fan club. Always eager to welcome back their prodigal daughter."

His fists clench, a trace of anger breaking through his stoic facade. "You were one of us, Lia. Loyalty should mean something to you."

Lia's laughter rings out, a sound that cuts through the tension. "Loyalty? Is that what you call it when you're forced to follow orders like a puppet?"

He takes a step closer, his voice low and dangerous. "You had power. You had purpose."

Lia's eyes flash with defiance. "And now I have something better. Freedom."

The scourge's gaze intensifies, his words laced with a bitter edge. "You were our best. I thought you believed in our cause."

Her retort is swift and unapologetic. "Your 'cause' is built on oppression and lies. Funny how that didn't quite make it into the recruitment pamphlet."

He clenches his jaw, his voice growing colder. "You can't outrun your past, Lia."

Lia's tone is mocking, her words a challenge. "And you can't catch up with us. Seems like we're at an impasse."

As he takes another step, his voice drops to a low, dangerous whisper. "You think your little rebellion will change anything?"

Lia's voice is steady, her gaze unyielding. "It's already changing me. And I think that's what scares you the most."

Their verbal dance continues, a battle of wills and words. The tension in the air is palpable, a clash of two opposing forces that can't be resolved with a simple conversation. And as they exchange barbs and accusations, the past hangs heavy between them, a reminder of the choices that brought them to this moment.

"Lia, we need to focus," I interject urgently, my eyes darting towards the approaching sounds of hooves getting louder. "The rest of them will surround us any moment now."

Lia's eyes remain fixed on the scourge in front of us, her anger fuelling her words. "Oh, I'm focused, believe me. Just enjoying a little heart-to-heart with our charming friend here."

The scourge's grip tightens on his sword, his patience clearly wearing thin. "You always did have a gift for words."

Lia's retort is quick and laced with bitterness. "And you always had a talent for following orders, no matter how twisted they were."

I glance towards the horizon, the sight of galloping horses drawing nearer. "Lia, we don't have time for this. We need to find a way out of here."

She finally tears her gaze away from the scourge and glances at me, a spark of defiance still in her eyes. "Don't worry, we'll find our way. Just need to make sure our dear guest here has a proper farewell."

The sound of hooves grows deafening, and I feel a sense of urgency that's hard to ignore. "Lia, please, we can't take on all of them. We need to move, now!"

The sight that meets my eyes sends a chill down my spine – the rest of the scourge are closing in on us, forming a circle around our position. We're surrounded.

But Lia remains stubborn, her taunts continuing as if the encroaching danger is nothing more than a distant thought. "Oh, how delightful. Seems like the whole party is here."

My heart races as I step closer to her, my voice low and urgent. "Lia, they've got us surrounded. We need to find a way out, now."

She waves a dismissive hand, her focus solely on the scourge in front of us. "Oh, don't you worry. I've got this all under control."

I can't believe her audacity in the face of such peril. "Lia, this isn't the time for games. We're outnumbered."

She finally tears her gaze away from the scourge and turns to me, a smirk playing on her lips. "Outnumbered? Well, isn't that just how I like it?"

The rest of the scourge draw nearer, the tension in the air thickening with each passing moment. Lia's bravado might be impressive, but it's also incredibly dangerous. "Lia, please, we need to come up with a plan, and fast."

She glances around at the encroaching figures, her confidence faltering just slightly. "Right, a plan. Well, how about we dazzle them with my charm? Or perhaps a rousing speech about the power of sarcasm?"

I grip her arm, trying to make her understand the severity of the situation. "Lia, this is serious. We're running out of options here."

She finally seems to grasp the gravity of the situation, her gaze flickering to the scourge who have now formed a tight circle around us. "Fine, let's get out of here. But don't think this is over, boys."

As we start to edge our way backwards, Lia's taunts die down, replaced by a focused determination. The encircling wall of scourge draws tighter, and I can feel the weight of the danger pressing in from all sides. In this dire moment, it's clear that our only chance is to escape this tightening noose of danger before it's too late.

The scourge in front of us takes a step closer, his sneering grin visible even in the fading light. "Well, well, what's this? The mighty Lia has run out of witty retorts?"

Lia fixes him with a glare, her earlier sarcasm replaced by a simmering anger. "Oh, don't you worry, I've got plenty left for you."

He chuckles, a sound that's dripping with condescension. "Is that so? Seems to me like you're all out of tricks."

I can feel the tension building in the air, a charged atmosphere that's ready to explode at any moment. Lia's fists clench at her sides, and I can see the battle of words escalating into something more dangerous.

"You know, I used to be just like you," the scourge continues, his tone mocking. "Full of fire, thinking I could change the world with my defiance. But look where that got me."

Lia's eyes narrow, and her voice is laced with a bitterness that's hard to miss. "Oh, believe me, I'm well aware of where it got you."

His laughter echoes through the stillness, a harsh sound that seems to reverberate off the savannah itself. "You think you're so different now? That you've somehow managed to escape the fate that's inevitable for people like us?"

Lia's retort is sharp, her voice dripping with disdain. "You don't know the first thing about me."

The tension is palpable, a storm waiting to break. The rest of the scourge watch with a mixture of amusement and curiosity, as if they're waiting to see who will break first in this verbal showdown. But I can't let it come to that – we need to find a way out of this trap before it's too late.

"Lia, we can't stay here," I whisper urgently, tugging at her arm.

The circle of Scourge tightens around us, a suffocating ring of shadows and steel. Fear pulses through me like a relentless drumbeat, each beat matching the thud of my heart. It's as if the air itself has thickened, suffused with the weight of their presence.

My eyes dart to the leader of the Scourge as he dismounts from behind us. The bloodied sword in his hand gleams maliciously in the fading light, a cruel promise of the violence he's capable of. The metallic scent of blood and the sharp tang of anticipation mingle in the air.

But then, I steal a glance at Lia, standing beside me. Her demeanour is remarkably calm, a tranquil island amidst the storm of tension. It's as if she's embraced the impending danger, accepted it as just another facet of the harsh reality she's been navigating for so long.

I can't help but marvel at her composure. Is it genuine confidence, or a mask carefully worn? My own pulse is racing, my breath coming quicker as my mind races to find a way out of this trap.

The encircling Scourge watch us with calculating eyes, their masked faces betraying nothing.

And yet, amid the turmoil of fear and uncertainty, Lia stands steady, a symbol of resistance against their intimidation. It's as if she knows something I don't, as if her experience has taught her to stare into the face of danger and refuse to flinch.

The leader of the Scourge dismounts, his bloodied sword glinting menacingly in the fading light. The tightening circle of Scourge around us leaves me feeling trapped and vulnerable, my heart racing in response to the impending threat. In stark contrast to the dire situation, Lia's composure remains remarkably steady. She exudes an air of calm confidence, a calmness that seems almost seductive in the face of danger.

As the leader approaches Lia, their interaction becomes a dance of power and defiance, each word a brushstroke on an intricate canvas of tension.

The leader's voice carries a hint of malice, a cruel smile twisting his lips. "Well, well, if it isn't our little runaway Lia. You thought you could escape us forever, didn't you?"

Lia's response is delivered with a subtle lean, her voice laced with a sultry confidence. "Oh darling, forever is such a strong word. But I've certainly enjoyed the break from your charming company."

The leader's grip on his bloodied sword tightens, his threat evident in his words. "You've always been a feisty one, haven't you? But you know what they say about defiance, Lia. It's a trait that needs... correction."

Lia's raised eyebrow and suggestive smile show her defiance isn't shaken. "Mmm, correction, you say? Is that your euphemism for your violent tendencies?"

His eyes narrow, his tone growing darker. "Watch your tongue, Lia. Your wit won't save you from the fate you deserve."

She steps closer, her movements fluid and deliberate. "Oh, my dear, it's not my wit that's meant to save me. It's your inability to truly understand what it means to be free."

His voice turns into a low growl. "You were one of us, Lia. You know the consequences of your betrayal."

Her soft chuckle holds a touch of silk brushing against steel. "Ah, but it's precisely because I was one of you that I know how hollow your promises are. How you've traded true purpose for blind obedience."

His patience frays, his sword inching closer. "You'll regret your words, Lia. You can't outwit us forever."

With a lean, she draws closer, her breath brushing his ear as her words take on a seductive tone. "Regret? My sweet, there's so much I regret in this world. But standing up to you? That's not one of them."

In a moment that defies expectations, Lia's lips meet the leader's, a kiss that's equal parts daring and enigmatic. The world seems to pause, caught in the tension between their lips, a silence that echoes with the weight of defiance and an undercurrent of something more.

The leader's initial shock melts into a mixture of surprise and confusion, his grip on his sword slackening momentarily. As their lips part, a flicker of vulnerability crosses his eyes, a chink in the armour he so meticulously maintains. The encircling Scourge exchange perplexed glances, unsure how to interpret this unexpected turn of events.

Lia's gaze meets the leader's, her expression holding a knowing edge. "You see, I never wanted to escape you completely. Just the chains you've wrapped around your own soul."

His eyes narrow, a war raging within him as he struggles to comprehend the conflicting emotions this encounter has stirred. He steps back, his stance wavering between anger and something akin to disbelief.

The leader's fury simmers beneath his clenched jaw, his eyes ablaze with a mix of indignation and a smouldering desire to regain control. He steps forward, his bloodied sword held at a dangerous angle.

"Enough of your games, Lia. Your little charades won't save you now," he spits, his voice laced with venom.

Lia tilts her head, a smirk playing on her lips. "Oh, darling, you mistake my intentions. I'm not here to be saved. Rather, I'm here to offer you a glimpse of what you've denied yourself for so long."

His grip on the sword tightens, his knuckles turning white. "You think you can sway me with your tricks? You're nothing but a traitor, a deserter."

Lia's laughter dances through the charged air, a melody that both intrigues and infuriates. "Deserter? Or perhaps just someone who learned to dance to a different tune? You used to know that tune too, remember? The one that played in the hidden corridors of our past."

The leader's eyes flicker with a mixture of anger and confusion. "Don't pretend to know me."

Her voice drips with seduction, a honeyed lilt that seems to stir something beneath his veneer of control. "Oh, but I do know you. I know the man you were, the one who believed in something more than just blind allegiance."

His sword trembles, wavering for a moment as doubt dances across his features. "You left us. You betrayed us all."

Lia takes a step closer, her gaze unyielding. "Or perhaps, I found a way to escape the betrayal that consumed you."

He shakes his head, attempting to push aside the tendrils of doubt that Lia's words have sown. "This changes nothing. You will still face the consequences of your actions."

Lia's lips brush against his ear as she leans in, her voice a whispered promise. "Oh, I welcome the consequences, darling. But just remember, they won't only be mine to bear."

Lia's lips, a tantalizing promise of defiance, brush against his once more, a dangerous dance of seduction that draws him closer despite his better judgment. But just as their lips are about to seal another forbidden connection, the leader's arm raises, his sword poised for a final, deadly strike.

In a moment that defies the constraints of time, Lia's movements become a fluid blur of intention. Her kiss, infused with a cocktail of allure and power, remains unbroken even as she catches his wrist with an iron grip, suspending his arm in mid-air, the blade mere inches from her own head.

Their lips remain locked in a desperate fusion, a struggle between attraction and the danger that surrounds them. Lia's eyes, pools of unwavering determination, meet his gaze with an almost playful challenge, as if to say, "Is this all you have?"

The leader's fury mingles with shock, his arm trembling within Lia's grasp as he grapples with a force that transcends the physical.

With a calculated twist of her body, Lia breaks free from the seductive embrace, her lips parting from the leader's in a breathless separation. The air around them seems charged with an electric tension as she moves, fluid and fierce.

In the blink of an eye, Lia's hand darts towards the hilt of his sword, fingers closing around the grip with a lethal grace. In a seamless motion, she yanks the weapon from his grasp, the blade gleaming wickedly in the harsh light.

The leader's shock turns to a roar of fury as he realizes his weapon has been turned against him. Before he can react, Lia's movements become a blur of precision. She pivots on her heel, the stolen sword a seamless extension of her intent. With the grace of a dancer and the precision of a predator, she lunges forward, the blade finding its mark with a sickening accuracy.

The metal pierces through armour and flesh, a swift and brutal conquest. The leader's eyes widen in an agonized realization, his cry of rage transforming into a guttural sound of pain. The blade slides free, leaving a vivid trail of red in its wake, and he crumples to the ground, a fallen conqueror brought low by the very weapon he once wielded.

Lia stands over him, her chest heaving with exertion, her eyes a blazing testament to her defiance. Blood drips from the blade in her hand, a crimson reminder of her lethal determination. The Scourge surrounding them are frozen in stunned silence, their loyalty shattered by the unforeseen reversal of fate.

As the leader's body lies motionless on the ground, the weight of Lia's actions settles upon the air. The savannah seems to hold its breath, as if the very earth is aware of the pivotal moment that has transpired. And amidst the tension and the chaos, Lia stands as a singular figure of power, a woman who has turned the tide with a single, decisive stroke.

The once formidable leader's body lies sprawled on the savannah's unforgiving ground, a testament to the swift and brutal end that fate has dealt him. His eyes, once filled with arrogance and dominance, now stare lifelessly at the boundless sky above. The crimson stain of his own demise mingles with the wet earth, a chilling reminder of the violence that has transpired.

Amidst this tableau of death and triumph, Lia's form trembles with an inexplicable force. The blade in her hand reflects the stark reality of what she has just done, and a disbelieving tremor courses through her. Her eyes, wide with a mix of shock and horror, focus on the weapon that brought about this fate.

But it's not just the blade that captures her attention. A searing sensation, like the sting of a thousand fire ants, erupts at the base of her neck. A sudden, guttural scream tears from her throat, a raw and primal sound that pierces the heavy air. She clutches at the source of the pain, her fingers encountering something that wasn't there before.

As the echo of her scream dissipates into the distance, her eyes widen in disbelief at the sight her fingers find. A wound, glowing with an eerie light, has materialized on the back of her neck. It pulses with an otherworldly energy, its serpentine tendrils of light winding around her skin like a malevolent living thing.

Lia's breath comes in ragged gasps as she grapples with the reality of what this wound signifies. It's a transgression, a mark of retribution, an undeniable proof of her act against her former kin. She stares at it as if expecting it to vanish, to be nothing more than a cruel trick of her imagination. But the searing pain and the ethereal glow are all too real. Blood, dark and viscous, trickles from the wound on the back of Lia's neck, mingling with the rain-soaked earth. The wound pulses with an eerie light, its glow intensifying with each passing second. It's as if the mark itself is alive, a malevolent entity feeding on Lia's anguish and pain.

The scourge encircle us, their figures cast in stark relief against the backdrop of the savannah. Their blades gleam with a deadly promise, each swing of the weapon a symphony of impending doom. The air is thick with tension, a palpable miasma of danger that hangs over us like a dark cloud.

Lia's scream pierces the air, a raw and agonizing sound that seems to resonate with the very heartbeats of those present. It's a scream that carries the weight of her suffering, a culmination of all the pain she's endured and the torment she's faced. Her voice wavers between anguish and defiance, a last stand against the impending darkness.

The sound seems to echo across the open expanse, bouncing off the trees and the distant horizon. It's a cry that demands attention, a desperate plea for release from the torment that courses through her veins. It's a scream that speaks of vulnerability and strength in the same breath, a testament to the resilience of the human spirit even in the face of the cruellest fate.

As her scream fades, the silence that follows is deafening. The scourge stand poised, their weapons ready, their eyes fixed on Lia with a mixture of vindictive glee and grim determination. The world seems to hold its breath, waiting for the final blow, the moment when the scourge's vengeance will be realized.

Lia's actions are a symphony of urgency and precision. In a swift, fluid motion, she springs onto the back of the leader's horse, her movements almost choreographed. Her eyes lock onto mine, intense and unwavering, as she shouts, "Get on!" Her voice cuts through the chaos, a lifeline in this maelstrom of danger.

Without a moment's hesitation, I scramble onto the horse behind her, my heart racing in time with the frantic beat of hooves on the rain-soaked ground. I grasp onto Lia's waist, feeling her determination coursing through every fibre of her being. The blade, the very embodiment of the leader's violent intent, glistens ominously in her hand.

With a fierce determination, Lia thrusts the bloodied sword into the air. The blade arcs gracefully before gravity reclaims its hold, and it descends in a deadly arc towards the scourge that have encircled us. The blade's descent is both a threat and a proclamation, a testament to the power of defiance even in the face of overwhelming odds.

Panic ripples through the scourge as the sword's trajectory becomes apparent. Shouts of alarm and panicked neighs of horses fill the air, their disciplined formation unravelling like a fragile web caught in a storm. The blade's cruel descent severs their unity, shattering their cohesion into a frantic scramble for safety.

As the blade strikes the ground with a resounding thud, the dispersing scourge create a temporary opening, a gap in their ranks born from the chaos Lia has orchestrated. In that split second of opportunity, Lia urges the horse beneath us into motion, her grip on the reins unyielding. The horse responds with a surge of raw power, muscles flexing beneath its sleek coat.

We charge forward, propelled by a mixture of adrenaline, desperation, and the undeniable instinct for survival. The world becomes a blur of rain, grass, and the pounding of hooves, each beat a rhythmic defiance against the encroaching danger. The scent of damp earth mingles with the sensation of wind whipping against my skin, an intoxicating concoction that heightens my senses.

As the pounding of hooves carries us away from the encircling danger, the rain-soaked savannah stretches out before us, a landscape transformed by the fierce current of our escape. Lia's grip on the reins is unyielding, her determination a palpable force in the air. The horse beneath us gallops with a wild grace, its breath a rhythm that matches the beat of our racing hearts.

The cries of the scourge fade, swallowed by the expanse that now separates us. Yet, amid the surge of adrenaline and the urgency of our flight, a question lingers like a shadow in the back of my mind. What lies ahead for us in the unknown lands beyond this tumultuous chase? The answer is as uncertain as the future that unfurls before us, a chapter yet unwritten in the story we're weaving together. And so, with the relentless savannah stretching onward and the taste of freedom mingling with the tang of rain, we gallop forward, leaving the echoes of danger behind but the weight of our choices ever present.

12

Promiscuous

In the days following our narrow escape from the scourge, Lia and I find ourselves back on track towards AshWays. The memory of the confrontation lingers, and we often steal glances at each other, silently acknowledging the danger we narrowly evaded.

As we continue our journey, we engage in a conversation about Lia's recent wound. She explains that the pain it causes is a unique consequence of her past as a Scourge. Each time she commits a transgression against their code, the wound acts as a reminder, amplifying the pain with each new offense. It's a cruel reminder of her past, a mark of the life she once led and the choices she now opposes.

We ride silence for a while, the weight of our individual burdens hanging heavy in the air. The landscape around us shifts, the savannah giving way to a more varied terrain as we draw closer to AshWays. The air is thick with anticipation, a mixture of apprehension and determination guiding our steps.

In our shared journey, we find solace and understanding, despite the secrets and pain that lie between us. As we inch closer to the enigmatic city, we are both acutely aware that our alliance will be tested, our strength challenged, and our convictions pushed to their limits. But for now, in the face of uncertainty, it's the unity between us that provides the glimmer of hope we need to persevere.

"Does it hurt?" I finally break the silence, my voice laced with concern as I glance at Lia's wound.

She offers a half-smile, her eyes distant for a moment. "More than you can imagine. But pain has become an old companion, a reminder of my past and my defiance."

I nod, not needing her to elaborate. The weight of her transformation from Scourge to ally is heavy, and I can't help but admire the strength she carries within her.

"And what about you?" Lia's gaze turns towards me, her eyes searching mine. "How are you holding up?"

I shrug, trying to mask the pain and exhaustion that are slowly seeping into every inch of my body. "I'm alright. Just a bit tired."

Her lips twitch in amusement. "Ah, the classic 'I'm-fine-but-I'm-really-not' response. You really think you can fool me with that?"

I chuckle softly, appreciating her ability to read me. "Well, I guess I can't hide anything from you."

"That's the spirit," she replies with a wink. "But seriously, don't push yourself too hard. We're getting closer to AshWays, and we'll need all the energy we can muster."

I nod in agreement, my thoughts already wandering to what lies ahead. AshWays, the city of euphoria, is bound to be a challenge. The idea of a place where joy is manufactured and enforced is both fascinating and deeply unsettling. But it's a challenge we've chosen to face together, riding through the changing landscape on our horse.

The surroundings shift again, and I can see the outline of a sprawling city on the horizon. My heart quickens, a mixture of excitement and trepidation swirling within me. I steal a glance at Lia, who seems lost in her own thoughts, her expression a mixture of determination and something else I can't quite decipher.

As we ride on, I can't shake the feeling that our journey is far from over. The road ahead will test us in ways we can't predict, and the secrets that have yet to surface could change everything. But with Lia by my side, I find a renewed sense of purpose and the courage to face whatever challenges await us in AshWays.

After about an hour of riding, Lia gracefully dismounts from the horse, a mischievous glint in her eyes as she turns to me.

"Alright, partner in crime," she begins with a smirk, "let's have a reality check here. Sneaking one person into AshWays would be like trying to teach a fish to climb a tree. But two? Well, that's like throwing a whole parade."

Her words elicit a chuckle from me, as they often do. "So, our chances of a stealthy entrance are slim to none, then?"

Raising an eyebrow, she feigns mock surprise. "Oh, I'd say we're dancing around 'none' quite enthusiastically. But worry not, my friend, I've got a plan."

I lean against the horse, curious and amused. "I'm all ears."

Lia paces a little, her hands moving animatedly as she speaks. "Imagine this: AshWays is all about those who ooze euphoria, right? So, we're going to embrace our inner euphoria, my friend. We'll be walking, talking, beaming embodiments of ecstatic joy."

A laugh escapes me. "You mean, we pretend to be the happiest beings on the planet?"

Her grin widens. "Exactly! We'll dance through the streets, smile till our cheeks ache, and burst into songs of unbridled elation."

Shaking my head, I'm still chuckling. "Lia, have you lost your mind?"

Clapping her hands in excitement, her eyes sparkling, she retorts, "On the contrary, I've found a way to waltz through AshWays without anyone blinking. We'll be so outrageously, unimaginably joyous that they'll think we're part of a circus."

Wiping away a tear from laughing, I regain my composure. "Do you honestly believe this can work?"

Lia shrugs, a grin playing on her lips. "Well, it's an experiment worth testing, don't you think? And at the very least, we'll give the locals something to gossip about."

As the laughter subsides and we stand there, discussing our eccentric plan, I can't shake off the feeling that whatever AshWays holds for us, we'll be facing it together, with a shared determination and a healthy dose of whimsy.

With the decision made, we leave the horse behind, both of us acknowledging the impracticality of bringing it along. Our feet now firmly on the ground, we proceed on foot, the sun descending swiftly and surrendering the sky to the grasp of night.

Lia's voice slices through the encroaching darkness, excitement tinting her tone as she whispers, "We're getting close, my friend. Can you hear it?"

Straining my ears, I soon discern the distant cacophony of joy, laughter, and music. The collective euphoria of AshWays echoes through the air, reaching out to us even before we set eyes on its illuminated silhouette.

A few more minutes of brisk walking, and there it is – AshWays. The city sprawls before us, a shimmering utopia in stark contrast to the night sky. Neon lights weave ribbons of colour through the air, casting an iridescent glow upon the towering buildings. The city's towering gates, more colossal than even those of Fleshbourne, stand as a testament to the grandeur within.

The sheer luminosity of AshWays is almost blinding, and I squint against its brilliance. It's as if the city is trying to outshine the stars above, to create its own universe of light amid the darkness.

Lia's voice is soft with awe as she mutters, "Welcome to the 'city of euphoria,' my friend."

The muffled beat of music reaches us, and the air hums with the ecstatic energy that emanates from within AshWays. It's a stark departure from the solemn silence of the savannah, a living, breathing entity that pulses with life and celebration.

But beneath the radiant façade, I can't shake the sense that there's something deeper, something concealed beneath the surface of unbridled joy. AshWays might be a beacon of light, but just like the Scourge-infested streets of Fleshbourne, it harbours its own enigmatic secrets.

As we stand on the cusp of this bustling metropolis, the contrast between the city's brilliance and the obsidian sky above mirrors the choices ahead of us – to blend in, to uncover the truth, or perhaps, to reclaim the freedom that both of us have been deprived of for far too long.

****

As we approach the outskirts of AshWays, Lia's excitement seems to magnify. She glances around, a sly grin playing on her lips.

"You know, my friend, blending in here means embracing a whole new level of... shall we say, style?" she quips, her eyes glinting mischievously.

I raise an eyebrow, unsure of what to expect. My curiosity is soon met with surprise, though not exactly the kind I had hoped for. Lia begins to undress, pulling her shirt off in one swift motion, revealing a bralette that's far more revealing than anything I've seen in a while. She then proceeds to rip her trousers, transforming them into a pair of extremely short shorts. I can't help but feel my cheeks flush with a mixture of embarrassment and discomfort.

"Are you serious?" I manage to sputter out, my voice a mix of disbelief and something that might be akin to horror.

Lia chuckles, seemingly unfazed by my reaction. "Oh, come on! It's all part of the local fashion. And believe me, we need to blend in as best we can. AshWays isn't exactly known for its conservative attire."

I avert my gaze, feeling rather exposed myself in my normal clothes. "But isn't this a bit... much?"

Lia's laughter is rich and throaty. "Trust me, my friend, when in AshWays, do as the AshWaysians do. It's not just about the clothes, it's about the attitude. We need to look like we belong here, like we're ready to join in on the endless revelry."

"Just... don't expect me to pull off those... shorts," I mutter, my cheeks still aflame.

Lia smirks and gives me an exaggerated once-over. "Hmm, you're right. They might not be your colour."

As we continue walking, I can't help but shake my head, marvelling at the lengths we're willing to go to fit in – even if it means embracing fashion choices that make me cringe. AshWays might be a realm of vibrant lights and euphoric celebrations, but it's clear that it operates on a set of rules that are entirely its own.

As we step over the threshold into AshWays, it's as if we've entered a completely different dimension. The atmosphere is thick with the scent of excitement and the pulsating rhythm of a city that never sleeps. Neon lights paint the air in surreal hues, casting an otherworldly glow on everything they touch. Laughter and music intertwine, creating a symphony of joyful chaos that fills every corner.

People swarm the streets, each dressed in their own version of the outlandish attire that Lia now wears. The concept of modesty seems to have been left at the city gates. Men and women alike sport revealing outfits that are more akin to works of art than functional clothing. Tattoos cover every visible inch of skin, transforming bodies into canvases of intricate designs and vibrant colours.

Eyes are wide with euphoria, their expressions exaggerated, as if they're living in a constant state of exhilaration. Money is tossed carelessly into the air, fluttering down like confetti in a never-ending celebration. Glasses filled with every imaginable colour of liquid are raised high, as if to toast to the never-ending night.

Amidst this kaleidoscope of sensory overload, the city itself stands as a monument to extravagance and excess. Towering skyscrapers adorned with holographic billboards reach towards the sky, competing for attention with each other. Bridges woven from what seems to be a fusion of metal and glass span the gaps between buildings, connecting different layers of this vertiginous metropolis.

The streets are alive with a kinetic energy that seems to thrum through every inch of pavement. Markets filled with exotic wares spill out onto the sidewalks, their vendors haggling with customers in a symphony of diverse languages. The air carries the scent of an eclectic mix of cuisines, from savoury to sweet, as food carts line the streets, their vendors dishing out tantalizing delicacies to eager patrons.

As I take in this dazzling, chaotic scene, I can't help but feel overwhelmed by the sheer vibrancy of AshWays. It's a city of extremes, where every emotion is heightened, every experience intensified. And amidst it all, Lia and I stand, dressed in our outlandish outfits, ready to immerse ourselves in this bewildering realm of euphoria and enigma.

In the heart of AshWays, the city's frenzied energy seems to seep into our very beings. Lia, ever the chameleon, fully embraces the spirit of the place. Her shirt discarded, her attire barely more than a hint of fabric, she navigates the swirling crowds with a devil-may-care grin. Every step she takes seems to exude a kind of unrestrained confidence that draws people towards her like moths to a flame.

As the night wears on, I watch with a mixture of amusement and disbelief as Lia throws herself into the intoxicating atmosphere. She dances wildly with strangers, her laughter riding the waves of music that crash over us. Her lips meet unfamiliar ones in kisses that are fleeting but fiery, as if she's trying to taste every flavour the city has to offer. Her actions are bold, audacious, and as uninhibited as the city itself.

And then there's me, caught in this whirlwind of revelry. I've had a few drinks, enough to feel the warm haze settle over my thoughts, but not enough to lose all sense of reality. I find myself chiming into the ecstatic chatter of the locals, sharing in their laughter and their exaggerated tales. The city's euphoria is infectious, and it's hard not to get swept up in it.

Amidst the chaos, I exchange stories and experiences with those around me, my words tinged with a blend of wonder and incredulity. I'm an outsider, a stranger in this vibrant tapestry of life, yet for a moment, I feel like I belong. The boundaries of convention seem to blur, and I find myself joining in the spectacle, dancing to rhythms that were once foreign to me.

As the night wears on, the boundary between reality and revelry becomes increasingly blurred. The city pulses with a rhythm that matches the beat of our hearts, drawing us further into its embrace. Lia and I, in our own ways, have become part of this enigmatic world, swept away by its intensity, its hedonism, and its promise of endless ecstasy.

Amid the vibrant chaos of AshWays, I find myself engaged in snippets of conversations with the locals. Their words are a mix of wild enthusiasm and seemingly boundless excitement. Some are so absorbed in their own euphoria that they barely register my presence, while others fixate their attention on Lia, their gaze lingering a little too long, their intentions all too obvious.

"Hey there, stranger," a man with a broad grin and eyes glazed over by the city's atmosphere addresses me. "You with that fiery one?" His nod towards Lia is accompanied by a suggestive grin.

I offer a wry smile in response, playing along with the spirit of the place. "Oh, you've noticed her, huh? She's quite the firecracker."

He chuckles, a hearty sound that resonates with the revelry around us. "Firecracker indeed. I'd happily spend a night with her."

I raise an eyebrow, suppressing a flicker of annoyance. "You wouldn't be the first one to say that."

He claps me on the back, still grinning. "Well, cheers to you, my friend. You're a lucky one tonight."

I nod, masking my irritation with a practiced grin. "Lucky indeed."

As the night unfolds, similar encounters occur, each person's gaze on Lia carrying the same unspoken proposition. While my insides might churn with a mixture of protectiveness and frustration, I keep my outward demeanour affable. I laugh with them, share in their jests, and nod in agreement when they suggest the allure of a night with her.

Lia's infectious laughter rings through the air as she drags me away from the pulsating crowd and into the shelter of a dimly lit corner, shadows playing across her flushed face. Beads of sweat dot her forehead, evidence of the fervent dancing that she's been swept into.

"Did you see that guy's technique?" she quips, her voice dripping with playful disapproval as she swipes her hand across her lips.

I chuckle, leaning against the cool stone wall behind me. "Oh, you mean the one who practically devoured your face?"

She lets out an exaggerated shudder, a playful twinkle in her eyes. "Exactly! I mean, sure, I'm all for being open-minded and embracing local customs, but there's a fine line between enthusiastic and invasive."

We share a knowing laugh, the contrast between her carefree exterior and her shrewd observations not lost on me. As she takes a deep breath, her laughter fading, I can't help but admire the way she navigates the absurdity of AshWays with a sense of grace and her own brand of humour.

"You know," she begins, her tone shifting to a more contemplative note, "it's easy to get lost in all of this. It's like the city's offering an escape from reality, but at the same time, it's trapping everyone in a different kind of facade."

I nod in agreement, the distant sounds of revelry and the intermittent glow of neon lights serving as a backdrop to our conversation. "It's a paradox, isn't it? An escape that's also a cage."

She leans against the wall beside me, a wistful smile tugging at her lips. "Exactly. And as much as I enjoy playing along, I can't shake the feeling that there's something darker beneath the surface."

Her words resonate with a truth that I've been feeling as well. AshWays might be a city of euphoria, but it's built on a foundation of manufactured joy, and behind the neon-lit façade, shadows linger.

"I think we need to be careful here," I say, my voice low, my eyes scanning the revellers who pass by, their laughter and wild gestures masking something deeper. "This place might be more dangerous than it appears."

Lia's gaze meets mine, and for a moment, the levity in her eyes fades, replaced by a shared understanding of the precarious situation we've found ourselves in. The disorienting blend of ecstasy and unease that defines AshWays is a puzzle we must navigate if we're to uncover its secrets and make our presence known without getting ensnared by its allure.

But for now, as the city continues to throb with life around us, we stand side by side in the hidden corner, a temporary respite from the kaleidoscope of emotions and experiences that AshWays offers.

In that moment, the atmosphere around us seems to shift. A man, his features barely registering in my peripheral vision, pulls Lia into an embrace, his lips finding hers in an almost predatory kiss. My initial instinct is to look away, to give them the semblance of privacy amidst the frenetic dance of the North. But as I steal a glance, I'm met with a surprising twist.

Lia's initial expression of shock and disgust quickly transforms. A knowing glint sparks in her eyes, and the lines of her lips soften. Her fingers, which had been poised to push him away, now find purchase on his shirt, her body leaning into his with a deliberate surrender. It's as if she's slipped into a role, playing a part in a script I'm not privy to.

A faint smile tugs at the corners of my lips, and I avert my gaze, giving them the illusion of privacy. It's an odd mixture of emotions that stirs within me – relief that Lia has a handle on the situation, curiosity about the intricate dance she's performing, and perhaps a tinge of awkwardness at being a bystander to this carefully choreographed scene.

My attention shifts to the swirling lights of the North, letting the pulsating music and the laughter of the revellers fill the space between my thoughts. Lia's act is a reminder that AshWays is a city of masks, of personas that shift and change with the flicker of a moment. And in the midst of this extravagant masquerade, I find myself wondering – who are we, truly, amidst the enigmatic currents of this dystopian haven?

****

The dawn light creeps in through a cracked window, casting a muted glow over the unfamiliar room. The air is thick with the aftermath of euphoria – the remnants of a night that had blended into the surreal, the wild energy of AshWays still vibrating in the walls.

Lia stirs beside me, a groan escaping her as she slowly props herself up on her elbows. Her features are etched with the aftermath of the night's revelry – her eyes heavy-lidded and bleary, her hair tangled in disarray. It's a stark contrast to the vivacious woman I've come to know, and I can't help but feel a hint of sympathy as she winces, one hand pressed to her throbbing temple.

"Ugh," she mutters, her voice a raspy murmur. "Tell me we didn't partake in some sort of dare involving copious amounts of AshWays' finest poison."

I stifle a chuckle, shifting to lean against the wall. "I'm fairly sure we didn't. But then again, last night's events seem like something out of a fever dream."

She casts me a droll look, her lips twisting into a wry smile. "You're telling me."

As if on cue, a wave of nausea washes over her, and she rushes towards a nearby basin just in time to empty the contents of her stomach. I offer a reassuring pat on her back, keeping my amusement in check as the remnants of her excesses find their release.

"We were lucky to find this place," I mention as she finally straightens, her face pale and drawn.

She nods, wiping her mouth with the back of her hand. "Yeah, lucky for the person who owns this place too, since they're now playing host to a pair of unexpected guests."

I glance around the room, noting the distinct lack of concern for privacy. "Doesn't seem like anyone's too bothered about personal space around here."

Lia snorts, a mixture of amusement and annoyance in the sound.

"No kidding. The people here wouldn't bat an eye if we redecorated their living room."

The distant sounds of the city's euphoria continue, the revelry undisturbed by our presence. It's a stark reminder of the carefree chaos that pervades AshWays, a place where personal boundaries are as fluid as the neon lights that adorn its streets.

Lia gingerly slides back down onto a makeshift bed, her head still resting against the wall. "Remind me to never drink again. Or at least not until we're far away from this madness."

I can't help but chuckle. "Considering how quickly you embraced the madness, I think the 'never drink again' part might be easier said than done."

She smirks, though her eyes betray the remnants of discomfort. "Oh, hush. I'll be right as rain in no time. Just need to let my liver catch up to the shenanigans."

As she closes her eyes, seeking a respite from her hangover, I find myself lost in the sheer absurdity of our situation. Here we are, navigating a city that thrives on the extremes of pleasure and recklessness, while we inch closer to our goal of the West – a place that's promised to be a different shade of this intoxicating tapestry. The lines between reality and this euphoric illusion blur, leaving me wondering if, beneath the neon lights and the manic laughter, lies a deeper truth waiting to be unveiled.

I lean against a wall, my gaze flitting between the vibrant chaos of the room and Lia's dishevelled form. In her disarray, she's an embodiment of AshWays' unpredictable spirit – a fierce dancer amidst the whirlwind of euphoria and excess.

Lia's complaints about the raucous nightlife flow like a river, her words laced with her signature sarcasm. She details her encounters with the locals, painting vivid vignettes of men who seemed more interested in their own bravado than anything else. Her expressions shift from distaste to reluctant amusement, her own recounting of the night's antics eliciting a reluctant chuckle from me.

As the morning light seeps through the cracked windows, casting fragmented rainbows on the walls, Lia's voice weaves through the air, blending with the city's distant melodies. In this mismatched room, surrounded by AshWays' unfiltered authenticity, I find myself navigating the thin line between reality and the surreal, just as I am in this enigmatic city. And with Lia's tales of the previous night and her irreverent commentary, the room becomes a haven of shared stories in the midst of the city's fervour.

While the vibrant pulse of AshWays throbs beyond the room's confines, I wait patiently in the bedroom as Lia ventures into the shower. The sound of water splashing against the tiles mingles with her occasional exclamations, a concoction of surprise and pleasure. Her slight screams pierce through the air, each one a testament to the healing warmth of the water meeting her wounds.

Minutes stretch, and soon, the bathroom door creaks open, steam billowing out. Lia steps into the room, bare skin painted with a rosy flush from the steam-kissed shower. Her sarcasm, never far from her lips, is a steady accompaniment.

"I've decided I might as well stroll back out onto the streets like this. Seems like something these locals would fully embrace," she quips, her words laced with that biting humour I've come to expect. Her unabashedness about her body, even in the midst of this eccentric city, is another facet of her that blends seamlessly into AshWays' nonconformist ethos.

Her gaze sweeps over me, her lips curling into a playful smirk. "Well, have fun in the shower. I'm sure the walls here have heard their share of your pained groans by now."

I roll my eyes, managing a half-smile despite the twinge of discomfort that her remark invokes.

Under the invigorating cascade of water, my body initially

protests the intrusion, my wounds reacting with a sharp sting. But as the warmth envelops me, a soothing balm gradually spreads, coaxing my aching muscles into a reluctant relaxation.

I step out of the shower, the sensation of the cool air contrasting with the lingering warmth on my skin. Drying myself off with a towel, I wrap it around my waist, my comfort zone significantly narrower than Lia's when it comes to sartorial audacity.

As I re-enter the bedroom, I find her perched by the window, her gaze seemingly fixated on the lively street below. Her voice holds a tone of incredulity as she speaks, her disbelief echoing through her words.

"It's like they're immune to exhaustion, hangovers, and even self-awareness," she muses, shaking her head in mock exasperation. Her sharp observations come woven with humour, a defence mechanism against the overwhelming oddities of AshWays.

Her gaze flicks to me as I enter the room, wrapped in my towel, a faint smirk playing on her lips. "You know, I've been conducting an unofficial study, and I'm starting to believe these locals are fuelled by some sort of never-ending libido potion. It's like they're on a mission to defy the laws of basic human energy reserves."

Her laughter is infectious, and I can't help but join in, the sheer absurdity of the situation finding a strange camaraderie between us. In the midst of this surreal city, where pleasure seems to have taken a sharp turn into obsession, Lia's wit is a beacon of sanity.

As we step back into the colourful chaos of AshWays, I can't help but feel like an outsider in a fever dream. The streets are alive with a frenzied energy, a whirlwind of laughter, music, and a palpable sense of liberation. It's as if the inhabitants of this city have surrendered themselves to the whims of hedonism, moving with an unapologetic freedom that defies convention.

Lia's choice of attire, or lack thereof, seems perfectly in tune with the audacious spirit of AshWays. She wears her nonchalance like an accessory, while I, still feeling a touch more reserved, have followed her lead by shedding my shirt. Her infectious confidence is a buffer against the bewildering scene around us.

The cityscape is a vivid tapestry of neon lights, pulsating with an otherworldly glow. The architecture, a collision of futuristic innovation and eerie decadence, stands as a testament to AshWays' extravagant excess. The streets are a sea of bodies, each movement an uninhibited expression of desire and euphoria. Money floats through the air like confetti, discarded as if its value is merely an afterthought.

Lia's observations capture the essence of it all as she murmurs to me, "It's like the entire population is untamed and unhinged, surrendering to every whim with a fervour that's equal parts fascinating and alarming."

But her demeanour shifts as we encounter the locals up close, her tone transforming from sardonic to sweet and accommodating. Her interactions are marked by smiles and pleasant exchanges, a stark contrast to her commentary moments ago. It's as if she knows how to navigate the currents of this city, morphing from observer to participant with a practiced ease.

As we navigate the streets, I can't help but marvel at the duality of Lia's presence - her commentary hinting at a certain detachment from the chaos, while her interactions reveal an adeptness at blending into the intoxicating rhythm of AshWays. And in this sprawling carnival of excess, I find myself both captivated and bewildered, unsure of whether to revel in the spectacle or seek refuge from its relentless intensity.

Lia's frustration is palpable, a simmering undercurrent beneath her practiced smiles and forced pleasantries. Her determination to reach the western part of AshWays is evident, and yet, at every turn, she's intercepted by the ebullient locals. They pull her into their midst, their laughter ringing in her ears as they engage her in their wild revelries. She plays along, laughing when she must, dancing when prompted, all the while shooting me fleeting glances that are a mixture of exasperation and amusement.

For my part, I'm not immune to the attention either. As we make our way through the boisterous crowds, I'm repeatedly accosted by admiring women who seem undeterred by my own awkward attempts at politeness. Their advances are unrelenting, their eyes wide with the same euphoria that seems to be AshWays' prevailing currency. I can only offer strained smiles and curt nods, doing my best to disentangle myself from their enthusiastic grasp.

The clash between Lia's determination and the city's overwhelming atmosphere creates a peculiar tension, as if we're both caught in a whirlwind that threatens to sweep us off course. Amidst the relentless fervour of the locals, Lia's guise of enjoyment starts to blur the lines between acting and reality, and it's hard to discern where her discomfort truly begins. Each encounter with the locals seems to be testing her resolve, a battle of wills that she's navigating with a mix of stubborn determination and skilful diplomacy.

A local woman sidles up to me, a mischievous glint in her eyes. "Well, aren't you a handsome one? Lost in the whirlwind of AshWays, are you?"

I chuckle, glancing around at the frenetic activity that engulfs us. "Yeah, it's definitely a bit overwhelming."

She smirks, her gaze lingering on me. "You're not from around here, are you? I can tell by that look in your eyes. The city's got you all tangled up."

I smirk back, amused by her perceptiveness. "You could say that. It's quite a... unique place."

Her playful demeanour remains as she leans in a bit closer. "Oh, 'unique' is one word for it. But I have to say, you look like you could use a little... distraction."

I raise an eyebrow, intrigued. "I'm just trying to navigate my way through this ecstatic chaos."

Her tone grows more suggestive. "Well, lucky for you, I'm an expert in showing newcomers a good time. And I'm sure you've got a few secrets to share, too."

I can't help but grin at her audacity. "Secrets? What kind of secrets are we talking about?"

Leaning in even closer, she adopts a sultry tone. "Oh, you know, the kind that can make your stay here unforgettable. Let's just say I'm a connoisseur of experiences."

My grin widens, and I decide to play along. "I appreciate the offer, really, but I'm here on business. Got a destination in mind and all that."

She pouts in a playful, yet alluring manner. "Business? In Ash-Ways? You're missing out on all the fun, handsome."

I chuckle again, shaking my head. "Well, maybe some other time. Right now, I've got a mission to accomplish."

Her smirk remains as she studies me. "You're a tough one, aren't you? But mark my words, you won't be able to resist the pull of AshWays for long."

I return her gaze, a challenge in my eyes. "We'll see about that. Good luck with your... endeavours."

As we part ways, her laughter lingers in the air, mingling with the city's relentless euphoria.

Lia watches the interaction with an amused twinkle in her eye. As the local woman moves away, she raises an eyebrow at me. "Well, well, aren't you the charmer? Making friends already?"

I chuckle, shaking my head. "Just trying to blend in, you know."

Lia smirks, a hint of mischief in her tone. "Ah, yes, blending in. Because shirtless is definitely the latest fashion trend in AshWays."

I roll my eyes, unable to stifle my own laughter. "Well, when in Rome, right?"

She grins, the sarcasm practically dripping from her words. "Right, of course. Just remember, Rome also burned to the ground, so be careful."

Lia and I push forward through the vibrant chaos of AshWays, our determination to reach the West propelling us forward. The streets pulse with an intoxicating energy, the revelry of the city's inhabitants forming a cacophony that fills the air. Neon lights streak across the sky, casting an otherworldly glow over the scene.

Despite our weariness, we do our best to blend in with the ecstatic crowd. Every now and then, a surge of laughter or a burst of music makes us forget our fatigue, if only for a moment. But the constant sensory assault takes its toll, and I can see it in the way Lia's shoulders occasionally slump or her eyes flicker with a hint of exhaustion.

We exchange a knowing look, a silent acknowledgment of our shared weariness. We might be pushing forward, driven by our goal, but our bodies are beginning to protest. It's as if AshWays demands your full engagement, your complete immersion. Anything less, and you risk being swept away by its unending wave of euphoria.

We share a silent understanding and decide to slip into another unoccupied house. Like the first, we figure this one is likely to be empty, as the city's inhabitants seem far more preoccupied with their own pursuits than with what happens within their walls. It's as if AshWays itself is a living organism, pulsating with its own rhythm, and the individuals that make up its body are lost in their own intoxicating dance. With a mixture of weariness and relief, we enter the quiet confines of the house, seeking a brief reprieve from the unending frenzy outside.

We ascend the creaking stairs, the faded carpet muffling our footsteps. The house seems to wear its age like a cloak, each step a reminder of the stories it holds. The bedroom exudes a sense of forgotten coziness, with worn curtains filtering the city's neon glow and a slightly musty scent that hints at the passage of time. The bed, though slightly sagging, promises a respite from the city's unremitting energy.

As we settle onto the bed, I can feel the exhaustion creeping in, a heaviness that's been building with every step we've taken through the city's vibrant chaos. The soft creaking of the floorboards downstairs mingles with the distant hum of music and the occasional burst of laughter, creating an auditory tapestry of AshWays' ceaseless revelry.

Lia's complaints, however, carry a different tone this time, stripped of the usual playful sarcasm. Her voice is tinged with raw frustration, the weariness of navigating through a city that seems to refuse silence, the wear and tear on her patience palpable. It's a reminder that beneath her witty exterior, Lia is grappling with the same fatigue that's etching lines on my own face.

"I mean, seriously," she mutters, her brows furrowing in irritation. "Does this city ever take a breath? It's like it's fuelled by perpetual euphoria and decibels."

I nod, the rhythm of her words a reflection of my own thoughts. "It's overwhelming, to say the least. I'm not sure how the locals manage to keep up this pace."

Lia lets out a frustrated exhale, her fingers absently tracing patterns on the bedspread. "And don't get me started on the constant offers for drinks and... other things. It's like they're on a never-ending quest to keep the party going."

"Agreed," I reply, stifling a yawn. "It's almost as if they're afraid of any moment of quiet or stillness."

She turns her head to look at me, her gaze heavy with shared understanding. "I guess that's what happens when a city's built on unbridled hedonism."

We share a moment of quiet contemplation, the city's symphony of revelry filtering through the walls as a reminder of the world just beyond. The weariness that has settled into our bones underscores the urgency of our mission, to find the quieter haven in the West, away from the relentless pulse of AshWays' euphoria.

The door swings open, and for a heart-stopping moment, time seems to freeze. The owner of the house stands in the doorway, his eyes widening as he takes in the sight of us on his bed. Panic rushes in, my mind racing to formulate an explanation, an apology perhaps, for intruding into his space.

Before any words can escape my lips, the owner's expression transforms. A wide grin splits his face, and he raises his hands in an almost welcoming gesture.

"Oh, don't mind me!" he exclaims, his voice carrying an almost gleeful tone. "Just a couple of weary souls looking for a place to rest, eh?"

Lia's sarcasm drips from her voice as she mutters to me under her breath, "Oh, how silly of us to mistake this stranger's bedroom for a cozy inn."

I manage to suppress a chuckle, casting a wry smile in her direction. The owner, seemingly unfazed by our presence, strolls into the room, his eyes twinkling with amusement.

"Really, though," he continues, a mischievous glint in his eyes, "AshWays is all about the unexpected. And if that means unexpected guests, well, why not?"

Lia shoots me a glance that conveys both exasperation and a hint of amusement. I can't help but agree with her silent sentiment. The owner's easy acceptance is both baffling and oddly fitting for a city that seems to thrive on unapologetic chaos.

"Thank you for your understanding," I finally manage to say, a note of gratitude in my tone.

The owner waves a dismissive hand, still grinning from ear to ear. "No need to thank me! Just keep enjoying the city, my friends. Life's too short for rigid plans and quiet moments."

"Wait!" I call out before the owner can disappear completely, my curiosity getting the better of me. He turns back with an expectant smile, clearly not bothered by our lingering questions.

"How far is it to the West?" I inquire, hoping to gather some much-needed information about our impending journey.

The owner's eyes twinkle as he considers my question. "Ah, the West, you say? Not too far, my friends. If you make your way through the heart of AshWays and then venture beyond the bounds of the North, you'll find yourselves there in no time."

Lia can't seem to contain her impatience any longer. She lets out a theatrical sigh, accompanied by a not-so-subtle eye roll. "Well, isn't that just the most riveting piece of information we could've hoped for."

The owner chuckles, clearly amused by her lack of enthusiasm. "My apologies if I've ruined the suspense for you, my dear. But trust me, the West has its own unique surprises waiting for you."

"What surprises do the West have?" I find myself asking, my curiosity now fully piqued. The owner's cheerful demeanour remains intact, his eyes glinting with a mixture of mischief and knowing.

"Ah, the West," he begins, his voice taking on a sing-song quality, "is a place where survival takes on a whole new meaning. You see, my friends, the people there have embraced the notion of 'survival of the fittest' to its fullest extent."

I exchange a puzzled look with Lia, who seems equally intrigued and repelled by the idea. The owner continues, his words painting a rather grim picture.

"It's a land of challenges, where every day is a test of strength and cunning. The people of the West engage in a dance of danger, where they murder each other in the most creative and ruthless ways. It's a game of dominance, you could say."

Lia's patience reaches its limit, her sarcasm giving way to a blunt annoyance. "Wow, what a paradise you're painting there. Murderous festivities and all."

The owner's attention shifts to Lia, and he leers with an unsettling familiarity. "And what a charming addition you'd be to their little games, my dear. With a body like that, you'd surely turn a few heads... or perhaps lose them."

I can practically feel Lia's patience snap like a taut wire. Her voice drips with venom as she retorts, "How about you keep your charming commentary to yourself, and we'll be sure to navigate our own way through the West, thank you."

The owner's smile falters slightly, taken aback by Lia's unapologetic assertiveness. With a defeated shrug and a mocking bow, he finally takes his leave, leaving us alone once more.

Lia lets out a huff of exasperation, her frustration evident. "Seems like even in this place, some things never change."

I can't help but chuckle, a mix of relief and amusement washing over me. "Indeed. But at least we have a clearer picture of what lies ahead."

With the unsettling revelations about the West still swirling in our minds, we settle back into our temporary sanctuary, contemplating the challenges that await us beyond the bounds of AshWays.

Lia's frustration permeates the room as she begins to pace back and forth, her steps punctuated by her agitated muttering.

"Unbelievable. Murder as a form of entertainment? What kind of twisted society is this?"

Her voice is a mixture of anger and disbelief as she continues her tirade, her words a torrent of furious expressions. "And they call Fleshbourne oppressive? At least there, the cruelty was hidden behind layers of refinement."

Rhetorical questions pour from her lips, each one more exasperated than the last. "How can they revel in such madness? How can they be so blind to their own savagery? Is this what 'euphoria' means to them?"

I simply listen, allowing her frustration to pour out. There's a fire in her eyes, a fierce determination to resist the twisted reality of AshWays. I understand her anger; it mirrors my own unease about the city.

Lia's pacing gradually slows, her breathing steadying as she collects herself. She turns to me, her eyes searching for some form of understanding in my expression. "Can you believe this, though? Can you wrap your head around the fact that this is their version of 'life'?"

I meet her gaze, my own thoughts aligning with her incredulity. "It's beyond anything I could have imagined. But it also makes our purpose here all the more important. We need to find a way through this, to the West, and hopefully away from all of this madness."

Lia's eyes soften as they lock onto mine, a mix of determination and vulnerability within them. "You're right. We can't let ourselves get lost in their chaos. We have a purpose, and we'll find a way out of this mess."

Lia's frustration propels her out of the bedroom, her steps heavy and determined. The muffled sounds of cupboards opening and closing reach my ears, and I watch as she reemerges, a knife gripped in each hand. She tosses one to me, the blade glinting in the dim light of the room.

"Just in case we need them," she says, her tone firm and resolute.

I catch the knife, its weight foreign in my hand, and for a moment, I'm struck by the gravity of the situation. We're in a city that revels in madness, where survival is measured by ruthlessness. The knives serve as a stark reminder of the dangers that surround us, a tangible representation of the lengths we might have to go to ensure our escape.

I glance up at Lia, her eyes sharp and determined, a mirror of the weapon she holds. In that moment, I see not just the sarcasm and wit that she so often displays, but also the strength that underpins her spirit. We might be navigating a city of chaos, but we're not without our own defences.

"Thanks" I respond.

13

Blood Soaked Wealth

The passage of days finds us forging ahead, our footsteps a steady rhythm against the unpredictable backdrop of AshWays. As we venture further, the urban chaos starts to fade, giving way to a different landscape entirely. The familiar signs of the West begin to manifest, revealing a striking contrast within the city itself.

It's a bizarre transformation. The West exists within the same city, yet it's a world apart. The telltale markings become more prominent as we move, leading us through a subtle shift in surroundings. The dense urban environment gives way to pockets of greenery, as if the city itself is gradually succumbing to nature's embrace.

The transition is both surreal and refreshing. The city's core seems to radiate with an eerie energy, while around its edges, a verdant world unfolds. Tall buildings still rise in the centre, but they're flanked by lush woods and forests that sprawl outwards. The contrast is astonishing – the concrete and steel harmonizing with the wild foliage in a way that shouldn't make sense, yet somehow does.

Our journey leads us deeper into this intriguing convergence of city and forest. The air shifts, carrying hints of nature's perfume alongside the distant echoes of AshWays' manic revelry. It's as if two worlds exist side by side, separate yet intrinsically linked.

Lia and I exchange glances, silently acknowledging the strangeness of our surroundings. With each step, we're venturing further into this enigmatic realm – a place that defies the boundaries of convention and dares us to uncover its secrets.

Lia's observant nature doesn't miss the fact that we're not exactly dressed for the wilderness. She shoots me a wry smile, a hint of sarcasm tugging at her lips.

"Well, look at us," she remarks dryly. "Navigating the untamed wilds of the West, practically dressed for a stroll in the park."

I chuckle softly, glancing down at our city-appropriate attire that now seems absurdly inadequate. "I guess our urban chic isn't cutting it here."

Her eyes sweep over the landscape, taking in the urban-meets-wilderness scenery. "Not sure our bare skin will be much of an armour against the rumoured murderous tendencies of the West. And let's not forget the charming thorns waiting for us in those forests."

I raise an eyebrow. "Thorns, huh? Just what we need to complete our adventure."

Lia lets out a dramatic sigh. "Absolutely. Because nothing screams 'epic quest' like battling thorns with our fashionable lack of armour."

As we stand on the threshold of the West, my mind races with possibilities. The urban meets wilderness dichotomy is fascinating, and I can't help but be drawn to the idea of exploring these unfamiliar surroundings. I turn to Lia, a spark of mischief in my eyes.

"You know," I begin, "we could always follow the tried-and-tested strategy from our time in AshWays' North. Sneak into a few houses, 'borrow' some clothing – I mean, who would notice, right?"

Lia eyes me with a mixture of scepticism and amusement. "Ah, yes, because the locals in this part of the city are sure to be just as carefree about their belongings as our friends up North. Nothing says 'blending in' like raiding someone's wardrobe."

I grin, my tone playfully innocent. "Hey, if it worked once, it might just work again."

She raises an eyebrow, her lips quirking in an indulgent smile. "Oh, the logic is impeccable, truly."

We share a chuckle, the idea a temporary distraction from the uncertainties that lie ahead. The notion of infiltrating the homes of the West's inhabitants may be bold, but it's a reminder that adaptability is key in this vibrant and eccentric city – no matter which part of it we find ourselves in.

As we approach the first house in the West, it becomes apparent that our plan to borrow clothing might not go as smoothly as it did in the North. The doors are securely locked, and Lia's muttered sarcasm under her breath is a testament to her growing frustration.

"Well, isn't this just a delightful turn of events," she mutters, her tone dripping with dry humour.

I shoot her a wry grin. "Looks like the 'borrowing' strategy has hit a small snag."

She rolls her eyes, gesturing towards a slightly ajar window. "Guess we'll have to rely on our climbing skills this time."

I chuckle, and together we manage to carefully clamber through an open window, landing inside the house with hushed thumps. The interior is dimly lit, the decor simple but cozy. We tread softly, moving through the house in search of any clothing that might suit our purpose.

Lia glances at me with a mischievous glint. "Remember, we're just 'borrowing'."

I raise an eyebrow, mirroring her grin. "Of course, it's all in the name of temporary fashion."

In a flurry of urgency, Lia and I hurriedly rummage through the wardrobe, flinging clothes in all directions in our search for suitable attire. My fingers finally close around a shirt and a jacket, a combination that seems to fit the mysterious aura of the West. On her end, Lia appears to have found something similar.

We find a couple of sets of clothing that seem fitting for the West's atmosphere – dark and practical. As we change into the borrowed attire, there's a sense of accomplishment in our resourcefulness. Even in a city as wild and unpredictable as AshWays, we've managed to find a way to adapt and navigate.

"Now we just need to hope that the original owners don't return too soon," I remark with a chuckle.

Lia smirks, adjusting her new attire. "Oh, I'm sure they won't mind contributing to our cause."

As we hastily slip into our 'borrowed' clothes, a sudden sound from downstairs freezes us in our tracks. The creak of a door swinging open sends a jolt of panic through our veins. We exchange wide-eyed glances, and in a split-second decision, we both scatter to find hiding spots, our hearts racing.

I find refuge behind a heavy velvet curtain, pressing my back against the wall, heart thudding loudly in my chest. The adrenaline surges through me, drowning out all other sound except for the rush of blood in my ears.

From my concealed vantage point, I see Lia disappearing into a closet, the door left slightly ajar. Her face is a mix of tension and determination as she holds her breath, listening intently.

Footsteps echo on the wooden floor below, muffled voices in conversation. I strain to catch any words, but they're indistinct, mere murmurs that add to the tension that hangs in the air.

The atmosphere in the room shifts abruptly as the door swings open once more, revealing the homeowner, his face a portrait of shock and anger. In his hand, a gun gleams ominously, a chilling reminder of the potential danger we're facing. His gaze darts around the room, taking in the chaos of clothes strewn haphazardly.

He strides forward, his voice rising in a torrent of furious words that I struggle to comprehend fully. The intensity of his anger is palpable, even from my hidden position. He points at the scattered pile of clothes, then sweeps his arm around the disarrayed room, his accusations clear even without understanding the language he's speaking.

The room trembles with tension, a fragile balance between danger and desperation. Lia's stifled sneeze breaks the suffocating silence, and the homeowner's attention jerks towards the source of the sound. His eyes narrow, suspicion etched across his face as he whips around, the gun's barrel following the movement of his head.

Before he can react, before the chaotic symphony of his emotions can translate into action, Lia explodes from her hiding spot like a coiled spring suddenly released. The world slows in those harrowing moments, a series of vivid images etched into memory.

Lia's body propels forward, a blur of determination and urgency. She doesn't hesitate, doesn't waver. The knife she had stashed earlier flashes through the air, a glint of deadly intent. Time seems to stretch as the knife hurtles, and then it thuds into its target with a sickening impact.

The homeowner's grip on the gun falters, his eyes widening in a mixture of shock and pain. His fingers fumble, the weapon slipping from his grasp to clatter on the floor. The room erupts in chaos, his strangled attempt at a shout choked off by the gurgling sound that escapes his throat.

He stumbles back, clutching at the knife that protrudes from his neck, blood surging from the wound in a crimson tide. His hands flail in a futile attempt to staunch the flow, his eyes bulging with a mixture of panic and realization.

Lia doesn't falter, doesn't pause. Her movements are precise, calculated. She crosses the room with swift strides, her gaze unflinching as she retrieves the fallen gun. The homeowner's eyes lock onto hers, a mix of defiance and desperation swirling within.

With a quick motion, Lia disarms him, the gun now in her possession. She steps back, maintaining a safe distance, her gaze never wavering from the dying man before her. His struggles weaken, his movements slow, until he finally slumps to the ground, his breathing growing shallower with every passing moment.

The room seems to hold its breath, the air heavy with the weight of what has just transpired. Lia's chest heaves as she surveys the scene, her expression a mixture of relief and grim acceptance. The seconds stretch on, the only sound in the room the ragged gasps of the dying man.

With a mixture of haste and nervousness, I rush over to the fallen man, my movements quick and purposeful. His body lies still, his eyes glazed over in a permanent emptiness. I search through his pockets, my fingers working swiftly to extract whatever valuables I can find.

The air is thick with tension as I rifle through his belongings, each rustle of fabric seeming to echo in the silence that surrounds us. My heart pounds in my chest, the weight of the situation heavy on my shoulders. It's a grim task, scavenging from a life so abruptly ended, but the necessities of survival compel me forward.

Coins jingle in my hand as I extract them from a pocket, their cold metal a stark reminder of the reality we find ourselves in. I also find a few small trinkets, items of sentimental value to him but now just potential sources of currency for us. It's a macabre dance, this balancing act of morality and necessity.

Lia watches from a distance, her expression a mixture of detachment and readiness. We don't linger, the urgency of our escape gnawing at the edges of our consciousness. With our ill-gotten gains secured, we both retreat from the house, leaving behind the life that has been extinguished within its walls.

The sunlight outside seems harsh, casting stark shadows across the street. The world moves on, oblivious to the turmoil that has unfolded behind closed doors. We move swiftly, the weight of what we've done settling heavily upon us as we continue on our journey through the twisted landscape of AshWays, a city that revels in its own chaotic ecstasy.

****

Frustration boils within me like a tempest, my emotions finally finding their release in a heated outburst. "Why in the world did you think dragging us to this hellish place was a brilliant idea?" My voice carries a blend of anger and exasperation, fuelled by the swirling mess of emotions that have been building within me.

Lia's eyes flash with a mixture of irritation and resignation. "AshWays was the closest city on the path to where we need to be," she retorts, her own patience stretched thin. "And the west seemed like a decent enough pit stop. It was the only place that promised some respite from the maddening crowd of the north."

I run a hand through my hair, struggling to temper the storm of emotions within me. "You mean to tell me that this murderous wilderness was your idea of a 'respite'?"

Lia's frustration matches mine, her tone sharp. "I didn't exactly know the extent of how... well, murderous the west could be, okay? It's not like this place comes with a tourist guide." She pauses, her expression softening slightly. "I thought we could catch our breath here, away from the blinding euphoria of the north. I didn't anticipate this."

My anger simmers, mingling with a gnawing sense of guilt. I exhale sharply, my frustration now tinged with remorse. "I get it,

Lia. I do. We're in this mess together. I just... this whole situation is overwhelming."

Lia's gaze softens as she steps closer, her voice gentler now. "Believe me, I didn't want this either. But we're adaptable. We'll find a way through this, just like we've managed so far."

I let out a resigned sigh, the weight of our circumstances pressing down on me. "We better find a way, because I'm not sure how much more of this I can take."

Lia reaches out, placing a comforting hand on my shoulder. "We will. We've come too far to give up now." Her words carry a weight of determination that resonates deep within me, giving me a sliver of hope in the midst of the chaos that surrounds us.

Leaving behind the unsettling scene of the house, Lia and I step into the shadowy embrace of the surrounding forest. The air feels thicker here, heavy with the scent of damp earth and decaying leaves. Every step we take is muffled by a carpet of fallen foliage, and the ground beneath our feet is uneven, the terrain a mix of roots and hidden crevices.

The forest stretches out before us like an ancient realm, its dense canopy casting a twilight shroud over the landscape. The towering trees, gnarled and twisted, reach towards the sky like skeletal fingers. Shafts of muted sunlight filter through the leaves, casting dappled patterns on the ground that seem to writhe and shift as if alive.

The sounds of the city are left behind, replaced by the hushed symphony of nature. The occasional rustle of leaves, like whispered secrets, creates an eerie soundtrack. Birds hidden within the canopy call out in haunting melodies, their voices carrying a mournful echo.

As we delve deeper, the darkness grows more pronounced, the forest embracing us with its cool embrace. My fingers brush against the rough bark of a tree, and I can feel the centuries of growth etched into its surface. The air is thick with moisture, a hint of earthiness that clings to every breath.

Amidst the muted symphony of the forest, a sudden snap of twigs draws our attention. Lia and I share a fleeting glance, our instincts urging us to seek cover. We press ourselves against the rough bark of a massive tree, our breaths held in anticipation. As I cautiously peer around the trunk, my eyes land upon a figure emerging from the shadows.

The woman steps lithely through the undergrowth, her form a dance of grace amidst the gnarled surroundings. She wears a cloak of dark snake skin, its patterns shimmering in the dappled sunlight that filters through the canopy. The scales seem to meld seamlessly with her surroundings, casting her as both a part of the forest and a predator within it.

Her lithe body moves with a fluidity that speaks of familiarity with these woods. A bow is slung across her shoulder, and a quiver of arrows adorns her back like a crown of deadly beauty. Her skin is bronzed, a testament to a life lived amidst the elements. Sharp eyes, the colour of amber, sweep the terrain with keen awareness, absorbing every nuance of the environment.

Tangled locks of raven-black hair cascade over her shoulders, and a few feathers are woven into her strands, a connection to the avian companions of the forest. Her attire is simple yet purposeful, a union of practicality and an unspoken communion with the wilderness.

As she moves, her steps leave no trace, her presence a whisper in the wind. She seems to navigate the forest's secrets effortlessly, as if she and the woods are one entity, sharing an unspoken language.

Unaware of our concealed presence, she continues her journey, a lone figure amidst the ancient trees, a guardian of the shadows, a huntress of both prey and truth. And as I watch her, I am struck by the raw power and untamed beauty she embodies, a living embodiment of the enigmatic forest that surrounds us.

Lia's voice brushes my ear in a hushed whisper, laden with

caution. "We need to be careful," she murmurs, her words a reminder of the precariousness of our situation. "We don't know these westerners, and they could end us in an instant."

Her eyes, still fixed on the woman in the distance, reflect the gravity of her words. The realization of our vulnerability in this unknown territory hangs heavily in the air, mingling with the earthy scent of the forest. Our every movement is a carefully orchestrated dance with the shadows, our senses attuned to the rhythms of the woods and the stranger who navigates them.

Lia's fingers graze my arm gently, a silent agreement between us to remain concealed and watchful. We are intruders in this domain, foreigners to its mysteries. And as the woman with the bow continues to tread her silent path, we hold our breath, aware that one misstep could lead to consequences we dare not fathom.

After the woman's figure becomes a mere memory among the trees, we venture forth cautiously, our steps purposeful yet wary. The forest seems to close in around us, its secrets and shadows merging into an enigmatic tapestry. Soon, the dense foliage gives way to the soft murmurs of flowing water.

Before us lies a river, its expanse wider than we anticipated, its waters reflecting the dappled sunlight like liquid glass. The rush of its current speaks of a hidden power, a force of nature that cannot be underestimated. Lia and I exchange a glance, uncertainty mirrored in each other's eyes.

"This complicates things," Lia mutters softly, her voice carrying a tinge of frustration. I nod in agreement, both of us grappling with the challenge that now stands before us. The urgency of our quest and the unfamiliarity of these woods weigh heavily on our shoulders.

The river's song is a constant backdrop as we stand at its edge, contemplating our options. It's as if time has suspended in this forest sanctuary, and the rhythmic lapping of water against stones is the only measure of its passage. With a sigh, I turn to Lia, seeking a solution in her eyes.

"We can't let this stop us," I say, my voice resolute. "There must be a way across."

Lia's gaze narrows in thought, her determination etched in the lines of her expression. "We'll need to find a shallower point or something to aid us," she suggests, her mind already at work on the problem. "Let's follow the riverbank and see if we can come across a better spot."

And so, we set off along the river's edge, our footsteps weaving a silent symphony with the gentle susurrus of the water.

As we move along the river's bank, the serenity of the forest takes an unsettling turn. Scattered among the underbrush and nestled in the crevices of rocks are human skulls, their empty sockets staring at us with a hollow gaze. The pungent scent of decaying flesh taints the air, mingling with the earthy aroma of damp leaves.

Pools of darkened blood stain the ground, an ominous testament to the savagery that has unfolded here. The once tranquil atmosphere feels charged with a grim energy, as if the very earth holds the memories of the violence that has occurred.

I can't help but make a disgusted remark, my voice low and laced with a mixture of revulsion and disbelief. "These people... they don't just murder, they revel in it. What kind of morality do they hold in these twisted woods?"

Lia's face is a reflection of my own repulsion, her eyes taking in the macabre scene before us. "Survival of the fittest takes on a whole new meaning here," she replies, her voice grim. "It's as if the forest itself has absorbed their brutality."

The wind rustles the leaves above us, its whisper a haunting chorus to the sombre scene. The forest seems to close in around us, as if it bears witness to the horrors that have transpired on its sacred grounds. We continue to tread carefully, the weight of the knowledge of these brutal customs hanging heavily on our shoulders.

Each step becomes a dance with caution, a dance that takes us further into the heart of this unforgiving wilderness. The river's gentle song contrasts starkly with the darkness that surrounds us, a reminder that even in the midst of such cruelty, nature's rhythm continues unabated.

The forest canopy gives way to a sudden clearing, and at its heart stands a tower that seems to pierce the very sky. Its ancient stones rise in solemn elegance, reaching towards the heavens with an air of both mystery and grandeur. The tower is tall, its height accentuated by the absence of any other structures nearby.

Carved from weathered stone, the tower's surface is etched with intricate patterns and symbols, some of which have faded over time, leaving behind only the traces of forgotten stories. Vines and ivy cling to its walls, nature's claim on a structure that has stood for ages. The tower's base widens slightly, its architecture reminding us of a bygone era, a testament to the craftsmanship of those who built it.

Narrow windows are scattered at irregular intervals along the tower's sides, their dark openings like watchful eyes that peer out onto the surrounding forest. As the sunlight filters through the leaves above, it casts dappled patterns of light and shadow onto the tower's surface, creating an ethereal dance that seems to breathe life into the ancient stones.

The air around the tower is charged with a sense of anticipation, as if it holds secrets waiting to be unveiled. The clearing itself, framed by the towering trees, seems to hold its breath, allowing the tower to stand as a silent sentinel, a beacon in the midst of the wilderness.

We approach cautiously, a mixture of awe and trepidation in our hearts. The tower's presence is a reminder that even in the depths of this enigmatic forest, there are echoes of the past that still resonate. As we draw nearer, the weight of its history and the stories it holds seem to envelop us, leaving us with a sense of reverence for the mysteries that await within its ancient walls.

I suggest seeking refuge within the tower. Given that the westerners' homes are not within the forest itself, this towering structure might provide a safer haven. Its sturdy walls and the sense of isolation it offers from the eerie surroundings seem like a preferable alternative to venturing further into the unsettling depths of the woods. With a shared nod, Lia and I decide to cautiously approach the tower and see if it holds any entrance or passage that could grant us shelter from the disturbing sights and sounds of the forest.

As we draw closer to the tower, it becomes evident that there is no easily accessible entrance on the ground level. Lia lets out a cynical chuckle, her voice laced with sarcasm as she observes the situation.

"Well, well, isn't this just our lucky day?" she quips, her eyes fixed on the tower's imposing exterior. "A tower with no welcome mat. How thoughtful of them."

I can't help but roll my eyes, the tension of the situation momentarily lightened by her humour. "Yeah, it's like they knew we were coming and decided to roll out the thorny welcome wagon."

Lia smirks, her gaze shifting upwards to where the tower stretches into the sky. "Guess it's time to show off our rock climbing skills. Who needs doors anyway?"

With a wry grin, I look up at the tower as well. "Right. Because scaling ancient towers is just another item on our thrilling to-do list."

As we prepare to ascend the tower's rough exterior, Lia's dry humour continues to offer a strange sense of camaraderie amidst the eerie atmosphere of the forest. The tower awaits, promising refuge from the unsettling forest and, perhaps, more enigmatic discoveries hidden within its walls.

With a shared determination, Lia and I begin our ascent up the tower's weathered walls. The rough texture of the stone presses against our palms and fingertips, the surface cold and uneven. Each foothold requires careful consideration, as we navigate the irregular pattern of jutting stones and crevices. The forest's eerie stillness is broken only by the sound of our laboured breaths and the faint rustling of leaves below.

Lia's movements are a combination of grace and strength, her lithe form finding purchase on even the smallest of ledges. Her muscles ripple beneath her skin as she flexes and stretches, her focus unwavering as she climbs. Her sarcastic remarks seem to have temporarily given way to a fierce determination, her eyes fixed firmly on the ascent.

I follow closely, my hands and legs finding their place on the stone wall through trial and error. The strain in my muscles is palpable, each upward reach a reminder of the physical demands of this climb. Yet, alongside the discomfort, there's a rush of adrenaline, a sense of accomplishment as we steadily conquer the tower's height.

As we rise, the forest below gradually transforms into a mosaic of green and brown, the canopy of leaves offering intermittent glimpses of the ground. The air grows cooler with each upward step, the height granting us respite from the forest's oppressive humidity.

Lia's voice breaks the rhythmic sounds of our climbing, a mix of exertion and excitement. "You know, they should add this to the list of 'fun' activities in AshWays. Tower climbing, anyone?"

I manage a breathless laugh, the tension in my muscles momentarily easing. "Oh, absolutely. Alongside 'dodging arrows' and 'skull collection.'"

Lia's laughter joins mine, the sound echoing off the tower walls. "Ah, the stuff of epic adventures."

The higher we climb, the more distant the forest becomes, its sounds and scents fading. The tower's stones become smoother, evidence of the passage of time and countless climbers before us. Our progress is steady, a testament to our determination to conquer whatever challenges this tower might hold.

Finally, after what feels like an eternity, we reach the tower's summit. Breathing heavily, we stand at the top, overlooking the forest and the landscape beyond. The view is both breathtaking and surreal, a reward for our efforts and a reminder of the vast world that lies ahead.

With a mixture of caution and anticipation, Lia and I manage to slip through the tower's window, the glass pane offering a last-minute sting as it scrapes my cheek. The room we enter is a stark contrast to the natural beauty of the forest outside. The sight before us is chilling, shocking, and fills the air with an oppressive sense of dread.

Our eyes widen as they take in the scene that greets us – a gruesome tableau of death. Bodies lie piled upon one another, their twisted forms frozen in various states of agony. The stench of blood and decay hangs heavy in the air, almost suffocating. The walls are spattered with crimson, a grotesque mural that seems to mirror the violence that occurred within this space.

Lia's hand instinctively tightens around mine, her gaze locked on the horrific display. The room itself feels like a macabre crypt, the silence broken only by the distant sounds of the forest and our own shallow breaths.

"What... what happened here?" My voice barely rises above a whisper, as if speaking too loudly might awaken the nightmare before us.

Lia's response is equally hushed, her words carrying a mixture of shock and unease. "I don't know, but it's clear that this tower holds more secrets than we anticipated."

As we take cautious steps further into the room, our eyes scan the surroundings, seeking any clues that might unravel the mystery of this grim scene. The bodies show signs of violence, but the nature of that violence remains a haunting puzzle. The room's eerie stillness feels like a heavy weight, suffocating any attempt at rational thought.

Amid the horror, a glint of something catches my eye – a reflection of light against a metallic surface. My gaze falls upon a dagger, its blade gleaming in a pool of dim light. Without a word, I bend down and retrieve it, my fingers closing around the hilt with a mix of trepidation and resolve.

Lia's hand on my shoulder brings me back to the present. Her eyes, wide with a combination of fear and determination, meet mine. "We can't stay here," she says, her voice steady despite the unease that lingers in the room.

Lia's eyes catch a glimmer in the dimness of the room's corner. Her cautious steps echo softly in the grim space, the squelching sound of her boots against the blood-stained floor seeming strangely muted against the weight of the scene around us. I follow her, a mix of curiosity and caution driving my movements.

As she draws closer to the source of the glimmer, the form begins to take shape – a box, ornate and beautifully crafted. It's a stark contrast to the horror that surrounds us, a small island of opulence in this sea of death. Lia's gloved hand reaches out, her fingers tentatively brushing against the surface of the box.

Carefully, almost reverently, she lifts the lid. A soft gasp escapes her lips as the contents come into view – a cache of gold and jewels, their radiance an almost surreal sight against the backdrop of the room's darkness.

My gaze shifts from the glittering treasure to Lia's face, where a mixture of astonishment and wariness plays out in her expression. The sight is breathtaking, yes, but in the context of this grim tower, it's also deeply unsettling. The idea that such precious wealth co-exists with the horror of the room is a paradox that defies easy explanation.

"Gold and jewels," Lia murmurs, her voice low and tinged with a hint of incredulity. "In the midst of all this death..."

I nod, my mind racing to piece together the puzzle. The box, the riches – they stand as a stark testament to the duality of the world we find ourselves in. Beauty and horror, opulence and violence, existing side by side.

Lia closes the lid of the box, the soft click breaking the silence that has settled around us. Her gaze meets mine, and in that exchange, we both seem to acknowledge the weight of what we've discovered. This is a world that doesn't neatly conform to our expectations, where even the most wondrous and the most terrible things can exist in tandem.

"We should take some of it," Lia finally says, her tone a mix of practicality and contemplation. "It might come in handy."

I offer a silent nod, recognizing the truth in her words. In a world as unpredictable as this, having resources could mean the difference between life and death.

With the weight of the decision we've just made settling in our bags, we secure a handful of the precious gems and gold, tucking them away for a future that's as uncertain as the present. The weight of the treasure is a stark reminder of the choices we've been forced to make in this unforgiving world.

Our focus shifts back to the tower's window, our intention to leave suddenly interrupted by movement beyond the glass. Our hearts seem to skip a beat as our eyes lock onto the figure making their way up the tower's exterior. Another soul navigating the same treacherous path we did, drawn perhaps by the same glimmer that caught Lia's eye.

We exchange a quick, wordless glance, our expressions a mirror of surprise and wariness. Who could this be, and what brought them to this place? The forest below us seems to hold its breath, the stillness broken only by the distant rustle of leaves. In this tense moment, the tower feels like a trap, its confines suddenly closing in on us.

Lia's hand tightens around the edge of the window frame, her knuckles white against her skin. The urgency of the situation fuels our decision-making, propelling us into swift action. Without a word, we retreat from the window, our movements nearly synchronized as we assess our options.

"The roof," Lia whispers, her voice barely audible. I nod, understanding her plan. The roof might offer us a chance to remain hidden, to observe this unexpected newcomer without revealing ourselves. As we make our way upward, the tower's interior seems to close in around us, the walls echoing with the anticipation of an encounter that could change the course of our journey.

Gritting our teeth, we ascend the tower's staircase with a cautious determination. The air grows thick with tension, our senses heightened as we reach the roof. Peering through gaps in the stone, we catch sight of the figure's ascent, their movements deliberate and purposeful.

My heart pounds in my chest as we huddle on the rooftop, hidden in the shadows. Our fingers grip the cold stone beneath us, and we hold our breath as the figure draws nearer, their face obscured by the ascent. Who are they, and what do they seek in this tower of death and treasure?

The newcomer's figure emerges at the pinnacle of the tower, casting an enigmatic silhouette against the backdrop of the sky. A woman stands there, a striking juxtaposition of strength and vulnerability. Bloodied and wounded, she presents an image of defiance, her unwavering gaze a testament to her determination.

Her attire, though torn and dirtied, is marked by a unique blend of practicality and style. A long leather coat clings to her form, a garment that once held an air of distinction but now bears the signs of struggle. Beneath it, a tattered shirt hints at a life led on the edge, while her fitted trousers suggest a readiness for action.

The woman's features are sharp, etched with the lines of a life filled with experiences both harsh and rewarding. Her eyes, a piercing shade of hazel, reflect a fierce resolve that matches the glint of the knife she holds in her grasp. A strand of raven-black hair falls defiantly across her brow, adding to the overall impression of a warrior unyielding in the face of adversity.

But it's the sight of the knife lodged in her back that lends an air of grim authenticity to her appearance. It tells a story of a life steeped in danger, of battles fought in the shadows. And yet, despite the wound, her stance remains unyielding, her eyes locked onto the world around her with an intensity that suggests a mind perpetually in motion.

With each step she takes, her movements resonate with a careful grace, a fluidity born of experience. The woman's aura is one of determination, a survivor's spirit that refuses to be extinguished, even as the blood trickles down her side. As she raises her own knife, her intention is clear: to face whatever challenges await her with unwavering strength, and perhaps even a glimmer of hope.

14

We Are Thieves

Lia's hushed voice trickles through the tense air, carrying her characteristic touch of dry humour. "Well, isn't she a bundle of sunshine? Bleeding, armed, and on a treasure hunt. What a charming combination."

As the woman's gaze sweeps the room, her actions measured and deliberate, Lia's words seem almost to echo in response to her scrutiny. A corner of her lips twitches upward in a faint smirk as she continues, her voice pitched just low enough to remain discreet. "Do you think she's contemplating whether the thief has good taste in gems?"

Her eyes flit to me for an instant, the glint of amusement dancing in her gaze. It's as though she finds a peculiar entertainment in the situation, as grim as it may be. Lia's tone remains sardonic, her observations delivered with a mixture of curiosity and underlying sarcasm. "You know, there's something profoundly poetic about scavenging for riches amidst all this... splendour."

I can't help but crack a faint smile, despite the tension of the moment. Lia's ability to find humour in the most unlikely circumstances is both a source of exasperation and comfort. As the woman's search intensifies, her movements growing more urgent, Lia's wry commentary weaves a thread of levity through the uncertainty. It's a reminder that even in the direst situations, a touch of sarcasm can be a surprising source of resilience.

Lia's demeanour shifts imperceptibly as the woman inches closer to the tower's staircase. The air seems to thicken with tension, and her eyes follow the woman's movements with a watchful unease. The usual sarcasm that often accompanies her words takes a backseat, replaced by a heightened sense of awareness.

I can feel Lia's tension reverberating in the space between us, her usually sharp wit temporarily subdued by the gravity of the situation. As the woman's steps echo against the stone, Lia's fingers tighten their grip on the edge of the windowsill, her gaze fixed on the approaching figure. It's a rare glimpse of vulnerability in her, a reminder that even the most seemingly unflappable can be affected by fear.

The room's atmosphere seems to shift, mirroring Lia's growing anxiety. It's a palpable reminder that beneath her layers of wit and sarcasm, she's just as human as the rest of us, susceptible to the unpredictable turns of fate. As the woman's silhouette looms nearer, Lia's eyes flicker between her and me, a silent acknowledgment of the potential danger that now stands just a breath away.

Lia's voice cuts through the tension like a blade, her words hanging heavily in the air. "There's no backing out now," she murmurs, her eyes locked onto the woman who inches closer to the tower's staircase.

Before I can respond, Lia rises to her feet, her movements deliberate and calculated. Her decision is swift, a testament to her instinctual nature. A sense of urgency seems to fuel her actions, propelling her forward without hesitation. The woman's attention snaps to her like a magnet, and Lia's presence fills the room with an electric charge.

In the space of a heartbeat, the atmosphere transforms from one of silent anticipation to a frenetic dance of danger. Lia's movement is met with immediate response as a knife is hurled towards her, slicing through the air with a deadly accuracy. Lia's reflexes kick in, her body swaying with a graceful agility that narrowly avoids the blade's lethal trajectory.

The knife's momentum carries it forward, embedding it in the wall with a resounding thud. The room seems to hold its breath for a moment, the tableau frozen in time. Lia stands there, a figure of defiance, her gaze locked onto the woman who now holds a knife in her hand.

The standoff crackles with an intensity that's hard to ignore, the air heavy with the unspoken threat that hovers between them. Lia's decision to take action has plunged us into an unpredictable dance, where every movement could determine our fate.

Lia's voice drips with sarcasm, a volatile mix of anger and taunting. "Nice throw," she spits, her words slashing through the charged atmosphere like a blade. Before the echoes of her voice can fade, she launches herself towards the woman with a ferocity that's both awe-inspiring and terrifying.

The clash is immediate, their bodies colliding in a maelstrom of movement. They grapple, a tangle of limbs and desperation, and the room itself seems to become a battleground, where every surface is a potential weapon. The stench of iron from the blood-splattered surroundings mingles with the heat of their exertion, creating a nauseating and eerie ambiance.

Their struggle takes on an almost primal quality, as if the very essence of survival has been distilled into this intense clash. Lia's movements are fuelled by a raw determination, her years of survival training evident in the way she anticipates the woman's every shift and twist. It's a dance of aggression and evasion, a symphony of panting breaths and guttural grunts.

They roll and thrash, each attempting to gain the upper hand. Fingers claw at fabric and skin, nails leaving red trails in their wake. The room seems to close in around them, the walls echoing their fierce struggle. Blood mixes with sweat, forming a grotesque palette that paints their bodies with a macabre artistry.

Their eyes lock for a brief second, a collision of defiance and desperation. In that fleeting connection, the weight of their shared circumstance hangs heavily. This is a battle that transcends physicality – it's a clash of wills, of determination, of the unrelenting force of two survivors refusing to yield.

With a final surge of energy, Lia manages to gain an upper hand, her movements fluid and calculated. In a swift motion, she forces the woman onto her back, pinning her to the floor. The woman's knife clatters to the ground, a cruel reminder of the weapon's failed purpose.

Lia's voice, strained but resolute, cuts through the chaos of their struggle. "Get out of here!" she commands, her eyes locking onto mine for a brief second, a silent plea laden with urgency. Without hesitation, I scramble to my feet, my heart pounding in my chest.

The woman's anger is palpable, her movements fuelled by a desperate determination. She lashes out, attempting to swipe at Lia even as Lia's knees effectively immobilize her arms. The air is thick with tension, the room a crucible of conflicting emotions and agendas.

Lia's features are a mask of grim determination as she battles to keep the woman pinned. Her strength, a product of years spent surviving in a harsh world, holds the woman in place despite her struggles. It's a struggle of wills, a contest between two women who've each faced their own trials and emerged as formidable forces.

The woman's attempts to break free become increasingly frenzied, her frustration and desperation fuelling her struggle. But Lia's grip remains unyielding, a testament to her resilience and the deep well of determination that runs within her.

With a sudden and brutal manoeuvre, the woman manages to catch Lia off guard. Her kick lands with a sickening thud, driving Lia's knees up into her own waist. Lia's grip falters as pain radiates through her body, and she's forced to release her hold on the woman.

Lia stumbles back, her breath catching in her throat, a mixture of pain and frustration etched across her face. It's a momentary victory for the woman, a brief respite from the grips of Lia's determination.

Seeing this opening, I seize the opportunity, my own instincts flaring to life. Lunging forward, I channel all the fear and anger of our dire situation into a burst of strength. My momentum carries me towards the woman, who's still struggling to regain her footing after breaking free from Lia's hold.

My collision with the woman sends both of us crashing to the floor. It's a scramble of limbs and desperation, a fight for control in the midst of the tower's grim ambiance. The woman's knife gleams menacingly in the dim light, a stark reminder of the danger that hangs over us.

Our struggle intensifies, each of us driven by a fierce determination to emerge from this encounter intact. The room seems to close in around us, walls soaked in blood and death serving as a haunting backdrop to our fight. The air is thick with tension, punctuated by the sound of laboured breaths and the occasional thud as our bodies collide.

Lia, though momentarily weakened, isn't one to stay down for long. Through the haze of pain, her resolve shines bright, her eyes locked on our chaotic struggle. And as we grapple on the cold floor, the tower's eerie silence is shattered by the symphony of our fight – a desperate symphony of survival in a world where every moment could be your last.

Summoning her sheer willpower, Lia pushes through the pain and frustration. With a fierce determination burning in her eyes, she renters the fray. I feel her presence beside me, her movements synchronized with mine as we both strive to overcome the woman who now fights against both of us.

Our efforts combine, creating a formidable force against our opponent. We manage to pin the woman down, our combined strength overpowering her resistance. Despite her struggle, her energy starts to wane, her movements growing sluggish as exhaustion and pain take their toll.

The woman's pleas fill the air, a desperate and trembling voice that carries a hint of vulnerability. Her struggle seems to have shifted from physical to emotional, her words now a last resort in her attempt to escape the clutches of her captors.

Lia's grip falters for a moment, her expression briefly showing a flicker of doubt. But I remain resolute, my fingers firmly clenched around the woman's wrists, unyielding to her appeals. The room is heavy with tension, the echoes of our struggle still reverberating through the air.

The woman's cries continue, a mixture of fear and desperation that tugs at something deep within me. Yet, my resolve remains unwavering. I exchange a glance with Lia, a silent understanding passing between us. We've seen enough, suffered enough at the hands of others. This time, we hold the power.

****

The room was a tableau of uncertainty. The woman's muffled pleas contrasted with the tension hanging in the air. Lia's eyes met mine, and in that unspoken exchange, I sensed the gravity of the decision we had to make.

Lia sighed, frustration etching lines on her forehead. "This is a mess, isn't it? Just when we thought we were out of the frying pan..."

I nodded, my gaze still fixed on the woman struggling beneath us. "Yeah, it's complicated. But we have to figure out what to do with her."

The woman's eyes darted between us, fear mingling with pleading. Lia leaned closer, her voice low but unwavering. "Why did you attack us? What do you want?"

Her muffled response was unintelligible, lost within the fabric that Lia had stuffed into her mouth. Lia looked at me, a mix of frustration and doubt in her eyes. "Should we take that gag off? Can we trust her to talk?"

I hesitated, weighing the options. "We need to know her intentions. If she's willing to talk, we have to hear her out."

With a cautious nod, Lia removed the makeshift gag. The woman took a deep breath, her voice trembling. "I didn't mean to hurt anyone. I was just desperate – hungry and alone."

Lia's eyes narrowed, scepticism evident. "Desperation doesn't always lead to attacking strangers. Why should we believe you?"

I studied her face, searching for any sign of deceit. "What's your name?"

She hesitated before whispering, "Eva.... I know you took the jewels. Those are mine. You can't just come here and steal from me."

Lia's eyebrows shot up, a mixture of surprise and disbelief crossing her face. "You've got to be kidding me. You attack us, and now you're complaining about the jewels?"

Eva's voice wavered as she continued, "I've been alone here, struggling to survive, and you come in and take what little I had left."

Lia's patience seemed to be wearing thin, a spark of irritation flashing in her eyes. "You attacked us with a knife in your back. For all we know, you could be some sort of bandit."

Eva's tone shifted, an edge of defiance creeping in. "Oh, please. Bandit? Look who's talking – the thieves who ransacked my home."

Lia's lips curled into a sarcastic smile. "You really have a way with words, don't you? Attacking us, then accusing us of theft."

Eva's voice grew louder, anger now front and centre. "I was just trying to survive! You think you're better than me?"

I stepped between them, attempting to defuse the escalating situation. "Enough. We're not here to argue. We're willing to give back the jewels if that's what it takes to settle this."

Eva's eyes narrowed, suspicion still evident. "And what guarantee do I have that you won't just run off with them again?"

Lia's patience snapped, a sigh of exasperation escaping her lips. Without a word, she grabbed a piece of cloth from her bag and proceeded to gag Eva in a rather comedic manner. It was a strange sight – Eva's protests muffled by the cloth, her eyes wide with indignation.

Lia stepped back, a triumphant grin on her face. "There. Now you can't complain."

Lia's eyes shifted from the bound Eva to the two of us, a mix of frustration and exhaustion etched on her face. She gestured toward the blood-splattered floor and then pointed at our dishevelled appearances.

"Great," she muttered, her voice dripping with irritation. "We look like we just crawled out of a butcher's shop. This is just fantastic."

I couldn't help but crack a half-smile at her grumbling. "Well, you did say we needed to fit in with the locals. This might just give us an edge."

Lia shot me a sarcastic look, her eyes narrowing in mock annoyance. "Oh yes, because I'm sure the locals here are all about the 'freshly disembowelled' look."

"Yeah, you might have a point," I admitted, a chuckle escaping me. "Maybe we should find some water to clean up before we proceed."

Lia's expression softened slightly, her irritation giving way to a tired grin. "Water sounds like a godsend right now. Let's get this mess sorted out before anyone else decides to climb up here."

We turned our attention back to Eva, who was still gagged and bound on the floor. As bizarre as the situation was, it seemed that we were now presented with a new reality in the West – one where survival meant grappling with unpredictable challenges and making choices that could seem absurd at first glance...

15

Shadows Of Prestige

In the days that followed, a grim routine had settled over us. The once vibrant echoes of AshWays felt like a distant memory as we navigated the harsh reality of the West. We had taken down those who posed a threat, claiming their possessions as our own. The house we now occupied was a testament to our survival, a fortress built on the bones of those who had underestimated us.

The walls of the house held whispers of the lives that once thrived within them. Tattered remnants of clothing, now stripped of their owners, hung as eerie reminders of the past. The air was heavy with the scent of blood and sweat, an unsettling mix that seemed to seep into every corner.

****

The dim light of a few candles flickered across the room, casting dancing shadows on the walls. The air was heavy with a mix of exhaustion and accomplishment as we lay on the couch, surrounded by the spoils of our struggles.

Lia was tending to her wounds, her face twisted in concentration as she applied a makeshift bandage. I watched her, a sense of awe mingling with the exhaustion that had settled in my bones. The past few days had been a whirlwind of danger and survival, but in this quiet moment, it was as if the chaos outside couldn't touch us.

I shifted slightly on the couch, the soft creak of the old furniture breaking the stillness. Lia glanced up from her task, her gaze meeting mine. There was a glint of something unspoken in her eyes – a mix of weariness, determination, and perhaps a hint of vulnerability.

"These jewels," I finally spoke, my voice low as if not to disturb the fragile peace of the moment. "They're going to make things easier, aren't they?"

Lia's lips curved into a tired smile as she set aside the bandages and looked at the bags filled with gleaming gems. "Oh, absolutely. It's like we hit the jackpot in the midst of all this madness."

I chuckled softly. "I can't believe the kind of world we're navigating through. From the chaos of AshWays to this – a house full of goods we had to fight for."

Lia's smile faded slightly, replaced by a contemplative expression. "It's survival, in its rawest form. The only rule here is to come out on top, no matter what it takes."

I nodded, the weight of her words settling in the air between us. The world had become a harsh, unforgiving place, a reality that forced us to adapt, to make choices that we wouldn't have even considered in the past.

Lia's gaze shifted back to the jewels, her fingers absentmindedly tracing the edges of one of the gemstones. "But we're not like them, are we? We're not going to let this world turn us into monsters."

There was a quiet determination in her voice, a resolve that spoke of a deeper strength. As tired as we were, as beaten down by the world, there was still a flicker of something unbreakable within us.

"No," I agreed softly. "We won't let it."

Lia let out a sigh, her fingers absently toying with one of the jewels in her hand. "You know, as unbearable as the North of AshWays was, I think I'd take dealing with those obscene men over what the West turned out to be."

I couldn't help but chuckle at her exasperation. "Really? So, you're saying you'd rather fend off relentless advances than be surrounded by bloodthirsty locals?"

Lia shot me a mock glare, a playful fire dancing in her eyes. "I'd rather not be surrounded by either, thank you very much."

I leaned back against the wall, smirking. "Oh, come on now. I'm sure those locals appreciated your... charms."

Her eyes narrowed at me, but a mischievous grin tugged at her lips. "Oh, I'm sure they did. But I can't say I shared the sentiment."

I laughed, the sound echoing through the room. In the midst of the chaos and danger that had become our daily reality, these moments of light-hearted banter felt like a lifeline – a reminder that there was more to us than just survival.

Lia heads to the shower, her movements weary and determined. The memories of Fleshbourne are never far from our minds, the oppressive rules, the suffocating control. Guilt gnaws at me. We escaped, but others are still trapped within those iron walls, their lives bound by rules they didn't choose.

Sitting on the couch, I let out a sigh, a stolen jewel held loosely in my hand. "Lia," I call out, my voice rising above the sound of the running water, "do you ever think about the people we left behind in Fleshbourne?"

Her reply comes from the bathroom, a mixture of exhaustion and frustration woven into her words. "All the time. But what could we do, stay there and suffer too?"

I lean back, my gaze fixed on the ceiling. "I know, I know. We had to escape. Survival comes first. But it feels... unfair, you know?

We're here, safe to an extent, while they're still trapped in that nightmare."

Lia's voice cuts through, a sharp note of defiance lacing her words. "Don't think AshWays is any better. It's not the same oppression, but it's its own kind of twisted."

I furrow my brow, her words giving me pause. "What do you mean?"

The water stops, and after a moment, Lia emerges, her wet hair clinging to her skin. She meets my gaze, her eyes intense. "AshWays might not have the same strict rules as Fleshbourne, but it's a different kind of prison. The constant pursuit of pleasure, the obsession with euphoria – it's a distraction, a way to keep people in line without them realizing."

I frown, her words sinking in. "So, they're slaves to their own desires?"

Lia nods, her expression heavy. "Exactly. They're trapped in their own pursuit of happiness, too blinded to see the chains."

In the dim light, Lia's face is illuminated, and I see the weight of her words mirrored there. AshWays promises freedom, but it's a different kind of cage, one built on ecstasy and false choices.

"You're right," I concede, the realization settling in my chest. "Maybe there's no real escape, no matter where we go."

Lia's sigh is a mix of weariness and resolve. "But that doesn't mean we give up. We're not just running – we're fighting for change. We're tearing down systems, whether they're enforced by rules or desires."

Determination surges within me. "You're right, Lia. We can't run forever. We have to fight, for something better, for us and for them."

A small, tired smile tugs at her lips, water droplets glistening in her hair. "Exactly. So, let's rest. Tomorrow, we keep moving, keep fighting."

With those words, Lia heads back to the bathroom, leaving me alone with my thoughts. As the water starts again, I know that despite the twisted cities, despite the challenges, we have each other. And that's a strength that can overcome any obstacle.

****

As the first rays of dawn infiltrate the room, casting a warm glow, my eyes flutter open. I find myself sitting up on the bed, the soft sheets tangled around me. Beside me, Lia sleeps, her features relaxed in slumber. I stretch my limbs, the stiffness of sleep slowly fading away, and I swing my legs over the edge of the bed.

Careful not to disturb Lia, I rise from the bed and make my way towards the window. The world outside is slowly awakening, the hues of morning painting the sky with soft pastels. A new day, a new beginning.

After a moment of contemplation, I decide it's time to start the day. I tiptoe through the room and head downstairs. The wooden floorboards creak faintly beneath my steps, and I make my way to the small kitchen area.

As I gather the essentials for breakfast – a couple of eggs, some bread, and a few pieces of fruit – I can't help but reflect on our journey so far. From Fleshbourne to AshWays, it's been a relentless pursuit of freedom, a fight against oppressive systems, both blatant and subtle.

I crack the eggs into a pan, the sizzle of cooking filling the air. Lia's words from the previous night echo in my mind – the twisted nature of AshWays, the illusory chains of pleasure and euphoria. It's a reminder that our fight isn't just against physical foes, but against the very concepts that bind people's minds and souls.

The aroma of cooking eggs begins to fill the small kitchen, and I turn my attention to the slices of bread, placing them in the toaster.

The simple routine of preparing breakfast offers a sense of normalcy, a moment of respite amidst the chaos of our journey.

As I place the cooked eggs on a plate and retrieve the toasted bread, I can hear faint rustling upstairs. Lia must be waking up. I set the breakfast on the table, taking a deep breath.

The soft padding of footsteps announces Lia's presence in the kitchen. I turn to see her, a genuine surprise lighting up her features as she takes in the scene before her. A playful grin tugs at the corner of her lips, and she offers a light-hearted comment that dances with a touch of morning sarcasm.

"Well, well, if it isn't the early riser of the century. Did the sun rise from the west today?" Her voice is infused with a blend of surprise and amusement, a testament to our shared history of late mornings and hurried breakfasts.

I chuckle, feeling a sense of satisfaction in having the upper hand this time. "Believe it or not, I managed to beat you to it this time. Thought I'd give you a taste of what it's like to wake up with the birds."

She pretends to clutch her heart dramatically, her expression mockingly overwhelmed. "Oh, the shock! The horror! What's next, you'll be suggesting we eat lunch at noon?"

I shake my head, a smirk playing on my lips. "Let's not get ahead of ourselves. Breakfast is already quite an achievement for me."

Her laughter fills the room, a sound that's become all too familiar and comforting. As she approaches the table and takes a seat, I can't help but appreciate the simplicity of this moment – two weary travellers, sharing a meal, taking respite before the world outside demands our attention once more.

"So, what's on the menu?" she asks, her tone lighter than it's been in days.

"Eggs, toast, and a side of morning triumph," I reply with a wink, serving her a plate of breakfast.

She raises an eyebrow, a playful glint in her eyes. "You're really milking this, aren't you?"

I join her at the table, the warmth of companionship infusing the air around us. "Absolutely. It's not every day I get to gloat about being up before you."

She takes a bite of the eggs, her expression shifting from teasing to genuine appreciation. "Well, I have to admit, you might just have a future as a morning person. These eggs are surprisingly good."

I grin, a sense of contentment settling over me. "Well, I aim to please."

As we eat our breakfast and exchange light-hearted banter, I can't help but be grateful for these moments – a pause in our journey, a chance to savour a slice of normalcy amidst the chaos.

I finally get to ask Lia about the civilization that might be our key to taking down the scourge. She puts down her fork, a thoughtful look in her eyes, as if retracing the journey, she once embarked upon.

"They're not too far from AshWays," she starts, her voice holding a hint of gravity. "When I first heard about them, I was still navigating the North of AshWays. I thought they might be our chance, a real resistance against the scourge."

I lean forward, my curiosity piqued. "What happened? Why didn't you go to them?"

A shadow passes over her features, a mixture of frustration and disappointment. "I made the mistake of stopping in the North of AshWays before reaching them. I thought I could find some supplies, maybe a place to rest for a while. But they caught wind of my history as a scourge."

Her words hang in the air, heavy with the weight of what she must have faced. I can only imagine the hostility she encountered, the prejudice that coloured her every move.

"They attacked you?" I ask, my voice low.

She nods, a mixture of sadness and bitterness in her eyes. "Yes. They didn't trust me, couldn't see past my past. I barely made it out alive. I had to fight my way through to escape."

I take a deep breath, processing the significance of her journey and the challenges she's already faced. "So, what now? How do we approach them this time?"

Lia's expression becomes determined, a fire rekindling in her eyes. "We need to be careful, strategic. They won't welcome us with open arms, that's for sure. We'll have to prove ourselves, show them that we're serious about taking down the scourge. And this time, I won't make the mistake of lingering anywhere else. We go straight to them, no distractions."

I can't help but admire her resilience, her unwavering commitment to the cause. "Sounds like a plan. But what's the name of this civilization?"

A small smile plays on her lips, a glimpse of hope in her eyes. "They're called the Havenreach. From what I've gathered, they're a diverse group of people from various backgrounds, united against the scourge's oppression. If anyone can help us, it's them."

I nod, feeling a mixture of determination and anticipation. The journey ahead won't be easy but knowing that there's a group out there fighting the same battle fills me with a renewed sense of purpose.

"Let's do it, then," I say, my voice resolute.

Lia raises her coffee cup in a silent toast. "To Havenreach, and to finally putting an end to the scourge's reign."

As our cups clink together, I can't help but feel a surge of optimism, a belief that with Lia by my side and allies like the Havenreach, we just might have a chance to make a difference.

Lia gathers our empty plates and utensils, her movements brisk and purposeful. She glances at me and raises an eyebrow with a hint of a mischievous smile. "No need to worry about washing these. I'm pretty sure the owners won't mind the mess. After all, we did kind of, well, you know," she trails off, the unspoken words hanging in the air.

I chuckle, a mix of dark humour and disbelief. "Yeah, I suppose they won't be coming back to complain."

She grins as she deposits the dirty dishes in the sink. "Exactly. So, no need to fuss over it."

With a final clink of dishes, she straightens up and turns to face me, her gaze holding a mixture of determination and anticipation. "Ready to get moving?"

I nod, a sense of resolve settling within me. "Absolutely. Let's not overstay our welcome."

Lia's smile widens as she heads towards the door, gesturing for me to follow. "Exactly my thinking. The sooner we're on the move, the better."

As we finish getting ready, pulling on our salvaged clothes and strapping on our bags, a sense of purpose settles over us. The weight of the upcoming journey is palpable, but there's also a glimmer of hope in the air.

I carefully unfold the map, its creases showing the wear of our travels, and scan its markings. Lia stands beside me, her gaze fixed on the map as well. Together, we step outside the house we've temporarily called home, greeted by the distinct ambiance of the West.

The surroundings are an intriguing contrast – the city houses, clustered together like forgotten relics of a bygone era, give way to the wild embrace of the forest. It's a patchwork of civilization and nature, an intricate dance between human structures and the untamed wilderness.

Lia exhales softly, her breath misting in the morning air. "It's something, isn't it? The way these two worlds collide."

I nod in agreement, a sense of reverence for the strange beauty that surrounds us. "Definitely. It's like nature and civilization are locked in this perpetual struggle."

She smirks, her eyes twinkling with a mix of amusement and determination. "Well, let's hope we can find our way through that struggle and come out on the other side."

The idea of our next move hangs in the air like a question mark. Lia's suggestion to travel through the south of AshWays seems like a practical choice, a way to avoid the dense and eerie forests of the West. Her eyes hold a mix of weariness and determination as she lays out her plan.

"We should head south," she says, her voice carrying a note of conviction. "The forests in the West were... unsettling, to say the least. I'd rather not venture through there again. Plus, the south is closer to Havenreach. We might find a smoother route."

I consider her words, the pros and cons of each option racing through my mind. The thought of those foreboding woods sends a shiver down my spine, but the unknown terrain of the south presents its own set of challenges. I can't help but voice my concerns.

"But Lia, we don't know what's waiting for us in the south either. It could be just as treacherous. And if we encounter any hostility from the locals, we might end up in a worse situation than before."

She nods thoughtfully, her gaze fixed on the path ahead. "You make a fair point. But I can't shake the feeling that we need to keep moving forward, even if it means taking a risk. Havenreach might hold the answers we're seeking, and I don't want to waste any more time than we already have."

I sigh, running a hand through my hair. Lia's determination is contagious, and a part of me wants to trust her instincts. After all, we've come this far by relying on each other's judgment.

"Alright," I concede, giving her a small smile. "South it is, then. But let's proceed with caution. We don't want to trade one set of dangers for another."

****

As we travel further into the South of AshWays, the landscape undergoes a remarkable transformation. The dense forest that surrounded us gradually gives way to the sprawling, electrifying cityscape that characterizes this dystopian world. Neon lights slice through the dusky air, creating a symphony of vibrant colours that dance along the edges of buildings and cascade from towering billboards. The streets are alive with a pulsating energy, a rhythmic beat that seems to synchronize with the collective heartbeat of the city's denizens.

Similar to the North we encountered before, this part of AshWays is a labyrinthine tapestry of streets and alleys, a bustling mosaic of life and technology interwoven in a cacophony of sights and sounds. People stream through the thoroughfares like currents in a river, their attire ranging from eclectic to outrageous, each person a unique expression of AshWays' eclectic culture.

The buildings are a fusion of the old and new, a testament to the city's complex history. Glistening glass structures rise alongside crumbling brick edifices, the past and future coexisting in this frenetic urban sprawl. Hovering vehicles whiz above, their lights casting fleeting shadows on the streets below.

The air is charged with a sense of anticipation, an underlying tension that seems to hum beneath the surface. It's as if every person here is driven by a relentless pursuit, each step a testament to their determination to carve out a space in this urban jungle. The aroma of street food wafts through the air, mingling with the metallic tang of machinery and the distinct scent of excitement.

As we traverse the streets, Lia and I become enveloped in the rhythm of the city. We blend in, just two more figures navigating this vibrant metropolis. Lia's gaze is both contemplative and watchful, her eyes taking in the surroundings with a mixture of familiarity and caution. We're acutely aware that beneath the glitz and glamour lies a city that doesn't easily reveal its secrets.

The South of AshWays, much like its Northern counterpart, is a world of contrasts, where opulence and desperation coexist in a complex dance. As we move forward, the weight of our mission and the uncertainty of what lies ahead serve as a constant reminder that we're walking a tightrope between survival and discovery, between the promise of Havenreach and the perils of this dystopian realm.

Lia's voice carries a note of exasperation as she gazes around at the familiar surroundings of the South of AshWays. "You know," she mutters, a touch of sarcasm lacing her words, "I was really hoping for a change of scenery. But it seems like AshWays has this uncanny ability to stay consistent, no matter where you are."

Her frustration is palpable, a reflection of her longing for something different, something that would deviate from the monotonous urban landscape they've been traversing. She kicks at a loose piece of debris on the pavement, her irritation manifesting in the way her brows furrow.

"It's like a twisted mirror, isn't it?" she continues, her voice tinged with a mix of annoyance and resignation. "Different parts of the city, yet the same underlying chaos, the same unapologetic frenzy. Just dressed up in different shades and neon lights."

Her words hang in the air, a commentary on the unchanging nature of AshWays despite the apparent shifts in its districts. She raises an eyebrow and gives a wry smile. "I guess the lesson here is that you can't escape the essence of a place, no matter how far you roam within its boundaries."

As Lia's gaze sweeps across the bustling streets and the eclectic mix of people, her expression softens, and a hint of nostalgia replaces her annoyance. "But hey," she adds with a shrug, "I've survived worse. And I've got you with me this time. So, let's embrace the chaos, shall we?"

In her sardonic tone and weary smile, there's an odd sort of acceptance, a grudging understanding that despite its shortcomings, AshWays is a part of her journey, a chapter in a story that's yet to be fully written. And as the city throbs with its own unique energy, Lia seems to reconcile with the fact that she's entwined in its tapestry, for better or worse.

16

Tangled In Luxury

The South of AshWays sprawls before us like a decadent dreamscape, a realm bathed in opulence and contrast. The familiar urban landscape, with its towering skyscrapers and neon-lit alleys, now takes on a surreal twist. Instead of the gritty, chaotic atmosphere of the North, the South is adorned with flowing streams of clear water, meandering lazily through the bustling streets. And here, in an almost fantastical spectacle, rivers of golden honey wind their way alongside the water, weaving a tapestry of liquid gold that catches the sun's rays and casts a warm, inviting glow.

As we navigate through this new landscape, my senses are assailed by a different kind of frenzy. The air is heavy with the scent of delicate perfumes and the subtle fragrance of exotic spices wafting from the myriad food stalls that line the streets. The hum of conversation is replaced by a melodic symphony of laughter and soft chatter, as the well-dressed residents of the South engage in leisurely conversations while savouring delectable treats.

The people here are a stark contrast to their Northern

counterparts. Clad in lavish silk gowns and luxurious velvet suits, the southerners exude an air of refined elegance. Their skin, adorned with intricate tattoos, becomes a canvas for both opulent jewellery and the marks of individual stories. Expensive watches glint on wrists, and necklaces with precious gems catch the light, creating a spectacle of wealth that's as much a part of their identity as the ink that graces their skin.

In this sophisticated realm, the chaos of the North is replaced by a different kind of chaos—one of indulgence and extravagance. Lavish parties spill onto the streets, where musicians play haunting melodies and dancers twirl in ethereal movements. It's a world of excess, where the mundane is transformed into the extraordinary, and the very essence of AshWays seems to shift from one district to another, as if the city itself is a living, breathing entity that adapts to the desires of its inhabitants.

As we navigate through this surreal domain, I am undoubtedly drawn into its peculiar allure. Yet, beneath the gilded surface, the city's undercurrents remain as potent as ever, a reminder that even amidst the most enchanting facade, danger and intrigue still lurk, waiting for the right moment to surface.

A southern local approaches us with an air of refined confidence. His attire, meticulously chosen, reflects the opulence of the South. A tailored velvet suit drapes his frame, its deep burgundy hue enhancing his commanding presence. The fabric shimmers with a faint sheen in the sunlight, and the intricate patterns woven into it hint at the artisanal craftsmanship that went into its creation.

A pristine white shirt peeks out from beneath the jacket, its collar perfectly aligned and secured with a diamond-studded pin. His tie, a work of art in itself, features an elaborate design that catches the eye without overwhelming the ensemble. The choice of a deep shade of emerald green adds a touch of vibrancy to the otherwise subdued palette of his attire.

His shoes, polished to a mirror-like shine, complete the look. Each step he takes resonates with a sense of authority and grace, embodying the sophistication of the city's southern district. And as his gaze locks onto us, his eyes reflect a knowledge and understanding that goes beyond mere appearances, suggesting a well-rounded individual who is accustomed to the complexities of the South's intricate social landscape.

"Good day, travellers," he greets us with a voice as smooth as silk. "I couldn't help but notice that you are new to our fair city. Might I be of assistance in any way?" His smile is warm, genuine, and holds a hint of curiosity.

Lia, ever the quick wit, responds with an exaggerated display of sophistication, her voice dripping with an almost comical level of refinement. "Ah, dear sir, we extend our sincerest gratitude for your gracious offer, but alas, we find ourselves most capable of navigating the intricate tapestry of AshWays' southern streets."

The local's courteous smile remains steadfast, seemingly unperturbed by Lia's theatrics. "Of course, madam. Should you find yourself in need of any guidance or information, do not hesitate to seek me out. I am at your disposal."

Lia nods graciously, a hint of amusement dancing in her eyes. "How kind of you, sir. We shall certainly keep your generous offer in mind as we meander through this exquisite realm of refinement."

As we continue on our way, I can't help but stifle a chuckle at Lia's playful mimicry. The local's genuine courtesy contrasts sharply with her exaggerated impersonation, making for an amusing and somewhat surreal encounter.

Lia's chuckle rings out, carrying a note of sarcasm. "Annoyingly pleasant, aren't they? It's like they've all been dipped in a vat of sugar syrup."

I nod in agreement, a wry smile playing on my lips. "It's almost surreal, the contrast between the two parts of AshWays. The North is wild and uninhibited, while the South is all refined manners and delicate sensibilities."

Lia rolls her eyes playfully. "Well, at least we won't have to worry about being dragged into impromptu street parties here. Though I'm not sure if I prefer that or the constant catcalls from the North."

****

As we step into the crystalline shopping mall, a breathtaking sight unfolds before us. The entire structure seems to be composed of meticulously cut and polished gemstones, reflecting and refracting the sunlight that filters in through the grand arched windows. The walls are adorned with elaborate mosaics crafted from sapphires, emeralds, and amethysts, creating a mesmerizing dance of colours across the floor.

The air is scented with the delicate fragrance of blooming flowers, while the soothing sound of a cascading water feature echoes softly through the vast atrium. Lavish shops line the walkways, displaying opulent wares that glitter and gleam under carefully calibrated lighting. Elegant mannequins draped in silk and velvet gowns pose regally in the storefronts, their jewelled accessories catching the light and casting kaleidoscopic patterns on the walls.

Well-dressed southerners peruse the boutiques, their conversations hushed and punctuated by the occasional delighted gasp or appreciative chuckle. Exquisite fabrics drape gracefully from racks, adorned with intricate embroidery and delicate beadwork. Sparkling jewellery catches the eye from behind glass cases, and the soft hum of activity blends seamlessly with the tranquil ambiance.

Lia's eyes widen as she takes in the splendour around us. "Well, isn't this just a sparkling slice of wealth?"

I chuckle softly. "Seems like we've stumbled into a realm where even the buildings are fashioned from treasures."

Lia playfully elbows me. "And here I thought the North was wild. These folks take luxury to a whole new level."

We continue our exploration of the crystal mall, marvelling at the sheer opulence that surrounds us, a stark contrast to the dilapidated streets of Fleshbourne and the unruly North of AshWays.

As we step into the shop nestled within the crystal mall, a wave of opulence washes over us. The shelves are adorned with intricately designed artifacts, ranging from delicate sculptures and fine paintings to exquisite jewellery and ornate clothing. Each piece seems to exude an air of refined elegance, drawing our eyes and holding our attention in equal measure.

Lia glances around, her expression a mix of amusement and mild exasperation. "Isn't it fascinating how they manage to turn even the mundane into a showcase of extravagance?"

I chuckle in agreement, my gaze sweeping over a display of intricately carved gemstone figurines. "Seems like subtlety is a foreign concept here. Everything demands attention."

Lia's lips curl into a wry smile. "Well, I guess if you've got it, flaunt it."

We move further into the shop, examining the exquisite fabrics of the clothing section and the intricate craftsmanship of the jewellery. While the quality is undeniable, Lia's undercurrent of scepticism is palpable.

She leans over and mutters to me, "It's like they're trying so hard to prove their wealth, even if it means turning everyday items into gilded statements."

I nod in agreement, acknowledging the perceptiveness of her observation. "It's as if every object here is shouting, 'Look at me, I'm expensive!'"

Lia smirks. "Exactly. Makes you wonder what they're compensating for."

The shopkeeper, a suave and impeccably dressed gentleman,

approaches us with a polite smile. "Greetings, esteemed guests. Is there anything I can assist you with today?"

I offer a courteous smile in return. "Thank you, but we're just browsing."

He chuckles softly, his voice carrying an air of practiced charm. "Ah, I can't help but notice that your attire speaks of a different origin. Might I venture a guess that you're not from the southern parts?"

Lia smirks playfully. "You're quite the perceptive one."

The shopkeeper's smile widens. "Well, your uniqueness is a breath of fresh air in this sea of familiarity. And I must say, your distinct sense of style could benefit from a southern touch."

I raise an eyebrow, my resistance already forming. "We're fine as we are, really."

He leans in slightly, his tone friendly yet persistent. "Allow me to assure you that our selection is unparalleled, a blend of elegance and refinement that could enhance even the most refined tastes."

Lia glances at me, amusement dancing in her eyes. "Enhance, huh?"

The shopkeeper's demeanour remains unswayed by our scepticism. "Absolutely. Our garments are tailored not just for comfort, but for making a statement. And I assure you, the statement will be loud and clear."

I glance at Lia, and she gives a subtle nod of agreement. "Fine, show us your collection."

The shopkeeper's eyes light up, and he motions us to follow him as he gracefully leads the way through the shop. With each display he presents, he elaborates on the intricate details, the luxurious fabrics, and the impeccable craftsmanship. While his enthusiasm is palpable, my initial frustration begins to wane, replaced by a reluctant appreciation for the artistry on display.

Lia casts me a sidelong glance, her lips curling into a half-smile that conveys a mixture of amusement and concession. "Well, if we're going to stand out, might as well do it with style."

I chuckle softly, nodding in agreement. "Seems like we're about to get a taste of southern refinement after all."

With a graceful snap of the shopkeeper's fingers, two assistants emerge from the shadows, their presence almost choreographed in its precision. The first, a young woman, steps forward with an air of elegance that matches the fine silk she wears. Her chestnut hair falls in cascading waves around her shoulders, perfectly framing her porcelain face. Her almond-shaped eyes hold a warm and genuine smile as she approaches us.

Her attire is a masterpiece of delicate embroidery, the fabric draping her form like a second skin. The intricate patterns seem to come alive with every movement, shimmering in the soft store lights. She carries herself with a refined poise, her every gesture a testament to her training in the art of assisting distinguished clientele.

The male assistant, standing slightly behind her, exudes an air of sophistication that speaks of confidence acquired through experience. His impeccably tailored suit, a deep shade of charcoal grey, accentuates his tall and commanding presence. His dark hair is neatly styled, and his sharp features are softened by an easy smile that seems to come naturally to him.

His role is clear in his stance – ready to assist, attentive to our needs, and yet maintaining a respectful distance. His gaze holds a hint of amusement, as if he's privy to some unspoken understanding, perhaps a knowing twinkle that life within these opulent walls has granted him.

Together, the two assistants form a harmonious pair, their contrasting qualities complementing each other perfectly. The woman's grace and warmth balance the man's composed demeanour, creating an inviting atmosphere that makes us feel strangely welcomed in this world of luxury.

The male assistant extends a courteous hand towards me, gesturing towards a separate area of the shop. "If you'll follow me, sir, I believe we have just the ensemble that would suit your taste."

I exchange a quick glance with Lia, who smirks playfully before turning her attention to the female assistant. "Well, my dear, I suppose I'll trust your judgment for now," Lia remarks, her tone laced with a hint of sarcasm.

The female assistant responds with a gracious smile, her voice carrying a pleasant melody. "I promise to make it worth your while, madam. We have some exquisite pieces that might just change your perception of southern elegance."

I raise an eyebrow at the male assistant, who maintains his courteous demeanour as he guides me through racks of luxurious garments. "Please, allow me to introduce you to the essence of southern fashion, where elegance meets comfort."

Lia's voice drifts over from where she stands with the female assistant. "Comfort? In these lavish fabrics?" she retorts with a hint of amusement, her voice tinged with curiosity.

The female assistant chuckles softly, her eyes gleaming with an understanding of Lia's scepticism. "You'd be surprised, madam. Our designs are not only pleasing to the eye but also tailored for utmost comfort. A harmonious blend, if you will."

I catch Lia's eye and offer her a playful grin before turning my attention back to the male assistant. "Well then, let's see what southern elegance truly entails," I remark, intrigued by the prospect of this unexpected shopping experience.

The male assistant leads me into a sprawling room, adorned with floor-to-ceiling mirrors that reflect the opulent array of suits and formal wear. The lighting is just right, accentuating the fine textures and exquisite details of the garments. It's a visual feast of colours, fabrics, and designs, each piece radiating a sense of luxury.

"These, sir, are our latest arrivals," the assistant announces with a polite smile, his voice carrying an air of genuine enthusiasm. "We have an extensive range of styles, each meticulously crafted to cater to diverse tastes."

I nod appreciatively, my eyes scanning the room with a mixture of curiosity and admiration. "Impressive collection," I remark, genuinely intrigued by the variety before me. "I have to admit, I wasn't expecting such a... lavish display."

The assistant chuckles softly, a gleam of pride in his eyes. "Southern fashion is renowned for its emphasis on quality, comfort, and of course, style. We believe that one's attire is a reflection of their personality."

As I browse through the racks, my fingers grazing the rich fabrics, he continues to explain the distinct features of each design. "Here, we have the classic tailored suits, perfect for formal occasions or business affairs. And if you're feeling a bit adventurous, we also offer more contemporary cuts and patterns."

My gaze falls upon a deep navy suit, its threads catching the light in a mesmerizing dance. "What about this one?" I inquire, my voice laced with curiosity.

The assistant steps closer, examining the suit with an expert eye. "Ah, a fine choice, sir. This particular piece is crafted from a blend of silk and wool, ensuring both elegance and comfort. The slim cut offers a modern touch, and the intricate stitching adds a touch of sophistication."

I can't help but run my fingers over the fabric, appreciating the craftsmanship. "And the accessories?" I inquire, glancing towards a display of ties, cufflinks, and pocket squares.

The assistant's smile widens. "Accessories, indeed. They are the details that truly make an outfit come alive. We have an exquisite range of ties, from traditional silk to more daring textures. Cufflinks in various designs, and pocket squares that can add a pop of colour or a touch of refinement."

I meticulously sift through the array of suits, each offering its unique allure and charm. The assistant's patient guidance helps me explore the subtle differences that set each piece apart.

The first suit I examine is a charcoal grey ensemble, its fabric finely woven, promising both comfort and sophistication. The jacket exudes a sense of understated elegance, while the trousers boast a tailored fit that speaks of timeless style.

Moving on, I come across a midnight blue suit, its colour rich and deep like the night sky. The lapels are adorned with a delicate pattern, adding a touch of whimsy to its formal aura. I can already imagine how the suit would catch the light during an evening event.

A daring burgundy suit captures my attention next. Its shade is rich and vibrant, a bold statement that contrasts the traditional blacks and greys. The assistant explains that such hues are not uncommon in the southern fashion scene, where self-expression is celebrated.

My fingers brush over the lapel of a classic black tuxedo, its simplicity and refined lines timeless. The assistant informs me that tuxedos are a staple for formal occasions, and this particular piece has been tailored to ensure a flawless fit.

Finally, I come across a dark navy suit, similar to the one I initially spotted. It beckons me, and as I examine it closely, I notice the intricate stitching that runs along the lapels, adding an unexpected detail to its otherwise classic design.

After careful consideration, I make my choice. The midnight blue suit resonates with me, its deep colour and subtle pattern capturing the essence of southern elegance. As I convey my decision to the assistant, he nods approvingly, his eyes reflecting a genuine satisfaction in helping me find the perfect fit.

"Now that you've chosen the suit, it's time to prepare your body," the assistant announces with a congenial smile. His words pique my curiosity, prompting me to inquire about this seemingly enigmatic next step.

Perceiving my slight confusion, he lets out a good-natured chuckle before elaborating, "Please forgive me if that caught you off guard. In the realm of southern fashion, grooming is regarded as an indispensable part of the entire ensemble. Just as a well-tailored suit enhances your appearance, careful grooming ensures that your overall presentation is nothing short of impeccable."

He motions gracefully toward an elegantly arranged area complete with a mirror. This space is adorned with an array of grooming products ranging from refined colognes to precision razors. "This section offers an array of grooming essentials that will complement your look. A precise shave, a hint of cologne, and meticulously styled hair—these are the components that contribute to the overall refinement of a gentleman's image."

As he imparts his insights, the connection between grooming and fashion becomes more pronounced in my mind. I realize that southern culture intricately weaves together these details to form a cohesive tapestry of personal presentation.

"Once you don your chosen suit," the assistant continues with a warm demeanour, "engaging in these grooming practices will bolster your confidence and enhance your presence. A well-groomed gentleman not only showcases his best appearance but also radiates a sense of self-assured elegance that leaves a lasting mark."

I graciously accept the offer and express my gratitude, but before I can finish, a good-natured chuckle escapes from the assistant's lips. Following the direction of his gesture, I notice a crystal door to his left. It becomes apparent that this is where I'm expected to proceed next. Understanding his unspoken cue, I offer a polite smile and nod of acknowledgment. It's evident that the southern sense of refinement encompasses not just the garments but the meticulous details that elevate one's presentation to an art form. With renewed curiosity, I head towards the indicated door, ready to discover what lies beyond.

****

After gently closing the crystal door behind me, I find myself in a peculiar yet lavish chamber. It's immediately apparent that this is a shower room, albeit unlike any I've encountered before. The opulence exuding from every inch of the space is nothing short of astonishing. The room is expansive, its grandeur emphasized by the play of light and crystal that reflects and refracts in every direction.

Against the backdrop of glistening tiles, an array of water jets emerges from the walls, each meticulously positioned to create a symphony of soothing cascades. The air carries a faint aroma, a mixture of invigorating scents that transport my senses to a realm of serenity.

As I take in the scene, my gaze is drawn to three men, each standing just outside the threshold of the shower doors. Clad in towels wrapped around their waists, their gestures are unmistakable – an invitation to step into the realm of relaxation that lies beyond. Their tranquil expressions and confident postures tell of a practiced routine, a ritual woven into the fabric of their daily lives. I approached cautiously, unsure of what to expect from this unconventional grooming experience. The man nearest to me greeted me with a smile that radiated genuine friendliness. "Welcome, sir," he said, his voice resonating with a soothing tone. "This is a part of our grooming tradition here in the South. We provide a thorough grooming experience for our clients, ensuring they look and feel their best."

I couldn't help but feel a mixture of curiosity and nerves as I glanced between the men. "Grooming experience?" I questioned, my eyebrows slightly raised. "I mean, I appreciate the offer, but I'm not quite used to this level of... well, luxury."

Another man chimed in, his chuckle putting me somewhat at ease. "No worries, sir. We understand it might be a bit different from what you're accustomed to. But trust us, it's an experience you won't forget."

With their words echoing in my ears, I made a decision. "Alright, I'll give it a try. But what exactly do I need to do?"

The third man spoke up, his demeanour friendly and inviting. "Just relax and enjoy, sir. We'll guide you through the process. Our aim is to ensure you leave here feeling refreshed and rejuvenated."

I nodded, my hesitation giving way to a sense of willingness. "Okay, I guess I'm in your hands then."

****

I stood beneath the warm streams of water, the gentle cascade creating a cocoon of comfort around me. The temperature was perfect, a soothing embrace that seemed to melt away the layers of tension that had accumulated over our journey. The steam rose, enveloping the space in a shroud of mist that added an ethereal quality to the scene.

As the men began their careful ministrations, their skilled hands moved with purpose, each touch deliberate and precise. I felt a slight blush creeping onto my cheeks, an instinctual response to the intimacy of the situation. My gaze flitted between their assured expressions, their focus solely on their task at hand. It was as if they were artists, working with the canvas of my body to create a masterpiece of relaxation and renewal.

Occasional flinches escaped me as their hands grazed over my wounds, a reminder of the battles we had faced. The discomfort was fleeting, replaced by a gentle reassurance as their touch continued, mindful of the areas that needed special attention. Despite my initial embarrassment, I found myself surrendering to their expertise, allowing their care to wash away my reservations.

The warm water continued to cascade over me, a steady rhythm that echoed the passage of time. The sensations were both invigorating and soothing, a paradoxical dance of emotions that mirrored the contrasts of the world around us. I closed my eyes, immersing myself in the moment, letting the sensations wash over me.

The steam swirled around us, creating an intimate ambiance that shrouded the space in a veil of privacy. It was as if the world outside had faded into obscurity, leaving only this sanctuary of warmth and care. The sounds of the water's gentle patter and the occasional murmur of conversation formed a soothing symphony that resonated in the background.

As the minutes stretched into a timeless blur, I couldn't help but reflect on the absurdity of the situation. Here I was, a stranger in a foreign land, being tended to by three men in a luxurious shower. The contrasts of our journey, from the rugged wilderness to the opulence of the South, were not lost on me.

In that moment, I allowed myself to let go of my reservations and embrace the unfamiliar. The men's expertise and their genuine desire to provide me with a moment of indulgence spoke volumes about the culture of the South. It was a lesson in the art of self-care, a reminder that even in the most unexpected circumstances, there could be moments of relaxation and rejuvenation.

As the water rinsed away the remnants of the past, I felt a renewed sense of vitality coursing through me. The embarrassment had faded, replaced by a deep gratitude for this unexpected respite. And as the steam continued to rise and the warm water enveloped me, I allowed myself to fully embrace the sensations, basking in the simple pleasure of the moment.

I step out of the shower, the warmth of the water still clinging to my skin. The steam begins to dissipate, revealing the clear outlines of the room once more. The men's attentiveness doesn't waver as they follow me, their expert hands now gently rubbing the towel over my body.

My initial sense of awkwardness resurfaces as their touch moves lower, the towel gliding over my thighs and lower regions. It's a reminder of my vulnerability, a moment of exposure that feels intensely intimate. Despite my attempts to maintain composure, a flush of embarrassment colours my cheeks, a silent acknowledgment of the intimacy of this ritual.

Their movements are practiced, each stroke of the towel deliberate and efficient. Their professionalism is evident, and yet the nature of the task makes it difficult to fully ignore the underlying sense of vulnerability. I shift my weight uncomfortably, my gaze momentarily averted as I grapple with my own self-consciousness.

In the midst of the physical sensations, I can't help but reflect on the cultural differences that have brought me to this moment. The customs of the South are a stark contrast to the ruggedness of the North, a reflection of the opulent lifestyle that permeates this world. And here I am, a foreigner amidst it all, navigating a realm of luxury that feels both foreign and strangely alluring.

As the men's motions continue, their touch is professional and respectful. Yet, their proximity and the nature of the task heighten my awareness of their presence. I find myself longing for the comfort of my own privacy, a space where I can grapple with the swirl of emotions that this experience has stirred within me.

Finally, the towel's gentle caresses come to an end, leaving me feeling oddly exposed despite the fact that I'm now dry and wrapped in the fabric. Their work is done, and I'm left standing here, the echoes of this unusual encounter lingering in the air. I meet their eyes briefly, offering a muted smile that attempts to convey gratitude and understanding.

In this moment, I realize that this experience is a part of the journey, a lesson in embracing the unfamiliar and confronting the boundaries of my comfort zone. And as I prepare to don the elegant suit that awaits me, I carry with me the memory of this unexpected moment of vulnerability, a reminder of the complexities of the world I'm navigating.

****

Stepping out of the shower room, I'm greeted by the familiar sight of the opulent room filled with exquisite suits. The steam has dissipated, replaced by the scent of cleanliness and the feeling of rejuvenation. Despite the lingering sense of vulnerability from the shower, I can't help but feel a newfound sense of freshness as I stand there, wrapped in the towel.

The male assistant's presence is a reminder that I'm not alone in this transformation. His eyes light up with enthusiasm as he regards me, a faint smile playing on his lips. His excitement is palpable as he gestures toward the array of clothing, his voice tinged with a sincere delight.

"Marvelous," he exclaims, his tone carrying genuine admiration. "You look simply marvellous."

His words are unexpected, and while I'm still grappling with my own self-consciousness, I find a hint of pride creeping into my demeanour. It's a strange blend of emotions — vulnerability and a burgeoning confidence, all mingling together in this unfamiliar setting. As I step closer to the array of clothing, the assistant is quick to extend his offerings — a pair of underwear and a vest. These seemingly mundane items hold a significance in this moment, a symbolic transition from vulnerability to empowerment. I take them with a nod of gratitude, a small gesture that carries more weight than I could have anticipated.

17

The Price Of Excess

With the array of clothing in my hands, the male assistant steps forward, his presence both reassuring and slightly surreal. He carries himself with an air of practiced elegance, his movements fluid and graceful. As he extends his assistance, his touch is gentle yet purposeful, guiding me through the process with a blend of expertise and consideration.

He helps me slide into the underwear and vest, his hands deftly adjusting the fit with an eye for detail. The fabric is smooth against my skin, a tactile reminder of the difference that even the simplest change can make. It's an odd sensation, allowing someone else to help dress me, yet his demeanour is so professional that any awkwardness quickly dissipates.

Then comes the suit jacket, and his guidance is particularly pronounced here. He expertly aligns the shoulders, ensuring a perfect fit that moulds to my frame. His hands brush against my skin, a fleeting touch that leaves a residual warmth in its wake. As he steps back, his eyes meet mine with a subtle approval, his lips curving into a brief but genuine smile.

"Almost there," he remarks, his voice soft and encouraging. "Just a few final adjustments."

He steps forward again, fine-tuning the collar and straightening the lapels. His attention to detail is remarkable, and I find myself feeling both grateful and impressed by his commitment to ensuring I look my best.

Finally, he gestures toward the full-length mirror, his voice imbued with a sense of pride. "Take a look. You're quite the transformation."

Turning toward the mirror, I'm met with a reflection that feels distinctly unfamiliar and yet undeniably intriguing. The suit fits impeccably, its tailored lines creating a silhouette that exudes confidence and a touch of sophistication. It's as if I'm looking at a different version of myself, one that has emerged from the ordinary and stepped into a world of opulence and refinement.

As I gaze at my reflection, a mix of emotions courses through me. There's a sense of amazement at how this experience has unfolded, a touch of self-consciousness as I see myself in this new light, and a growing sense of acceptance that I'm embarking on a journey of transformation, both in appearance and in understanding.

The male assistant's reflection stands behind me, his eyes holding an encouraging glint. "You wear it well," he says, a genuine compliment that adds a layer of reassurance to this unexpected moment.

Curiosity gets the better of me, and I find myself leaning slightly toward the assistant, my voice lowered as if sharing a secret. "Was Lia's experience similar to mine?"

The assistant's lips curl into a knowing smile, his eyes glinting with amusement. "Ah, your female friend," he replies, his tone a playful tease. "Well, women have their own rituals, often a bit more elaborate. A reflection of their complexity, perhaps."

He seems to deliberate for a moment before continuing, his tone light. "And speaking of connections, it's quite intriguing to see two travellers so closely intertwined. The nature of your bond is quite evident, even to an observant eye."

There's a mischievous twinkle in his gaze as he raises an eyebrow, a silent question that hangs in the air. It's as if he's unravelling a thread of curiosity, one that hints at the layers of our companionship and the dynamics that define it. Yet, he remains respectful in his approach, delicately acknowledging the connection without prying too deeply.

I chuckle softly, appreciating his tactful way of addressing the unspoken. "Travel tends to forge interesting bonds," I reply, my tone light and a touch enigmatic. "We've certainly shared our fair share of adventures."

His smile widens, an unspoken agreement passing between us. "Indeed, travel has a way of weaving stories that linger in memory."

As I turn back to the mirror, his words linger in my thoughts. There's an unspoken acknowledgment that Lia and I are not just solitary wanderers, but companions on a journey marked by its twists, challenges, and the moments of connection that seem to unfold naturally, no matter how unexpected the circumstances. And as I adjust the collar of the suit, I can't help but wonder what other stories this journey holds in store for us, waiting to be discovered as we navigate the intricacies of this world together.

With practiced finesse, the assistant guides me through an array of accessories, each piece adding a unique touch to the ensemble. He presents a selection of watches, each one a testament to craftsmanship and elegance. There are leather bands and polished metal, faces that range from minimalist to intricately detailed.

I take a moment to examine each one, weighing the options before making my choice. A classic timepiece with a black leather band and a sleek silver face catches my eye. It's a blend of modern sophistication and timeless charm, a reflection of the world I've ventured into. "This one," I say with a nod, a sense of satisfaction settling over me.

The assistant's eyes gleam with approval as he places the watch around my wrist, adjusting it with meticulous care. The touch is gentle, almost reverent, as if he's helping me don more than just an accessory but a piece of the world I'm navigating.

Next come the shoes, a collection that ranges from understated formal to contemporary flair. I opt for a pair of polished black shoes, their design both classic and versatile. As I slip them on, a feeling of completion settles in, as if each element of the outfit has contributed to a transformation.

The assistant steps back, a pleased smile gracing his features. "Exquisite choice, sir. It's a pleasure to witness such refinement."

The assistant and I return to the front of the shop, where the shopkeeper awaits us with an appreciative smile. "Ah, I see you're back," he says, his gaze sweeping over me with a sense of approval. "I trust everything went well?"

The assistant nods with a professional demeanour. "Indeed, sir. Our guest has chosen an ensemble that perfectly resonates with his style."

The shopkeeper's eyes twinkle with satisfaction as he turns to me. "You look absolutely splendid, my dear customer. I hope the experience has met your expectations."

I can't help but feel a mix of gratitude and amazement. The process has been more than just selecting clothes; it's been an immersion into a world of elegance and luxury, a world that contrasts so starkly with my previous reality. "I'm truly impressed," I reply, my voice carrying a blend of surprise and genuine appreciation. "Thank you for your assistance."

The shopkeeper inclines his head graciously. "It was our pleasure to serve you. Our establishment prides itself on delivering not only fine garments but also an experience that's tailored to our clients' desires."

As the female assistant enters the scene, a new wave of elegance seems to grace the air. The shopkeeper's face lights up with a warm welcome as he addresses her. "Ah, my dear, you've returned as well. I trust your experience has been equally satisfying?"

The assistant offers a graceful nod, her demeanour poised and refined. "Indeed, sir. Our guest's 'female friend,' as you put it, has undergone a transformation that perfectly complements her essence."

My eyes follow the shopkeeper's gaze as it shifts to the entrance, where Lia makes her entrance. The sight of her is nothing short of breathtaking. Her gown, crafted from the finest silk, drapes over her figure with an ethereal grace. The gentle hues of the fabric seem to accentuate her every movement, the soft swish of the gown's hem resonating with her steps. Lia's gown is a mesmerizing shade of deep sapphire blue, a hue that resonates with the richness of the ocean depths. The colour plays a fascinating game with the light, revealing layers of darkness and subtle variations as she moves. It's a shade that encapsulates both mystery and allure, inviting the eye to explore its depths just as the sea beckons to be discovered.

Her high heels add a touch of sophistication to her stride, a subtle confidence in every step. Makeup artfully applied highlights her emerald eyes, making them gleam with a captivating intensity. Her brown hair is styled in a way that balances the delicate and the daring, cascading in controlled waves that frame her features with a hint of wild allure.

What draws my gaze the most, however, are the adornments she wears. Jewellery, sparkling with opulence, graces her wrists and ears, each piece seeming to tell a story of opulence and grandeur.

Yet, amidst the opulent display, there's one piece that stands out—the pendant around her neck, the same pendant that caught my attention back at the ancient ruins.

Lia's presence is a marvel, a harmonious blend of sophistication and wild spirit, a balance between allure and enigma. She glides into the room, her presence a symphony of elegance, and for a moment, time seems to stand still as I take in the radiant beauty before me.

The male assistant grins mischievously, his eyes gleaming with playful intent. "Seems like your female friend has turned quite a few heads with that appearance," he quips, giving a subtle nod toward Lia.

Lia, never one to back down from banter, smirks and replies with a twinkle in her eyes, "Well, it's not every day the city gets a glimpse of genuine style."

The assistant chuckles, clearly enjoying the exchange, and glances between the two of you. "Well, the two of you certainly make quite the pair. If you ever need more fashion advice or assistance, don't hesitate to drop by."

Lia raises an eyebrow in mock contemplation. "Oh, I'm sure we'll be back for more fashion wisdom, just to keep up with the south's impeccable standards."

With a final shared smile, you both exit the shop, stepping back into the world of opulence and sophistication that characterizes the southern district of AshWays.

18

Eyes Of The Elite

Lia and I step onto the bustling streets of the southern district, and we exchange amused glances, our laughter bubbling up uncontrollably. The whole experience of being pampered and prepped feels so out of place in our usual lives.

Lia's eyes gleam mischievously as she starts, "Did you see the way they treated my nails? I swear, I thought my cuticles were about to get their own spa vacation."

I chuckle, unable to contain my amusement. "And those makeup artists! I felt like a blank canvas, waiting for them to create a masterpiece."

Lia bursts into laughter, her voice a harmonious note in the sophisticated surroundings. "And the pedicure! I half expected them to offer my feet a cup of tea and engage in some polite conversation."

We share a moment of genuine camaraderie, finding hilarity in the over-the-top extravagance we've just experienced. It's such a departure from our usual life and the challenges we've been facing.

"It's like we've entered a whole different dimension," I muse, still smiling.

Lia nods, her gaze sweeping over the elegantly dressed crowds. "That's AshWays for you. It's all about appearances here. But you know what they say, 'When in Rome...'"

We burst into laughter again, our voices melding with the hum of the city's high-society conversations. This moment feels like a fleeting escape, a chance to share some light-heartedness amidst the weight of our mission and the dangers we've encountered.

As we continue strolling through the opulent streets, it's hard to shake off the feeling that Lia and I are just a couple of outsiders, trying to navigate a world that's both enchanting and utterly foreign.

Lia and I stand in the midst of the vibrant southern district, the map in her hand a stark contrast to the elegance that surrounds us. Her brows furrow slightly as her emerald eyes scan the markings on the paper, her focus unwavering despite the distractions of the opulent streets.

After a contemplative moment, she finally lowers the map and gazes at me, a wry smile tugging at the corner of her lips. "You know," she starts, her voice a mixture of amusement and determination, "we could easily lose ourselves in this lavish maze. Just a few days' walk from Havenreach, they said."

I chuckle, understanding the unsaid invitation in her words. It's tempting, the thought of indulging in the grandeur that surrounds us, of taking a break from the hardships of our journey. But there's a shared resolve between us, a recognition of our purpose that has brought us this far.

"I won't lie, Lia," I reply with a smile of my own, "the idea of basking in southern luxuries is quite tempting. But Havenreach is our goal, our chance to find answers and allies against the scourge."

Lia nods in agreement, her eyes reflecting a mixture of

determination and something else – a longing, perhaps, for a simpler existence even in the midst of the city's grandeur. She slips the map back into her bag, as if sealing away the allure of the southern district.

"You're right," she concedes with a sigh, her gaze lingering on the elegantly dressed crowds passing by. "Let's save the indulgence for another time. Havenreach awaits, and who knows what challenges lie ahead."

****

As Lia and I navigate through the streets of the southern district, a sense of transformation accompanies each step. The opulence of our attire has caught the attention of the locals, their admiring glances and whispered compliments following us like a gentle breeze.

Men in well-tailored suits nod approvingly as we pass, their expressions a mix of acknowledgment and subtle envy. Women adorned in elaborate gowns offer us approving smiles, their eyes tracing the lines of our new attire with curiosity. It's as if the elegance of our appearance has earned us a newfound respect in this realm of sophistication.

Lia's silk gown rustles softly with every step she takes, the fabric gliding like liquid against her form. Her demeanour exudes a sense of confidence that matches her elegant ensemble. I watch as she engages in polite exchanges, her witty remarks and charming smiles eliciting nods of appreciation from those around her.

My own suit feels tailored to perfection, the smooth fabric hugging my frame in a way that commands attention. It's a stark departure from the rugged clothes we've been accustomed to. As I navigate through the crowd, I catch fragments of conversations – snippets of admiration and curiosity as passersby comment on our transformation.

The locals' complements create a subtle bond between us and this lavish world, a connection born from shared appreciation for the finer things. The recognition that we too belong, even if only for a brief moment, weaves a sense of belonging into the tapestry of our journey.

As we walk through the streets of the southern district, surrounded by the glitz and glamour, Lia's perceptive nature can't help but raise an eyebrow at the stark difference between our experiences here and those in the North and West of AshWays.

Her emerald eyes narrow slightly, and a small, thoughtful frown tugs at the corners of her lips. She breaks the silence, her voice carrying a hint of scepticism. "You know, it's strange. Nothing bad has happened to us since we entered the South. No aggressive locals, no life-threatening situations. It's almost like everything here is too... perfect."

I consider her words for a moment, matching her pace as we continue through the bustling streets. The contrast between the luxurious surroundings and the chaotic, dangerous territories we've traversed is undeniable. "You're right," I agree, my gaze flickering over the well-dressed locals and the serene ambiance. "It's quite the change from what we've encountered so far."

19

Cushioned Comforts

As the sun starts its descent, casting a warm golden hue over the southern district, Lia's frustration becomes palpable. Her usually determined and resourceful demeanour is giving way to a genuine exasperation, evident in the way her brows knit and her lips purse.

Her emerald eyes scan the surroundings, searching for any sign of respite. But unlike the North, where the streets were alive with revellers who wouldn't mind us claiming a hidden corner, and unlike the West, where we could overpower and claim an abandoned house, the Southern district seems to hold its luxuries close, leaving little room for wandering souls seeking a place to rest.

With a sigh, Lia throws her hands up in the air, her voice edged with annoyance. "This is ridiculous! It's like they've got everything figured out here, except for providing a place to spend the night. Who would have thought finding a shelter could be this difficult?"

I offer a sympathetic smile, understanding her frustration all too well. "It's definitely a change of pace from what we've encountered so far. But hey, at least we're not being chased by scourge or fighting for our lives against hostile locals."

Lia's eyes roll, her lips curling into a wry grin. "True, this is a different kind of challenge. I suppose I'd take the thrill of battling over this any day. At least that has a certain clarity to it."

We continue walking, the lively atmosphere of the Southern district almost mocking our predicament. Lia's gaze darts around, her determination unwavering even in the face of this unexpected obstacle. "We'll find something," she mutters to herself, more as a reassurance than a declaration.

I place a hand on her shoulder, offering a supportive squeeze. "We always do. And hey, if all else fails, we can just keep walking. Maybe the answer lies just around the corner."

Lia chuckles, her frustration beginning to give way to a sense of resignation. "You've got a point. There's bound to be a solution somewhere."

As the night sky deepens, the city's neon lights begin to illuminate the surroundings with their vibrant glow. Lia and I continue our search, the sounds of laughter and music serving as a stark contrast to our current dilemma. In this bustling oasis of wealth and opulence, we remain two wandering souls in search of a temporary haven, reminding ourselves that even in the lap of luxury, challenges persist.

Following the rivers of honey that snake through the streets like veins of liquid gold, we allow our steps to be guided by the enchanting current. The gentle aroma of sweetness wafts through the air, an olfactory delight that merges with the opulent visual display of this southern district.

Our journey leads us to the pinnacle of extravagance, an enormous house that stands as a testament to prosperity itself. Its grandeur is awe-inspiring, a symphony of architectural prowess, blending classic elegance with modern allure. The façade, adorned with intricate carvings and gilded accents, gleams softly under the ethereal glow of streetlights.

Our attention is soon captivated by a couple making their way toward the house. Their attire speaks volumes, a harmonious blend of sophistication and luxury. The man's suit fits him like a second skin, exuding tailored elegance, while a platinum watch winks discreetly from his wrist. Beside him, the woman's gown cascades in a shimmering cascade of sapphire silk, her jewellery gleaming with a brilliance akin to the stars.

As they approach the mansion, their interaction is a ballet of familiarity and shared affection. Words are exchanged with smiles that seem to emanate from the heart, gestures and expressions that hint at a deep connection. The man deftly produces a keyring, each key more ornate than the last, and the door obligingly yields to his touch.

The gentle cadence of our footfalls mingles with the distant hum of the city, a soothing backdrop to the unfolding scene. Lia's voice rises, a silken ribbon of sound that gracefully breaches the divide between us and the couple approaching the grand mansion. I move alongside her, a shadow eager to be part of the story about to unfold.

In the radiant glow of the moonlight, the mansion stands as a testament to affluence, its façade adorned with intricate details that shimmer like stars in the night sky. The couple, wrapped in an aura of quiet intimacy, appears poised to unlock the entry to their opulent abode. Their words, exchanged with a familiarity born of shared history, momentarily pause as their gazes fix upon the unexpected visitors.

Lia strides forward, her posture confident, her voice a melody that sweeps through the air, catching the couple's attention. I follow in her wake, my own steps a careful echo of her purposeful advance.

The couple's expressions shift from curiosity to polite interest, their countenances a study in graciousness as they momentarily set aside their keys and plans. Their conversation, a dance of phrases weighted with nuance and polished manners, unfolds with the grace of a waltz. The notes of their speech, composed of courtesy and sophistication, paint the canvas of our encounter.

In the midst of this exchange, Lia's offer emerges like a jewelled pendant unveiled from a satin pouch. The stolen treasures from the west, once a symbol of audacity, now lie humbly in her open palm—a currency of trust offered in exchange for sanctuary. The words she chooses weave a bridge between the realms we inhabit, expressing a yearning for a moment's respite, for a haven in the midst of foreign elegance.

And there I stand, a silent participant in this interaction, my presence a testament to the gravity of her request. The silence that stretches between Lia's offer and their response carries a weight of anticipation, my heart suspended between hope and uncertainty, each beat echoing within me like a distant drum.

Finally, their voices rise again, their words holding the delicate balance between contemplation and empathy. Their acceptance, delivered with measured consideration, encapsulates more than a mere transaction—it's an embrace, a gesture that binds our disparate worlds in a thread of shared understanding. The mansion, a monument to luxury, becomes a refuge, an embodiment of compassion that seeks to breach the chasm between their privilege and our journey.

As the conversation wanes, gratitude swells within me, a feeling as potent as a fine vintage discovered in the heart of a forgotten cellar. The couple, paragons of southern refinement, offer us not only their elegant home, but also a glimpse into the humanity beneath their polished exteriors. Beneath the veneer of luxury, a shared connection emerges, demonstrating that compassion knows no boundaries, and kindness can bloom even in the most lavish of gardens.

Lia turns back to me, her eyes alight with a mix of astonishment and relief. In the quiet exchange of words, in the acceptance of our plea, we find a moment of unity—a recognition that, regardless of the differences that may set us apart, the language of compassion is one that resonates universally.

With a gracious smile that mirrored the elegance of the couple's demeanour, Lia extended her thanks. Her words, a genuine expression of gratitude, carried a melody that harmonized with the warm night air. The couple, their eyes reflecting a kindness that surpassed their social standing, returned her smile with a nod of understanding.

As the words of appreciation lingered between them, like the gentle notes of a melody fading into the night, the couple gestured towards the mansion's ornate entrance. The threshold, once a boundary between worlds, now beckoned with an air of inclusion. With a gesture as regal as a royal invitation, they extended their arms, ushering us into their haven.

Lia and I exchanged glances, our shared history and journey etching a connection that surpassed words. The gesture, from these strangers who had now become benefactors, held a promise—an unspoken vow of refuge, a sanctuary amidst the hustle of the city. With a shared sense of gratitude, we stepped over the mansion's threshold, crossing into a realm of luxury that was, for this moment, ours to share.

****

The bedroom they bestowed upon us was a realm of opulence that seemed to stretch infinitely in all directions. The walls were adorned with gilded frames, housing artworks that whispered stories of eras long gone. A chandelier, its crystals cascading like frozen waterfalls, hung from the ceiling, casting a soft, warm glow that danced with the flicker of candlelight.

A plush, king-sized bed dominated the centre of the room, its velvet sheets inviting rest and reprieve. The intricate patterns of the headboard seemed to echo tales of bygone grandeur. Near the expansive window, thick curtains of deep crimson cascaded to the floor, a rich contrast against the moonlit night outside.

Lia and I stood there, momentarily silenced by the grandeur that enveloped us. Lia's eyes widened as she scanned the room, a silent acknowledgment of the reality that had unfolded before us. I could sense her amazement mingling with gratitude, a concoction that painted her features with a mix of awe and appreciation.

"This is... unbelievable," I whispered, the words barely more than a breath as they left my lips.

Lia's grin was infectious. "I know, right? It's like we stepped into a different universe."

The couple shared a soft chuckle, their eyes sparkling with a shared understanding of the awe that had overcome us. The woman gestured towards the bed, a gesture both gracious and warm.

"Please, make yourselves comfortable. Rest well, you've had quite a journey," she said, her voice a soothing lullaby that filled the air.

"Thank you," I managed to murmur, my voice conveying a depth of gratitude that transcended mere words.

As the couple left the room, the door closing with a hushed elegance, Lia and I stood there, still bathed in the ethereal glow of the room's magnificence. This, we realized, was a haven within a haven—a respite amid the splendour of the southern extravagance.

****

I gradually wake to the soft rustling of sheets, my eyes adjusting to the warm morning light streaming through the windows. Beside me, Lia is already up and about, her energy infectious even in the early hours.

"Morning, sleepyhead," she chimes, a mischievous glint in her eyes.

I manage a half-smile and yawn. "Morning. What's got you so lively?"

Lia's lips curl into a playful grin. "Well, our generous hosts are preparing a breakfast fit for royalty downstairs. Thought you might want to join me."

My stomach rumbles in agreement as I swing my legs over the edge of the bed. "You had me at breakfast."

As we make our way downstairs, the opulence of the mansion becomes even more apparent in the morning light. The grandeur of the place is almost overwhelming, and I can't help but feel a mixture of gratitude and awe.

Lia leads the way into a lavish dining room where the couple, who had welcomed us into their home, are already setting out an array of sumptuous dishes. The aromas of freshly baked pastries and brewed coffee fill the air.

"Good morning," Lia greets them with a warm smile.

The woman, dressed elegantly in a silk gown, smiles back. "Good morning to you both. We hope you slept well."

I nod in appreciation. "Very well, thank you."

The man, dressed in a finely tailored suit, gestures to the spread before us. "Please, help yourselves. We wanted to make sure you felt at home."

Lia's eyes light up as she surveys the feast before us. "This is quite the spread. Thank you so much."

As we sit down to eat, the couple joins us, and conversation flows easily. We exchange stories and learn about their life in the southern district of AshWays. It's fascinating to see a different side of this city, one that we hadn't encountered before.

"We've heard about your journey," the woman says, her tone empathetic. "It's not easy out there, especially in the west and the north. But you seem resourceful."

Lia chuckles, her demeanour a mix of gratitude and playful humility. "Well, we've had our fair share of adventures, that's for sure."

Curiosity sparks in the couple's eyes as they listen intently to our description of Fleshbourne. The contrast between the luxurious setting we find ourselves in and the dystopian reality of Fleshbourne is striking.

"I can't even fathom a place like that," the woman remarks, her tone a mix of disbelief and sympathy.

Lia nods solemnly. "Believe me, it's as oppressive and grim as it sounds. The buildings are crumbling, the air is heavy with despair, and the laws... well, they're more like chains than anything else."

The man's brow furrows in concern. "Weekly executions? That's unthinkable."

I sigh, the memories of the place still fresh in my mind. "Yes, it's a brutal way of maintaining control. The Scourge adds another layer of horror to it all. It's a cycle that seems impossible to break."

The woman's eyes darken, her gaze distant. "To live in such a place must be... suffocating."

Lia's voice is sombre. "It is. But that's why we're determined to reach Havenreach. It's a civilization that opposes the Scourge, a place of hope and resistance."

The man's expression shifts from concern to something akin to determination. "Havenreach... I've heard whispers of it, but never thought it could be more than a myth."

I nod, a sense of purpose coursing through me. "It's real, and it's where we're headed. We believe it's the only chance to turn the tide against the darkness that's taken hold in Fleshbourne."

The couple's eyes meet in a silent exchange, and I can see a shared understanding pass between them. The woman speaks softly, her voice laced with empathy. "Well, we admire your bravery. To escape such a place and seek out something better... that takes courage."

Lia offers a sincere smile. "Thank you. We're grateful for your hospitality. It's a reminder that not everyone is consumed by the chaos."

As our conversation continues, it becomes clear that while the couple may live in opulence, they are not blind to the suffering of others. Their kindness and genuine interest in our story are a testament to the resilience of human empathy, even in the midst of a cyberpunk city rife with contrasts.

The man's curiosity is evident as he leans in slightly, his gaze fixed on me. "Tell me, how did you manage to escape such a place as Fleshbourne?"

I take a deep breath, the memories of that daring escape resurfacing. "It wasn't easy, that's for sure. The key was timing and planning. I managed to slip away during one of the weekly executions, using the chaos and the distraction to my advantage. It was risky, and I had to navigate through the city's maze-like streets, avoiding the watchful eyes of the Enforcers."

The woman's eyes widen, clearly captivated by the story. "That sounds incredibly dangerous."

I nod, a mixture of pride and melancholy in my tone. "It was. But desperation can make you do things you never thought possible."

The man's gaze then turns to Lia, who has remained quiet throughout the conversation. "And what about you, miss? How did you escape?"

Sensing Lia's discomfort, I step in to divert the conversation. "You know, we're both really grateful for your kindness in letting us stay here. It's not often we come across such hospitality."

The woman smiles warmly, seeming to understand the shift in tone. "It's our pleasure. We believe in helping those who are trying to make a better life for themselves."

The man nods in agreement. "Indeed, and if you ever need anything, don't hesitate to ask."

I offer a thankful smile. "We won't forget your generosity."

As the conversation takes a lighter turn, I catch Lia's eye and give her a reassuring look. We both know that there are parts of our pasts that we'd rather keep hidden, but in this moment, surrounded by the warmth of the couple's hospitality, we can set those burdens aside and focus on the path ahead.

20

Disdain

As we step out of the couple's opulent mansion, Lia lets out a sigh, her frustration evident in her voice. "Did you see the way they were digging into my past like they were hunting for buried treasure? It's infuriating!"

I chuckle softly, understanding her annoyance. "Well, they were just curious. People tend to be nosy when they encounter strangers with interesting stories."

Lia rolls her eyes playfully. "Interesting is one way to put it. I'd rather they just assume I'm a mysterious traveller with a shady past. It's not like they need to know everything."

I pat her on the back reassuringly. "I get it. But remember, in a place like this, where everyone's practically dripping with curiosity, secrets are like magnets. They attract attention."

Lia huffs in exasperation. "Yeah, well, I'm not here to be some sort of enigma for their amusement."

We continue walking through the vibrant streets of the southern district, the honey-coloured streams flowing alongside us. As we blend into the crowd, I can't help but admire how Lia's fiery spirit remains unquenched, even in the face of relentless curiosity. It's just one more trait that makes her who she is - unapologetically herself.

As we stroll through the bustling streets of the southern district, the locals' compliments rain down upon us. "You two looked absolutely stunning yesterday!" a woman exclaims, her eyes shining with admiration.

Lia and I exchange amused glances, sharing an unspoken understanding of the irony. "Oh, thank you," Lia replies with a smirk. "We were just trying out our 'fancy city folk' costumes."

I chuckle and nod in agreement. "Yes, you know, it's all part of our world tour – one day in silk and velvet, the next in... whatever this is." I gesture to our more usual attire, a mix of practical clothing suitable for our journey.

The woman's smile falters for a moment, as if unsure whether we're being genuine. But then, she joins in our laughter. "Well, you both have a certain charm in any outfit, that's for sure."

Lia winks at her. "Well, we're aiming for 'charming' as our signature look. Good to know it's working."

The next few hours unfold like a series of persistent invitations, each stranger seemingly determined to introduce us to the opulent world of the southern district. "You simply must attend our soirée tonight," a man with a monocle insists, waving an ornate invitation as if it held the key to a secret treasure.

Lia and I exchange amused glances as we politely decline. "As tempting as that sounds," I reply, "we have a date with a different part of the city today."

A group of elegantly dressed women approaches us, their eyes gleaming with curiosity. "Would you care to join us for tea at the finest parlour in the district?" one of them asks, her voice dripping with honeyed charm.

Lia smirks and raises an eyebrow. "As much as we'd love to sip tea with the elite," she replies, "we're on a mission that involves a bit more adventure and a bit less refinement."

Despite our persistent refusals, the locals' invitations keep coming, each one more elaborate than the last. "A private cruise along the honey rivers, anyone?" a man in a captain's hat calls out, a velvet rope in hand.

I chuckle and shake my head. "Maybe next time, Captain. Duty calls."

As the hours tick by, the cityscape begins to morph and shift, a gradual transformation that mirrors our journey towards the edge of the southern district. The opulent buildings and bustling streets gradually give way to a more spacious landscape, the grandeur of the city slowly fading into the background.

The once-thronged streets start to thin out, the finely dressed locals becoming fewer and farther between. The elaborate architecture gives way to simpler structures, and the hum of luxurious activities is replaced by a more subdued ambiance. It's as if we're stepping away from a world of excess and entering a quieter, more down-to-earth realm.

The scenery undergoes a change too. Lush gardens and manicured parks give way to open spaces and meandering pathways. The rivers of honey become smaller, their flow less extravagant. Even the air seems to shift, carrying a different scent – one that's less fragrant with perfumes and more redolent of the earth.

With each step, the city's grip loosens, and we find ourselves at the fringes of the southern district. The once towering buildings now stand at a distance, their prominence diminished. The glamorous allure that surrounded us has softened into a more tranquil atmosphere, a hint of the world that exists beyond the city's lavish centre.

It's a reminder that AshWays is a place of contrasts, where the extravagant and the modest coexist, where grandeur and simplicity intertwine. And as we venture further away from the heart of the southern district, I can't help but feel a mixture of nostalgia and anticipation for what lies ahead – for the mysteries that the edges of this city hold, and for the journey that still stretches before us.

21

Lets Stop

The air in the outskirts of the southern district carries a different quality, less dense with the scents of luxury and more infused with a touch of natural earthiness. It's a subtle shift, a gentle reminder that beyond the opulence, there's a world that connects to the basics of life. The distant sounds of laughter and music are replaced by the soft rustling of leaves, a serenade by the breeze that carries a faint, refreshing scent of greenery.

Underfoot, the ground is no longer the meticulously paved walkways of the city centre. Here, it's a mix of cobblestones and uneven earth, an unpolished path that connects to the soil beneath. As we walk, our steps are accompanied by a gentle crunching, the sound of pebbles and soil yielding to our weight. It's a simple melody, a stark contrast to the orchestrated symphony of the city's streets.

The sunlight filters through the trees that line the path, dappling the ground with patterns of light and shadow. The warmth on our skin is no longer tempered by the towering buildings that cast their shadows – here, it's the touch of sunlight that's more direct, more intimate. It's a gentle caress that invites us to take in the surroundings with a more open awareness.

The landscape is changing too. The well-tended gardens and meticulously crafted statues are replaced by wilder, more untamed growth. The trees stretch their branches overhead, forming a natural canopy that filters the sunlight into dancing patterns. Birds add their own melody to the scene, their songs a reminder of the untamed life that persists even within the bounds of the city.

And as we continue forward, the grandiose architecture and glittering excesses of the city fade into memory. The surroundings become simpler, more raw, reflecting a different kind of beauty – one that's grounded in nature and the passage of time.

Then, ahead, the view shifts again. The exit gates of the southern district come into sight, a threshold that marks the end of this section of the city. They stand tall and sturdy, a symbol of transition and passage. As we approach, I can feel a sense of anticipation building, a mixture of excitement and trepidation for what lies beyond. The gates beckon, promising a new chapter, a new adventure, and a step closer to the elusive Havenreach that Lia seeks...

I stand beside Lia, gazing up at the imposing gates that mark the border between the southern district and the unknown beyond. The intricate design and craftsmanship are evident in every detail, a testament to the city's obsession with luxury and aesthetics.

"It's quite a sight, isn't it?" I say, my voice filled with a mix of awe and contemplation.

Lia nods, her eyes fixed on the gates. "It's almost as if they're saying, 'Step beyond this point, and you're leaving our world behind.'"

I chuckle softly. "Well, that's precisely what we're doing, isn't it?"

She gives me a sidelong glance, a playful smile tugging at the corner of her lips. "Always the realist, aren't you?"

I shrug, a grin tugging at my own lips. "Someone's got to keep our feet on the ground, especially in a world that seems so fond of floating."

Lia's gaze softens, and she turns her attention back to the gates. "You're right. And yet, there's something alluring about what lies beyond. Havenreach is out there, waiting for us."

I nod, my expression growing more serious. "True. But let's not forget that our journey might not end at Havenreach. There's still much to uncover, and I have a feeling we'll encounter challenges we can't even fathom yet."

Lia's eyes meet mine, and there's a determined glint in her gaze. "Challenges or not, we'll face them together."

"Always," I affirm, feeling a surge of gratitude for the partnership we've forged in this unpredictable world.

As we stand before the gates, ready to step into the unknown, I can't help but feel a mixture of excitement and apprehension. The city's grandeur and luxury are behind us now, replaced by the promise of adventure, discovery, and the pursuit of something greater. With Lia by my side, I'm ready to embrace whatever lies ahead.

As we cross the threshold of the grand gates, my anticipation rises, only to be met with the sight of an expansive savannah, much like the one that greeted us at the entrance to AshWays. My frustration bubbles up, and I can't help but exclaim, "You've got to be kidding me! Another savannah?"

Lia's laughter rings out beside me, her amusement evident. "Oh, come on! It's almost poetic, isn't it? A dramatic entrance and exit, surrounded by the same ol' scenery."

I shoot her a mock glare, unable to suppress a smile. "Poetic, maybe. But after everything we've been through, I was hoping for a change of scenery."

She places a hand on my shoulder, her tone gentler now. "Hey, don't let it get you down. Remember, it's not about where we are, but where we're going."

I sigh, the tension in my shoulders easing. "You're right, as always. It's just... I had this irrational hope that the outside world would be different somehow."

Lia chuckles, giving my shoulder a reassuring squeeze. "Well, the unpredictability of life doesn't necessarily come with a change of scenery. But who knows what's waiting for us beyond this savannah? Adventures, challenges, and maybe even a few surprises."

Her optimism is infectious, and I find myself grinning despite my initial annoyance. "You're an eternal optimist, aren't you?"

She winks, a mischievous glint in her eyes. "Someone's got to balance out your realism."

As we stride across the savannah, the sun casting a warm glow on the grasslands, I can't help but let out a dry chuckle. "You know, that horse we left outside AshWays would be really useful right about now."

Lia raises an eyebrow, shooting me a sly grin. "Oh, absolutely. Because navigating through the wilds with a horse was exactly what we needed back there in the city."

I smirk back at her, appreciating her wit. "Well, now we're out in the open, and a horse would be perfect for covering this distance."

Lia playfully nudges my shoulder. "Ah, the hindsight wisdom strikes again. But you do have a point. A horse would be great, if we had one."

Taking the map from Lia's hands, I unfold it and study the marked path. The simplicity of this gesture, the tangible connection to our journey, feels strangely comforting. I trace the route with my finger, mentally comparing it to the terrain we're traversing.

Lia's voice interrupts my thoughts, a mix of realism and caution. "Don't expect to be mesmerized by Havenreach. It's not like the opulence of the South or the chaotic extravagance of AshWays. It's a small civilization, focused on survival and unity."

I glance up from the map, meeting her gaze. Her emerald eyes hold a blend of determination and weariness. I can tell that, despite her reservations, Havenreach carries significance for her. It's not just another stop on our journey; it's a place where she believes we can make a difference, where our actions might matter.

I nod in understanding, carefully folding the map and tucking it away. "Well, as long as it's not trying to kill us, I'm willing to give it a chance."

Lia chuckles softly, the sound a mix of amusement and relief. "Trust me, it might not be a paradise, but it's a step away from the chaos we've been through. And that's worth something."

The sun hangs high in the sky, casting a relentless blaze across the vast savannah that stretches before us. The air shimmers with heat, distorting the distant horizon and creating an almost dream-like quality to the landscape. Waves of golden grass ripple in the warm breeze, their whispers creating a soothing undertone to the otherwise harsh surroundings.

Each step sends up a swirl of dust, mingling with the scents of earth and dried vegetation. The ground beneath our feet is firm and uneven, occasionally giving way to loose patches of sand. The sweltering heat seems to press down on us, creating a weight that's almost palpable. It clings to our skin, making the simplest movement an effort.

I can feel the sweat forming at my brow, the dampness at the back of my neck. My shirt sticks uncomfortably to my skin, and I run a hand through my hair, futilely trying to ease the sensation of being enveloped by the heat.

Lia walks beside me, her steps steady despite the challenging terrain. Her silk gown has been replaced with more practical attire, but even so, her elegance seems untouched by the harshness of the environment. Her emerald eyes, though shielded by sunglasses, radiate determination, a testament to her unwavering spirit.

As we continue, the distant horizon seems to shimmer, a mirage teasing the possibility of water or shade. But the reality remains unchanged – an unending expanse of grass and sky under the unrelenting sun. Our journey to Havenreach is a journey through this inhospitable land, a testament to our determination to find a place of refuge amidst the challenges of our world.

With the sun's intensity growing stronger by the minute, I cast a hopeful glance around the savannah, searching for even the tiniest oasis of shade. Lia's voice cuts through the sweltering air, her words dripping with her signature sarcasm. "Oh sure, let's just find some luxurious shade in this picturesque, shadeless wasteland," she quips, a playful glint in her emerald eyes.

I chuckle at her words, shaking my head. "Well, I was hoping for a five-star canopy and perhaps a personal fan, but I guess we'll have to settle for whatever scrap of shadow we can find," I retort, a wry smile tugging at my lips.

We continue to walk, eyes scanning the horizon for a spot that might offer a brief respite from the relentless heat. It's a bit of a treasure hunt, the prize being a few moments of relief from the sun's fiery grip. Finally, as if answering our silent plea, we spot a cluster of acacia trees in the distance. Their elongated shadows beckon to us like cool, welcoming havens in the midst of a desert.

Lia smirks at me, raising an eyebrow. "Well, what do you know? Our luck's turning around. Shall we see if this oasis offers a fruity drink with a little umbrella, too?"

I laugh, shaking my head. "One can only hope, Lia. One can only hope." With a shared chuckle and a new surge of determination, we quicken our pace, drawn toward the much-needed shade like sailors navigating toward the North Star.

22

Wounded Dreams

As we finally reach the shade of the acacia trees, a collective sigh of relief escapes our lips. The transition from the scorching sun to the soothing coolness of the shadow feels like a gift from the universe itself. With a mutual understanding, Lia and I settle down on the ground, letting the grassy earth cushion our weary bodies.

The quiet rustle of leaves above us creates a delicate symphony, a melody that blends seamlessly with the distant hum of the savannah. The trees' slender branches sway gently in the warm breeze, casting intricate patterns of dappled sunlight over our skin. It's a rare moment of tranquillity in the midst of our journey, a pause that allows us to catch our breath and soak in the beauty of the untamed world around us.

Lia leans back against the gnarled trunk of a tree, her eyes closed, a serene smile gracing her lips. The tension that had been etched across her features seems to melt away in the shade's embrace. I watch her for a moment, grateful for this chance to rest and simply exist in this moment of stillness.

"Feels like a different world, doesn't it?" I murmur, breaking the silence as my gaze sweeps over the landscape, from the golden grass beneath us to the vast expanse of the savannah stretching out into the horizon.

Lia cracks an eye open, her smile widening. "Yeah, a different world where our biggest concern is finding a spot of shade." She chuckles softly, her voice carrying a hint of playful nostalgia.

I join in her laughter, feeling the weight of our journey momentarily lift. The savannah stretches before us, a seemingly endless sea of grasses and rolling hills, yet in this pocket of shade, everything feels surprisingly manageable. As we sit side by side, basking in the gentle symphony of nature and the simple pleasure of each other's company, I can't help but feel a flicker of hope that maybe, just maybe, we'll find what we're looking for in this unpredictable wilderness.

The sun's warmth wraps around us like a soft embrace, and the gentle rustling of leaves overhead creates a soothing lullaby. The drowsiness that has been tugging at our senses finally takes hold, and before we know it, our eyes drift shut.

I slip into the realm of dreams, where the boundaries between reality and imagination blur. The savannah's golden hues and the whispering breeze become intertwined with my thoughts, creating a surreal landscape where time seems to stand still. In this half-conscious state, I catch glimpses of memories and desires, woven together like fragments of a tapestry.

Lia's presence beside me is a constant, an anchor that keeps me grounded even in the ethereal realm of dreams. Her steady breathing is a comforting rhythm that syncs with the heartbeat of the savannah itself. We are two wanderers, lost in our own journeys yet brought together by the threads of fate.

As the heat of the day continues to wrap around us, I feel the weight of fatigue and the allure of slumber. The boundaries between dream and reality blur further, until the sensations of the world around us and the realm of dreams become indistinguishable. In this hazy in-between, time stretches and contracts, and I surrender to the embrace of sleep.

The savannah's secrets remain hidden, its stories whispered among the swaying grasses and carried on the wings of birds. And as we drift into dreams, I can't help but wonder if those secrets might reveal themselves in the most unexpected of ways, perhaps even within the realm of our slumber.

My senses jolt awake at the ear-piercing scream that shatters the tranquillity of our shaded refuge. The world comes rushing back, and in an instant, I'm on my feet, heart pounding. My gaze snaps to Lia, and a surge of adrenaline courses through me as I see her struggling against a cloaked figure, a masked man who's trying to silence her cries with a firm hand. "Lia!" The single word carries a tidal wave of emotions — fear, anger, and a desperate need to protect her.

Lia's wide eyes meet mine for a fraction of a second, a silent plea for help. The cloaked assailant is draped in darkness, his identity concealed beneath layers of cloth and shadow. The mask obscures his face, rendering him a faceless spectre of threat. He's not alone; weapons glint against his shoulders, a grim testament to his intentions.

My mind races as I take in the scene — Lia's struggles, the determined pull of the cloaked man, the horse waiting a few meters away. There's a stark realization that chills my spine: this is a scourge, one of the enigmatic figures that haunt our world, an embodiment of terror and malevolence, and he has Lia...

To Be Continued....

Amaan Shabir is a world published author, who debuted with 'Scarred Visions' at 18 years old.

www.ingramcontent.com/pod-product-compliance
Lightning Source LLC
Chambersburg PA
CBHW070615310726
48982CB00001B/84

* 9 7 8 1 7 3 9 7 6 4 0 6 7 *